A Cuppa Trouble

The CafFUNated Mysteries

Book One A Caffeine Conundrum
Book Two A Cuppa Trouble

A Cuppa Trouble

Book Two in the CafFUNated Mysteries

By

Angela Ruth Strong

DEDICATION

Aimee, I'm so glad you were my very first friend
and that we are still friends today.

ACKNOWLEDGMENTS

I'm surrounded by so many people who have held my hand through hard times, cheered me on in good times, and forgiven my mistakes in confusing times. This list could get super long, so I'll keep it simple. Besides my family, friends, publisher, literary agency, writing group, church, and readers, who I will continue to thank with every book, there are two people I want to specifically acknowledge here:

Lissa Forrey is one of the best listeners I've ever met. It's only appropriate that she inspired my character Billie, who teaches communication skills to Tandy and Marissa in *A Cuppa Trouble*. I also appreciate how understanding she is when I accidentally call her "Billie" from time to time.

Paul Nobrega was a trainer for Focus Seminars. He not only taught me in the training room, but he's made himself available to help in my own personal growth...and in the growth of my characters. His philosophy is as brilliant as his live tweets on award shows.

I truly believe we become stronger when we are there for each other, meaning it's taken more than my husband to make me Mrs. Strong. Thank you all.

Chapter One

"I'M TURNING ON THE HEAT." TANDY rubbed her hands together while standing behind the brick counter tucked underneath the loft that would soon hold Marissa's frou-frou tea parties. "And I don't mean on the espresso machine."

Marissa flipped the sign from closed to open in the bay window of their new shop, Caffeine Conundrum, on their first day of business. "You may get the early crowd with all the Type A personalities to buy your coffee, but this afternoon, the dignified tea drinkers will come in to try my crumpets."

Tandy arched her eyebrows. She hadn't realized she was going into business with an elderly British woman. "You made crumpets? No wonder we don't have any customers yet."

Marissa wrinkled her nose at Tandy before staring out at the falling snow. "It's this weather. Beautiful but dangerous."

Marissa might as well have been describing herself. Tandy's business partner had already spilled water and slipped in the spill that morning. Tandy refrained from making any jokes because the large wet spot on Marissa's rear pretty much said it all.

"Someone's coming." Marissa turned and dashed straight into a chair. Thankfully she caught herself against a table and was able to join Tandy at the counter without injury.

Tandy pressed her lips together to keep from laughing as she peered outside to discern whether the first customer

Marissa noticed would be a coffee or tea drinker. "Oh…" She pointed toward the tubby man turning the corner. "He's wearing coveralls. He's mine."

Marissa tossed her long blonde waves over a shoulder. "You underestimate my skills as a sales lady."

Tandy rolled her eyes. Would the men of Grace Springs really start drinking tea because the hostess was gorgeous? She'd like to think better of men than that.

The door swung open with a gust of icy air, and the man in question stomped his feet on the mat.

"Jumpsuit George." Marissa greeted him with all the energy of all the green tea in all the world. "You're our first customer."

The man took off his gloves and looked around at the wood floors, white walls, brick accents, exposed beams, metal table tops, and fenced off corner for canine customers. "The place looks nice. I expected you to make it more girly, Marissa, but I'm glad you didn't. Then it would be awkward for me to stop in for my morning cup of joe."

Tandy adjusted the messy bun on top of her head, ready for business. "Large black coffee?"

"Yes, ma'am."

Marissa narrowed her eyes at Tandy before beaming up at their first customer. "The ground floor has more of an urban feel to it. Upstairs will be decorated with chandeliers and roses for those who appreciate classic taste. It'll open this weekend on Valentine's Day."

Tandy would avoid going upstairs at all costs, except, of course, for The Dating Game they'd be hosting on opening night as a fundraiser to fight heart disease. She and Greg would have to go up there to show the town that they were the closest couple in Grace Springs. Even if Marissa and her boyfriend were rom/com cover material.

She grabbed a mug. "For here or to go?"

"I need it to go." The man cleared his throat and faced Tandy, his hazel eyes widening in what she assumed to be relief that she'd gotten him out of talking about roses and Valentine's.

She returned the smooth white mug to its tray in favor of the paper cups they'd had designed with their company logo of a coffee bean next to a tea bag. "Headed to work?"

"Yep." The man removed his beanie to scratch his balding head. "This weather may be bad for your business, but it keeps me hopping. I already pulled a car out of the snow this morning, and I'm in the middle of towing it to the body shop. I can't believe anybody would try to drive a vintage Corvette in these conditions."

Marissa laughed. "Randon Evans?"

Warm steam condensed on Tandy's hand as she poured her favorite brew. From what she remembered of the local hipster's bragging, he'd purchased a vehicle based on it being rated best-in-snow. "I thought he drove a Subaru."

The tow truck driver shrugged. "He does, but it appears he doesn't know what to do with all the money he's making from his phone app software, so he started collecting cars. This one is really impressive. I checked it out for him before he bought it. It's the prototype built of the very first Corvette ever made. All steel body. Worth a pretty penny. A shame he left it stranded on the side of the road when it got stuck."

"Good night." Tandy couldn't imagine having such money, but she imagined that if she did, she wouldn't spend it on something so ostentatious.

A timer rang in the kitchen behind them, and Marissa pivoted on the stacked heel of her burgundy boot to check on whatever buttery-scented concoction she had baking. Crumpets couldn't smell that good, could they? "Wait one second, and I'll let you be the first to try my crumpets."

Maybe they were actually tasty, but once Marissa disappeared into the back room, the man rolled his eyes and muttered, "Do I have to try it?"

Tandy fitted a plastic lid to the cup and handed it to him. "I think I like you. I'm Tandy Brandt, by the way."

The man took the cup and sipped. "I think I *really* like you. I'm George Knibbs."

Marissa's boots click-clacked into the room, and she held out a shiny new plate with a small, thick, bubbly-looking pancake in the middle. "I call him Jumpsuit George because…" She motioned to his ensemble. "I surprisingly like the color of this jumpsuit. Navy is the new black, you know. Tandy, you should try it sometime."

Tandy clicked her tongue. "Black is the color of coffee. You can't go wrong with black."

George took another sip. Probably fuel to make a quick getaway. If the man didn't want to discuss Valentine's, then he definitely didn't want to discuss fashion. "Marissa, like I've been telling you, if anyone is going to try something new, you need to try a jumpsuit. They are comfortable, and also, if you're wearing a jumpsuit, it wouldn't matter if you spill tea on yourself. I've got an extra one out in my truck if you want."

Tandy turned sideways to face her business partner and grinned. "Yeah, Marissa. Try a jumpsuit."

Marissa shot her a pseudo scathing look before pretending to ignore her. "I don't want to keep you any longer, George, as I know you've got work to do. Shall I put this crumpet in a bag?"

George lowered his chin and voice. "Sweetie, I really don't want to try your fancy flapjack any more than you want to wear coveralls."

Marissa blinked. Or could she be fluttering her eyelashes? "But it's good. I know you'll like it if you try it."

"Back at ya."

Marissa stood taller. Her eyelash flutter hadn't worked. "Fine. Get me the jumpsuit, and I'll put the crumpet in a bag."

George tilted his head in what appeared to be confusion. Apparently he'd never thought this day would come. But then, neither had Tandy.

She shooed him into action. "Go, George, go. Before she changes her mind."

George shrugged a shoulder. "A deal's a deal." He set his coffee down and headed out the door to retrieve the coveralls in question.

Marissa leaned closer as soon as he was out of earshot. "Do you think he said that part about spilling tea because of the wet spot on my jeans?"

Tandy pressed her lips together to hold back the belly laughs rumbling around inside. "Perhaps. But even if he didn't, you have to consider how much money a jumpsuit could save you in dry cleaning."

Marissa eyed her up and down. "That's really why you always wear black, isn't it?"

Tandy twisted her lips in thought. She'd never considered wearing anything other than black, but if she wore a lighter color, would she suddenly realize she was as messy as Marissa? "You know if the jumpsuit is black, I'm gonna wanna wear it myself, right? It'll go with my motorcycle boots and leather choker."

Marissa's cappuccino brown eyes widened in horror.

The bell over the door chimed, and Tandy spun to see what color jumpsuit George had brought Marissa. Only it wasn't George at the door. It was Connor, wearing his tool belt and a hairstyle that either required a lot of hair paste or naturally looked that messy when he rolled out of bed. Knowing Connor, he'd never even heard of hair paste before.

Marissa clapped at the sight of her boyfriend. "This customer is mine." She grabbed a paper cup and opened the mini-fridge for milk. "Connor, I'm going to make you tea the way they make it in Chile. Miss Universe taught me at that pageant I judged last month. I want to know what you think before I add it to the menu."

Connor eyed the milk dubiously then slid a quick glance Tandy's way.

Tandy placed a hand on her hip. "He doesn't count as your customer if he doesn't pay."

"Connor counts double."

Marissa had no idea how true her statement was. Tandy grabbed a paper cup to combine regular coffee with a shot of espresso, knowing the beverage Connor really wanted to drink was called a Black Eye. Once the contractor finished their renovation, he wouldn't have an excuse to use a paper cup anymore, and the two of them wouldn't get away with their secret little exchanges.

Marissa worked beside her, steaming milk. "You giving yourself an extra shot of espresso to keep up with me?"

Tandy fitted the lid to her cup and held it by her heart rather than take a sip. "Everyone needs espresso to keep up with you." Especially Connor.

Marissa filled her cup three-fourths full with milk then added tea from a floral tea pot with a jarringly bright turquoise spout. She handed the cup to Connor and stepped back with a proud smile.

Connor nodded thanks, his gray eyes sparkling at Marissa. It was cute to see how much the man adored his girlfriend despite how different they were. He didn't even have to say a word for his infatuation to show.

Marissa nodded toward his hands. "Aren't you going to try it?"

Connor didn't move. "I don't want to burn my tongue." Impressive how quickly he came up with such a great excuse, though it could also be true.

A snort escaped before Tandy could stop it.

Marissa looked over her shoulder. "What?"

George returned. Saved by the bell.

Tandy pointed to the jumpsuit in George's hand. It was brown, which would almost be worse than black for her business partner. "Connor doesn't know what *you* are trying yet, Marissa."

The other woman's gaze landed on the garment folded in George's hands, and she visibly recoiled. "Connor has work to do in the loft." She stood on tiptoe to give him a quick peck on the cheek. "Go ahead, honey. I'll come up later to find out what you think of my tea."

Connor didn't go anywhere. He looked from person to person, and once George gripped the shoulders of the coveralls to let the legs unfold toward the ground, the confusion on his face morphed into curiosity. "I'm in no rush." He leaned against the counter.

Tandy joined him. As Marissa stepped toward George, they were free to switch cups behind her back. They did so with practiced precision. Connor soundlessly clinked his cup of coffee against the cup of tea in Tandy's hand and took a gulp.

His shoulders relaxed. Tandy knew that feeling well.

George held out the jumpsuit.

Marissa pinched the edges gingerly and lifted it away from her body like a dirty diaper.

The bell over the door chimed again, announcing Billie, the older Asian woman who owned the antique store across the street. "Wow, you girls are busy already, and it's barely seven a.m."

"Hi, Billie." Tandy didn't consider one paying customer to be the definition of busy, but Billie was always completely genuine in her optimism. Tandy loved her for it.

Marissa would love her even more for this distraction. "Yes, we are busy. George, I'll have to try your jumpsuit on later."

"Sure." George sent Tandy a smug smile. He obviously didn't believe Marissa for a second. "I've got to get back to work too. Congrats on the new shop, ladies."

Tandy waved. "Thanks, George. Nice to meet you." She would have preferred he stayed and made Marissa model for them, but as this was the grand opening of Caffeine Conundrum, she should focus on her job. She rounded the edge of the counter and lifted her cup toward the waste basket to free her hands for taking Billie's order.

"Tandy," Marissa hissed, stopping her in her tracks.

Tandy glanced up, her muscles flexing with a surge of adrenaline. Perhaps residual panic from when their lives were threatened in this very building a couple months ago. Though, at the moment, Marissa was likely only horrified by the thought of wearing a jumpsuit. "What?" Tandy asked anyway.

Marissa jutted her chin toward the cup in Tandy's hand, mistaking it for the cup of coffee she'd thought Tandy made for herself. "Aren't you going to drink that?"

Oops.

Connor covered his mouth as if to hide a grin then escaped up the stairs. If he let Tandy take the fall like this, she'd be better off giving him a real "black eye." But she'd have to deal with him later. Right now she needed to think fast.

What could she say? "I've already had two coffees this morning, and I'm starting to feel nervous." Completely true. Though her jumpiness wasn't from caffeine so much as from the thought of Marissa finding out what was inside her cup.

Marissa crossed her arms, her new jumpsuit hanging from one hand. "Do you not remember the rant you went on when I almost threw away a couple of your leftover coffee beans? You said it was wasteful, and we needed to cherish our goods the way we want our customer to cherish them."

Yes, Tandy had said that. But she hadn't been thinking of tea at the time. Of course, Marissa didn't know she was holding tea. "You're right." She pulled the cup back to her chest. Now what?

"What are you going to do with it?"

Tandy paused, but she didn't have a choice. She had to appease this monster to save Connor's soul. "Drink it?" she guessed.

"Only if you think it's worth drinking."

Gah. Tandy was cornered by her own words. Slowly, she raised the cup to her lips.

Would it be suspicious if she plugged her nose while sipping? Possibly.

Connor owed her big time.

With a deep breath, Tandy closed her eyes, curled her toes, and sipped the most...the most...the most satisfying drink she'd ever tasted. Rich. Silky. Liquid pleasure. Like crème brûlée in a cup.

It was that good.

Could Marissa's morning get any worse? First, she'd slipped in a puddle, then she stupidly agreed to try on a jumpsuit that resembled a paper bag, and now, Tandy was acting like their product didn't matter. Granted, Marissa would have thrown away the coffee herself, but Tandy was supposed to be selling the stuff. Would she continue to be this wasteful?

Speaking of waste, Marissa's little white paper bag that she'd given to George with a crumpet inside still sat on the counter. She'd agreed to try on the jumpsuit only if he tried the crumpet, but he hadn't kept his end of the bargain.

The bell over the door chimed, and she looked up in hopes George had returned.

Randon trudged in, his thick eyebrows low over dark, brooding eyes. Obviously, he wasn't having a good day either. Oh yeah. The Corvette.

"Hello, Randon." Marissa stuffed the jumpsuit behind the counter next to where she'd hidden the ugly boots Connor had given her as an early Valentine's gift. She didn't want Randon to see it and ask questions. She would have preferred not to speak to him at all since he was more likely to order coffee than tea—and because of their almost fateful date last Christmas. But Tandy was busy trying to talk Billie into ordering a Mexican Mocha under the argument that since Billie liked cinnamon in her apple cider then she'd also enjoy cinnamon with coffee. When Marissa got a second, she'd brew a cup of orange spice tea for Billie, and the woman would vow her allegiance forever. But at the moment, she had to make a similar offer to Randon. "Can I get you anything?"

Randon scraped a chair against the wood floors then landed in it with a thunk. "Can you get my car back?"

Marissa frowned. Why was he asking her about his car? "I can't, but Jumpsuit George can."

Randon studied her out of the corner of his eyes. "Why do you think that?"

Marissa tapped her chin. Maybe Randon didn't know George had found his car. "Because that's what George does when people get their cars stuck in snow."

Randon swiveled to face her. "My car isn't stuck in snow. My car was stolen."

Stolen. The word and its implications echoed through Marissa's mind. Her lips parted. "Oh." Her heart trilled. Did this mean what she thought it meant? "Jumpsuit George just stopped in for coffee after picking up your Corvette. He thought you abandoned it."

Randon jumped to his feet. "George was here? With my car? Is it okay?"

Marissa blinked, shook her head, and pointed out the window. "He parked around the corner. You didn't see him?"

Randon sprinted toward the door. "I came in the other way—from the police station."

Wow. Marissa had helped crack another crime. On her first day of business. She could see the headline now, *Tea Shop Owner Serves Solved Mysteries*. It could really boost her sales.

"I'm coming too." She grabbed the bag holding her crumpet off the counter and ran outside after him. She needed to be there when the news reporters showed up. Maybe they'd even get a photo of George eating her pastry. "Wait, Randon." Running in snow was not one of her talents.

Thankfully, Randon paused at the corner.

Her foot slipped twice, but she caught up to him without further incident…until she followed his gaze. Then her heart plummeted.

Not only was Randon's Corvette missing from the back of the tow truck, but George lay motionless in a mound of bloody snow.

Had their very first customer been murdered?

Chapter Two

MARISSA BURST BACK INTO THE OVERLY warm shop, her mind a blur of words she couldn't express. The growing crowd stared in expectation.

Tandy arched an eyebrow. "George didn't like the crumpet?"

If only. Marissa shook her head. She now had the right words to say, but she didn't want to say them. She didn't want them to be true.

Connor sipped his tea lazily in the loft above. "I'm sure your biscuits aren't that bad, hon."

She couldn't let their casualness continue. Not when she'd called Sheriff Griffin from Randon's phone, and the place was about to be surrounded by an ambulance and police cars. Most likely the coroner too, though Randon was still outside, trying to resuscitate the tow truck driver with CPR.

She shivered, suddenly cold despite the way she'd been burning up. "I think George is dead."

Tandy gasped. "From your—"

"No." Marissa closed her eyes in hopes of erasing the image of the man's blood. "It looked like he slipped and hit his head."

Tandy covered her mouth. Billie sank into a chair. Connor tromped down the stairs and wrapped his firm arms around her before she even realized he was there.

He pressed his lips to her temple. "This is why I bought you boots with better traction."

She was too saddened to point out that the boots Connor had bought her were a crime in themselves. Not that it mattered at the moment.

Sirens wailed in the distance.

A lump formed in Marissa's throat. She swallowed. "Randon's car is missing from the back of George's tow truck."

Connor pulled away to peer down at her face. "You mean it was stolen?"

Marissa met his gaze and bit her lip.

Tandy circled the counter to join them. "So George might have slipped when giving chase, or…?"

Marissa winced. "Or."

Connor took a deep breath, his chest pressing against her.

Emergency vehicles pulled to the curb outside the window, their flashing lights eerie in the dim morning light.

Tandy ran her hands over her face. Her eyes reappeared, their usual fire dulled by grief. "Did George have any family?"

Billy wiped at a tear. "He lived alone, but he was very loved."

Marissa had always enjoyed their visits. Even when he teased her about spilling tea on her clothes. "He has a niece in college. She comes to visit sometimes, but his employees are his family."

The front door swung open. The sheriff she'd once babysat stood there with his buzz cut, soft cheeks, and an authority he hadn't yet earned. Marissa and Tandy had actually solved his last case for him, but then the previous sheriff went and retired, so the kid got to pin a gold star to his shirt. "I don't want anyone leaving until questioned."

Marissa grimaced. She'd been questioned before. At least

this time she wasn't a suspect. She'd do everything she could to help. Even if that only meant brewing more tea.

She pulled away from Connor and stepped behind the counter to dig out her jar of chamomile tea leaves. They would help soothe nerves.

Tandy joined her, refilling a filter with her pungent coffee grounds.

The thought crossed Marissa's mind that the caffeine in coffee would make everyone more nervous, but at the moment she didn't have the heart to point out the error of Tandy's ways. If Marissa hadn't been so focused on their silly rivalry earlier, she might have paid more attention to George. She might have put on his ugly jumpsuit, causing him to linger in their shop a little longer. He might have stayed safe.

"I should have put on the jumpsuit."

Tandy lowered her bag of beans and squeezed Marissa's arm. "It's not your fault. None of us knew Randon's car was stolen. We didn't know there were car thieves in town. And even if we did, we didn't steal the car. We didn't hurt George."

Marissa sighed. It was good to hear her friend defend her, but words couldn't keep her from feeling the pain of all life's what-ifs.

Tandy dug a fist into her hip. "We need to buy a security camera."

Sheriff Griffin planted himself on the other side of the counter, eyes sharper than the stylus he used to make notes on his phone. "Billie installed security cameras recently, so we'll be able to check her footage. It won't have a clear view of George's tow truck, but we could possibly see the perp coming or going."

A feather of hope tickled inside Marissa's chest. Hope for justice. Though there was nothing just about George's death.

The bell over the door chimed. In breezed a middle-aged man wearing a blue FBI jacket over a tie. He might have been considered handsome if not for the rows of wrinkles under his V-shaped receding hairline. Thankfully, his critical gaze landed on Sheriff Griffin before it reached Marissa. He pulled out a piece of gum and stuck it in his mouth as he strode toward them.

The town sheriff cleared his throat twice. His chin puckered.

The FBI guy extended a hand. "Agent Nathan McNeil. I've been assigned to the car theft ring, and I'll be joining your investigation." His voice came out smooth and deep despite the wad of gum in his cheek.

"Agent McNeil?" Griffin added unnecessary pump action to their handshake. "It'll be an honor working with you. We had a murder right here last year, and I was able to track down the killer."

That wasn't how Marissa remembered the story. She glanced at Tandy who had her lips pressed firmly together, likely to hold back one of those witty retorts that had previously gotten her into trouble with the law.

Griffin continued. "With the both of us on this case, we'll have the perps behind bars in no time. I've been questioning witnesses who last saw George Knibbs, and we can also retrieve a surveillance video from the antique shop across the street."

Billie stood. "I'm not really sure how my surveillance system works. I better go call my son. He set it up for me."

McNeil nodded his curt approval.

Connor walked with Billie toward the door, a protective hand on her back. Probably asking if she wanted him to accompany her. He was sweet like that.

McNeil didn't care to watch the exchange. His scrutiny

remained on Marissa and Tandy. "You two are the women who solved the Virginia Pierce case, correct?"

Well, then. The FBI guy knew his stuff. Bad for Griffin, good for George.

"Yes," Tandy said.

Marissa nudged her with a shoulder. She didn't see the need for making the joint investigation harder on their local sheriff. Of course, Griffin hadn't once mistakenly arrested *her*. "We helped a little," she amended.

Tandy nudged back with equal force, except with Marissa, being a clumsy woman in heels, it was enough to tip her sideways. She caught herself on the counter and sheepishly regained her balance—a little farther away from Tandy this time.

Griffin narrowed his eyes in warning as if he thought she was goofing around to make him look bad.

Connor returned from walking Billie to the door, read Marissa's emotions, crossed his arms, and monitored the law enforcement officers.

McNeil never wavered from his intense study of her and Tandy. "I hope you can help this time." Deepening forehead wrinkles told her he had doubts. "What all did you see when you found Knibbs?"

Marissa took a deep breath before diving into her memories. What had she seen? It had been such a shock. "I...I saw George face down on the ground. There was blood, and Randon's car was gone, so I immediately assumed foul play. I don't remember anything else that would make me think that."

"Did you see...?" Griffin started in the small-town pace he was used to.

"Anybody else around?" McNeil snapped the question out faster.

"…anyone else?" Griffin finished.

Seeing the two trying to work together reminded Marissa of when she'd first joined forces with Tandy. Hopefully the law enforcement officers would also be able to balance each other out and become stronger as a team.

Marissa wracked her brain for clues. She reimagined the murder scene, though everything around George's lifeless form blurred in the background. Needing to calm her nerves, she reached blindly for the rest of the tea Connor had brought down from the loft earlier. She sipped the relaxing liquid.

A thought flitted through her mind. She focused to catch it like a butterfly in a net. It evaded her reach. She swiped again. So close. There it was. Yes. She knew what bugged her…

She stared at the cup in horror. She hadn't been drinking tea at all. The bitter dregs of coffee clung to her tongue. She must have grabbed Billie's cup by mistake. Though it really didn't taste like cinnamon.

"What?" Griffin demanded.

"What is it?" McNeil's tone bordered on cynical.

She looked up, knowing her answer would disappoint the others even more than herself. "I just drank coffee."

Tandy rubbed at the dull ache in her temples. It had been a long day. At least Marissa had been too out of it to realize she'd been drinking the coffee Tandy had secretly prepared for Connor. Her poor partner didn't need any more worries than that of being the first witness on a murder scene.

Marissa had a weird way of dealing with the stress though. She'd gone into overdrive, serving all their customers with the speed of Lightning McQueen. Unfortunately, it wasn't only her swift service that brought in more customers than expected on their first day.

The news of George's death had spread. The whole town turned up to hear firsthand what had happened, share in the mourning, and offer their own conspiracy theories.

Randon had been the worst. Even though the coroner left with George's body hours ago and both Griffin and McNeil had gone to the police station to analyze data and write reports, the hipster remained in their shop. He Googled car theft on his tablet as if he thought the FBI needed his help.

Tandy peeked over his shoulder to read an old article of a busted Ohio car theft ring where a group of men were caught breaking open the little black boxes that held keys at an auto dealership. Did auto dealerships still use those little boxes? She didn't know about that, though she did know automotive designers were constantly working to improve their anti-theft devices—a career that provided good job security since thieves were only ever a year or two behind in technology.

She knew this because her ex had chosen said job security over their relationship and relocated to Toledo. Of course, if he hadn't, Tandy never would have moved to Grace Springs. She never would have started her shop with Marissa or reconnected with Greg.

She glanced at her watch. Greg should have gotten off work a while ago. She didn't need support the way Marissa needed Connor comforting her in the kitchen while she baked, but it would have been nice if Greg had stopped in to check on her.

Tandy closed her eyes, ashamed of herself. She'd give Greg some of that grace she'd been learning about and assume he was stuck at work. He was, after all, an attorney. Another career with great job security that left her alone most of the time. Hmm...

Randon grunted. "These can't be the kind of thieves we're dealing with. My car is vintage and privately owned."

Tandy wasn't as alone as she wanted to be. She opened her eyes to get as far away from Randon as possible. The guy seemed more worried about his vehicle than the man who'd lost his life trying to tow it for him. She huffed and sent his stupid little screen a parting glare then—

She stopped. A name in the article snagged her attention. She refocused right as Randon scrolled to another screen.

"Wait. Go back."

"What? Why?"

She pointed. "I think I saw a familiar name." Could it be?

Randon moved his hand around the screen like a magic wand and the story reappeared.

Tandy scanned the article. No names. Maybe she'd been mistaken. Unless…

She lifted her fingers to the smooth surface and shifted the story sideways. There. The last line on the bottom of the bold list of culprits read: George Knibbs.

Randon leaped to his feet. "George wasn't saving my car. George stole my car. Call Agent McNeil."

Tandy cringed. She wished she'd found this information on her own. Now it would be used like ammo from the loose cannon that was Randon.

"Hold your fire." She raised a hand. "If George wanted to steal your vehicle, he wouldn't tow it here then come in and tell us about it. He didn't even know it was stolen."

Marissa bustled over. "Why do you think George stole it?"

Connor followed, his arms wide behind Marissa as if spotting a gymnast on the balance beam. Once she arrived safely, he stuffed his hands in his pockets.

Randon held up his tablet. "George went to jail in 1996

for stealing cars. That's too much of a coincidence."

Marissa cleared off the table next to them, seemingly unable to stand still. "I'm not so sure. It was a long time ago. He's been here for years, and there haven't been any other thefts that I know of."

Connor tilted his head. "You have to admit, it would be awfully ironic if he gave up his life of grand theft auto only to get killed by a car thief."

"I would use the word tragic." Marissa balanced a few too many mugs in one hand and plates in another.

Tandy agreed with the word tragic. It would also be a tragedy if Marissa broke all their dishes in her grief. Tandy reached to take some of the mugs and prevent any more disaster on their first day of business.

Connor emptied her other hand.

Marissa whirled, as if looking for something else to do. "Take it to the police if you want, Randon. I'm really busy here."

Connor lifted his eyebrows at Tandy. "I'll stay here with her if you want to go with Randon."

Tandy shot him a tight smile. "We could just call Griffin."

"Oh no." Randon pressed buttons on his tablet to take a screenshot. "I have to show this to the Feds. And we don't want to interrupt the investigation by making them come here again. It's only a few blocks away. I don't need you to go with me, Tandy." He grabbed his bright orange pea coat and fingerless gloves.

Tandy stood her ground, daring Connor with her eyes. What reason could he possibly have for wanting her to babysit the millennial?

Randon sauntered toward the door then studied his screen again. "I wonder if they would want me to use my skills on the 'dark web' to catch thieves. I could even go undercover. Do you think maybe the thieves knew the Corvette belonged to me, and they are only using it to lure me into helping them commit cybercrimes? I could, you know. Remember when the Ohio Power company had a blackout a couple of years ago? That was actually—"

"I'm not hearing this." Connor covered his ears. "Go. Please."

Tandy groaned. There were a million other things she'd rather be doing, but she'd go with Randon. Even if George was a criminal in his past life, he still deserved to have investigators track down his killer rather than get distracted by conspiracy theories.

Though once the murderer was locked behind bars, maybe Tandy could prod Randon into sharing his connection with a closed case involving Ohio Power and what had previously been labeled a terrorist threat. That would at least get her five to ten years of peace from him.

She reached behind the counter for her black moto jacket and gray scarf. See? She didn't *only* wear black. "I'll drive, Randon."

"My Subaru would be safer, but I'll let you drive since we're not going far, and that will allow me to keep looking up articles on George."

He also let her open the door for him. Not exactly a gentleman, but he'd probably make some feminist really happy one day.

Like she was happy. With Greg.

On her way back from the police station, Tandy would stop by the law office to fill Greg in on her day. If he was going to be working late again, she'd even offer to bring him coffee.

Randon trudged beside her, finally lowering his tablet to look around. "You drive a Volkswagen Beetle, don't you?"

"I do." She braced herself for a scathing reply.

"Where is it?"

Humph. That wasn't bad. She reached inside her pocket to push the lock button on her key fob three times. If she could remote start the engine and warm up the car, hopefully it would keep Randon from complaining the whole time.

She liked her little car. It had served her well. Even kept her safe during that run-in she'd had with a rockslide.

George's body shop had fixed it. They'd done a good job. It was too bad her car lived on while he did not.

Though was it alive? She hadn't heard her ignition turn over.

Pulling her car keys out of her pocket, she aimed them directly at...

A Range Rover.

She stopped. Squinted at the spot where the Range Rover sat. She must have parked behind the SUV.

"Uh..." Randon looked around. "I don't see a Beetle."

Tandy took another step forward. The spot behind the Ranger Rover appeared empty. In the morning's commotion, had she forgotten where she'd parked? "I thought..." She pointed to the spot. "...I parked right there."

Randon's eyes grew wide behind his plastic glasses frames. "Your car has been stolen too."

Chapter Three

Once again, Marissa had to deal with the sheriff and FBI agent in her shop. After her crazy morning, it would be too much to handle if she hadn't prepared by sneaking more of Tandy's atrocious espresso shots. She much preferred tea, but it didn't contain nearly the caffeine. Now she had enough energy to answer questions as well as clean up from the day's business, which was good, because Tandy wasn't being much help.

Her business partner had sunk into a chair the moment she'd walked through the front door. "Why does this kind of stuff happen to me? It was my car that hit the rockslide. Now it's my car that gets stolen."

Griffin and McNeil stood in front of her, both with arms crossed. Usually Griffin would have his phone out taking notes, but this time he seemed to be copying the FBI agent's stance like a five-year-old would his father.

McNeil chomped his gum. "Perhaps your car was stolen *because* it had been to the shop."

Griffin nodded like he agreed with the claim, though the wrinkling between his eyebrows suggested confusion.

"What do you mean?" Tandy asked so the sheriff didn't have to.

Marissa bussed the tables around the trio so she could overhear their conversation without slowing down. Her brain worked every bit as fast. Tandy's car had been in George's shop. If he were involved in the car theft ring, then his employees could have been making copies of their clients' keys. They'd also have addresses for where to track down the cars. As for Tandy, everyone in town knew she was starting a coffee shop that day and would be too busy to check on her car for hours.

McNeil held a hand wide as if the answer was obvious. "Randon's article revealed George was no stranger to car theft. If his body shop was the front for another ring, that could give someone the motive for murder."

Marissa didn't want to think ill of the dead. Yeah, George had been arrested before, but he'd seemed like a nice guy since she'd known him.

She juggled a cup and saucer. They clattered. Connor caught them.

A roomful of eyes turned her way at the commotion. Now that she had their attention, she could make her point. "We can't assume George is guilty simply because he made mistakes in his past."

The FBI agent sent her a skeptical scowl. "We can't rule him out either."

"Come on, hon." Connor motioned with his head toward the kitchen. "I'll help you wash dishes."

Marissa followed with a sigh. "I feel like they're missing something."

Connor stepped to the side so she could enter the back room first. "I'm sure they are. This is only the beginning of the investigation. Even if George was guilty, his murder is still wrong. The law enforcement officers are here to catch his killer."

"Or are they?" Randon challenged from his spot on a stool at the counter. With as long as he'd been there, they should start charging rent.

Marissa bit her lip. "What do you mean?"

Connor shook his head then disappeared into the

kitchen. Her boyfriend hadn't liked Randon since they'd met. Marissa wasn't the guy's biggest fan either, but if he knew something…

"The FBI got here really fast this morning, don't you think?"

The whole day was a blur, though she did remember Agent McNeil arriving shortly after Sheriff Griffin. Which meant he couldn't have come from Cincinnati. "Maybe he has a vacation home in Grace Springs."

"Yeah." Randon snorted. "And he'd give up his vacation time to investigate this?"

Marissa rested her elbows on the metal counter and leaned forward to keep him from talking so loudly. If he was going to say negative things about an FBI agent, it would be better if the man didn't overhear. "Why do *you* think he got here so quickly?"

Randon slid his narrowed gaze toward McNeil. "I think he was already investigating the car theft ring. I mean, the Feds don't get involved if it's only one car. Or one murder."

She hadn't thought about that. "Have there been other thefts in this area?"

"I don't know, but I'm going to find out." He slouched on the stool. "You know what really irks me, though?"

"That someone would kill George?" That's what irked her.

"That." Randon shrugged away the value of any life not his own. "And that the Feds wouldn't let the public know there were robberies going on. I mean, if I'd known, I would have charged the tracking device on my Corvette. I haven't been driving it in this snow, so I didn't think I needed it on."

Marissa stood up straighter and glanced at her business partner on the other side of the room. She was also slumping under the burden of a stolen vehicle. "And Tandy could have gotten an alarm installed on her car."

Connor strode out of the kitchen, a dish towel over his shoulder. "Do you want to give Tandy a ride home, hon? I'll finish up here."

Marissa met her boyfriend's gaze. He'd been so busy helping out and supporting her that he hadn't gotten anything done in the loft that day. If she let him continue to run himself ragged, he wouldn't finish in time for their grand opening on Valentine's. Plus, she still had an excess of energy shooting through her veins from her intake of caffeine.

"Oh, that's okay." She tugged the dishtowel from him and tossed it in the dirty towel hamper. "I've got to prep a few things for tomorrow. I know Tandy wouldn't mind waiting for me, but she looks wiped out. Do one of you guys want to take her home?"

Randon rolled his eyes. "It's too bad owning this shop doesn't make you ladies as much money as I make designing phone apps. Then she could afford a second car the way I do."

"On that note, I'll give her a ride." Connor unhooked his Carhartt jacket from a hook on the brick wall. "But I'm coming back here afterward to make sure you get home safely. I could even make you spaghetti for dinner if you want."

Marissa's anxiety settled slightly at Connor's offer. Spaghetti was the only thing her boyfriend knew how to make. But she'd take it. "That sounds like exactly what I need."

"Okay." He hugged her to his side but didn't follow up with a kiss. Probably because Randon was watching.

Oh well. Connor would be back soon. He could kiss her then. That would be the only right thing about this day.

This was the day Tandy had been looking forward to for months, yet now she couldn't wait for it to end. Though, at the moment, she didn't even know how she was going to get home.

"Sheriff Griffin, could I get a ride?" She'd ridden in the back of his cop car once before. Apparently, her life had not improved much since then.

"Sure, Tandy."

Agent McNeil looked at his watch. "If I leave now, I can interrogate the body shop employees before they close down."

"Except I can't," Griffin added. Obviously, an afterthought. "I've got to interrogate the body shop employees."

Tandy groaned and leaned back in her chair to stare at the ugly chandelier Marissa had insisted on keeping for her upstairs tea room. Anything above the first floor was Marissa's territory. It was silly and not a big issue compared with everything that had happened that day, but it was one more thing that made life feel out of control.

Tandy's jacket landed in her lap with a soft plop. She looked up from it to the man who had tossed it there.

Connor tilted his head toward the door. "Come on, kid."

Tandy glanced past him to where Marissa feverishly wiped off counters. She hadn't realized before what a neat freak her business partner was. "Is Marissa ready?"

"Nah." Connor pulled his keys out of his pocket. "I'll come back to help her after I take you home."

Again with the little things that felt huge. This simple gesture made Tandy want to break down in tears. Because

Connor didn't have to do that.

She grimaced at the thought of how Greg should have been the one to offer. What did it say that Marissa's boyfriend had to take care of both of them?

"Thanks, Connor, but let me call Greg first."

"No problem."

He didn't even sit down to wait. Like he knew she was going to get Greg's voicemail. At least the law enforcement officers were already headed out the door and didn't overhear her pathetic phone message.

"Hey, Greg. I know you're probably still busy at work, but I thought I should let you know my car was stolen. Connor has offered to give me a ride home. Maybe you could pick me up in the morning. Free coffee."

Ugh. Was she really dating a guy she had to bribe to stop by? She peeked up to gauge Connor's response.

He gave her an understanding smile. "Ready?"

She automatically dug her keys out of her purse. She'd need one to get into her apartment, but would she ever use the car key again? What else did she have in her car that she'd never see again? Her phone charger that Marissa always asked to borrow. Her new business cards. Her doggy car seat.

Cocoa would be there for her when she got home. Her loyal Pomeranian. At least she could count on him.

She'd bring him to work tomorrow. She'd left him behind for their first day in order to make sure everything went smoothly. That hadn't worked.

"Thanks, Connor." She stood. He held the door open, flipped the window sign to "closed," then waited for Randon to join them on the sidewalk.

Randon took off toward his Subaru, muttering something derogatory about the FBI.

Tandy grimaced at his back. "I should especially thank

you for not making me ride home with him."

Connor shot her a half smile. "After I tried to get you to take him to the police station earlier, I kinda owed you."

"There is that."

He opened the passenger door of his big truck. She climbed up, wishing it was Greg's Mercedes. And not because she cared about the vehicle. In fact, she'd rather Greg drive a lemon if it meant he could be there to give her a ride in it.

Connor climbed into the driver's side, letting her sulk in silence. He turned on the ignition and icy air burst from the vents. She swiveled them to point away from her already frozen fingers.

"Radio?" he asked.

She suspected from the size of his truck and the fact that he was raised on a farm that he might want to listen to country music. That would only make her day worse. "No, thanks. I just want my dog, my bed, and my electric blanket."

"I'll get you there as quickly as possible." He turned on his headlights and shifted into drive.

At the cross street ahead, a round, black car raced by.

Tandy bolted upright. Adrenaline pumped through her veins like she'd eaten a handful of chocolate covered coffee beans. "That looked like my Bug."

Connor stepped on the gas. "Does anyone else in town drive a black Volkswagen?"

"No." One local high schooler had a convertible yellow Bug, but most people in the area preferred American-made.

"It could be a tourist," he pointed out logically even as he spun the steering wheel to follow.

"Tourists don't drive like that," she responded with even more logic.

He grunted acknowledgment, eyes focused on the car

trying to disappear into the dark. "I know."

If someone stole her car, why would they be parading it through town? Were they kids on a joyride? She'd assumed that if George was involved in a crime ring that Sheriff Griffin would find the vehicle at the body shop. Oh… "They had my car at the body shop and had to sneak it out when Griffin arrived for questioning."

The Beetle turned at a side street. Connor flipped off his headlights then turned to follow. Tandy gripped the door handle as they eased into the inky blackness.

The red taillights ahead flashed dancing shadows against surrounding trees. They passed a couple of streets, and the woods grew thicker. Then the taillights swung onto a gravel side road.

Connor slowed.

Tandy dug her nails into the fabric seats and leaned toward her window to get a better look down that side road. "There's a house back there."

The driver of her Bug climbed out of the vehicle and pressed buttons on a keypad on the house to open an attached garage and park inside. She couldn't make out features in the dim light, but it could easily have been one of the auto body mechanics. If the police were suspicious, wouldn't they check the employees' homes too? How long could this guy store her car here?

Headlights illuminated them from behind, the bright light blinding in the rearview mirror. Connor's truck could be seen if they kept sitting there. But if they left, would they be able to find the place again? It was so dark.

Connor pulled forward and turned off the main road. The truck crunched into a small clearing, still hidden from their suspect's house by a grove of trees.

Tandy's heavy breaths puffed in the air. She fumbled for

her purse to call Griffin. Let him know she'd solved another case for him.

Connor sat at alert, ears almost visibly perked up the way Cocoa's did. His eyes scanned the dark shadows.

Tandy would let him play watch dog while she called the authorities. She pressed the button for her contacts. The resulting beep tore through the spooky silence.

"Wait." Connor held a hand to stop her.

She paused, though his wariness caused her pulse to thump louder than the beep had done.

Gravel crunched behind them. Tandy jerked to turn the direction of the sound.

The dark form of a man appeared from the street.

She gripped Connor's arm. "Go, go, go. Back out."

Connor shifted, but didn't step on the gas. "I'd run him over."

"He'll get out of the way."

The form grew larger. A flashlight beam bounced over the interior of the truck.

Was this the guy who stole her car? Was this the guy who'd murdered George?

Connor looked over his shoulder. "What if he doesn't move?"

Tandy reached across the bench seat to grab Connor's jacket and shake some sense into him. "What if he has a gun? What if he shoots at us?"

"Then I don't want to antagonize him." Connor shifted into park.

Tandy's heart shot tingles down her arms and legs. "Drive. What are you doing? What other choice do you have?"

Connor wrapped his big arms around her. Did he think he was Superman and bullets couldn't penetrate him? They were sitting ducks. Any criminal who found them here would know they were spying.

His nose nuzzled her temple. What in the world?

His mouth hovered by her ear, his breath less than pepperminty fresh. "Haven't you ever seen this in the movies?" he whispered.

Even if she was single and interested, this was not the time. She pushed Connor's chest. "I don't watch those kinds of movies."

Connor's muscles stiffened underneath her palms. "Spy movies."

Why were they talking about spy movies? Why was Connor acting like he wanted to kiss her? They'd been following a car thief who might actually be a killer, and now that they were caught, he could kill them too.

They needed to figure out a way to make this guy think they were here for some other reason. But why would anybody drive out into the woods at night and park unless…

"Spy movies!"

She grabbed Connor's face and kissed like her life depended on it. Because it did.

Chapter Four

TANDY CONTINUED KISSING WHILE UNBUCKLING HER seatbelt and climbing up to her knees. This way if the bad guy didn't buy their act and tried to hurt Connor, she would be free to climb into his seat and drive them to safety.

A rap on the window physically affected her the way a slap to her face might. Was Tandy feeling more scared or guilty? She cringed as she pulled away from her best friend's boyfriend.

Connor watched her, the whites of his eyes flashing in contrast to their dark surroundings. "You didn't have to really kiss me," he hissed.

Well, that would have been easier to explain to Marissa. If they survived. "I panicked."

"Yeah. At least you fogged up the windows." He turned to face their enemy, and as he rolled down the window, his edginess morphed into what looked like embarrassment, à la slouched shoulders and goofy grin. "Oh good, you're not a cop," he said as if the stranger was a conspirator and *they* were the lawbreakers.

The flashlight blinded Tandy. She lifted her hand to shield her face. She needed to act as nonchalant as Connor, but that felt impossible with her heart in her throat.

"You're on private property," the scary dude said. It was difficult to see what he looked like with the light pointed at her, but he sounded like he'd eaten gravel for breakfast. Had he come to Caffeine Conundrum and eaten a crumpet instead, he might not sound like such a bad guy.

Of course, he probably *was* there at breakfast time, but he had to leave before coming in because he didn't want anyone to suspect him of killing George.

"I'm sorry. We didn't know." Tandy squeezed Connor's arm as an outlet for her terror. She leaned forward to unite them like a team. If nothing else, they were two against one. But until the Batman impersonator realized they were against him, she'd pretend that she was hanging onto Connor out of infatuation. "If we leave, do you promise not to press charges?"

The dude flashed his light on her again. He wouldn't recognize her, would he? She'd taken her car to George's body shop, but she didn't remember meeting any employees who had a voice like this.

"Aren't you two a little too old to be parking?" the dude growled.

Um… He had a good point.

"Sadly, I still live with my parents," Connor confessed. "And she's got a boyfriend. So…"

Tandy frowned. The part about her having a boyfriend was true, but did Connor still live with his parents? That had to be an excuse.

The guy chuckled. "That *is* pretty sad."

Tandy laid her head on Connor's shoulder. "See why we don't want anyone to find out?"

The dude ran a hand over his head and looked the direction of the house where the Bug had been parked. It wasn't visible through the trees. That would work in their favor, right?

He stepped away. "Get out of here, and don't come back."

Tandy held her breath rather than exhale in one big whoosh. Such a reaction might be a tad suspicious. They were so close to freedom. She couldn't mess this up now.

Connor nodded. "Thanks, man. I really appreciate it."

"Yes, thank you." Tandy echoed. She grabbed her seatbelt and strapped herself in, ready for Connor to step on the gas.

Connor shifted then gave a friendly wave. The truck rolled backwards, and he had to do a three-point turn to direct it toward the street again. His window was still open, and the bad dude still watched, otherwise Tandy would have given a Dukes of Hazard type ye-haw.

Gravel crunched.

Her chest threatened to explode.

Connor gunned the engine, and they burst into the open.

Tandy scrambled for her phone and dialed. "I can't believe that happened."

"Which part?" Connor sounded so calm. Too calm.

"Any of it. Good thinking with the kissing cover. Though for Marissa's sake, you may want to lay off the onions." She held the phone to her ear, listening to the ring.

"For Marissa's sake, maybe we shouldn't tell her about this right before Valentine's."

The couple's history was reason enough to believe that Marissa would make mountains out of their make-out session, but the longer Connor waited to tell her about it, the more volcanic her eruption would become. "You can't keep it from her forever, Connor. Eventually you'll have to tell Marissa that we kissed."

"Tandy, is that you?" the sheriff's tinny voice blared in her ear. "You kissed Connor?"

Of all the times for Griffin to make a good detective.

"Sheriff, Connor and I found my stolen car. We followed it off 2nd Street into the woods. It's parked in a garage."

"I knew I heard a car engine start up when I got to the

body shop. Tell me where you are. I'm going to make the arrest without Agent McNeil."

Tandy dropped her head against the headrest. Why couldn't people work together? Why did there have to be so much competition and secrecy? "We'll wait for you at the church."

Connor nodded his understanding and pulled into the parking lot. She hung up. Then they sat and stared at the white steeple. At least the heater had finally warmed up the car.

"Griffin overheard me say we kissed."

Connor cringed.

Would the sheriff ask questions? Would it be in the morning newspaper? Had they just busted an international syndicate, and they'd be featured on Dateline? The only date show she wanted to be a part of was The Dating Game taking place in the tea house on Valentine's Day.

"I'm going to tell Greg. I'm sure he'll understand."

"He's logical like that, though I'm going to be uncomfortable around him now." Connor shifted in his seat.

Tandy gave a sad smile. "Maybe the fact that you and I have kissed will prod him into kissing me."

Connor ran a hand through his hair. "He hasn't kissed you yet?"

Tandy grimaced. She'd come up with lots of excuses for Greg. Like it had only been a little over a month since they'd reconnected. And he was really busy with work. And they'd been childhood buddies, so the transition from friends to more was tricky. But hearing Connor say it made their lack of romance sound pitiful. "Is that bad?"

"It's bad for me." Connor looked out his window. "Now it won't only be Marissa who hates me."

"Marissa won't hate you."

"Are you sure? She broke up with me over less."

Tandy twisted her lips. He had a point. "Too bad you're in love with her."

"Yeah."

"Too bad I'm falling for another guy who doesn't even have time for me."

"He's missing out."

Tandy smiled sadly. "Too bad I didn't feel anything romantic when I kissed you. Because you and I would make so much more sense as a couple."

"Ironic, isn't it?"

Maybe that would be too easy. The two of them would always be in agreement and never have anyone there to challenge them to grow. "Nothing personal. You're a pretty good kisser."

Connor laughed. "It was like kissing a brother though, huh?"

"Yep."

"Then you should be the one to tell Marissa. I'm afraid to even call her and let her know I'm not going to make it back tonight to cook her spaghetti."

Tandy groaned. The best thing she could do to convince Marissa she wasn't interested in Connor was to get more serious with Greg. She'd talk to Greg the next morning.

In the same way, Connor needed to be the one to talk to Marissa about the kiss. But she could help out with the spaghetti thing. She already had her phone handy. "I'll call her right now and tell her we found my car so she's not expecting you."

"Thank you, Tandy. That means so much I could kiss you."

Tandy punched his arm then punched in Marissa's number.

"What? Too soon?"

Marissa couldn't get home fast enough. Holding arms wide for balance, she baby stepped down the icy sidewalk. Connor had wanted to come back and walk her to her Jeep to make sure she made it home safely since there was a killer on the loose, but since he and Tandy currently had the bad guy cornered, Marissa should be safe.

She'd say extra prayers for Connor and Tandy's safety as she crawled into bed that night. And she wouldn't sleep until Connor called to let her know he'd made it home, as well.

Shivering, she glanced around at the deserted street. Only Mama's Kitchen remained open at this hour, and all the diners were inside. Should anyone intend to harm her, she'd be on her own.

She glanced across the street at Grandma's Attic to reassure herself she was protected. At least now if anything happened to her, there would be a clear surveillance recording of her face and a record of when she left her shop.

Billie's place looked darker than usual. Didn't the store owner usually leave a back light on inside? Tonight there wasn't even a silhouette of the antiques. The only light coming from that side of the street was the glint of streetlamps off glass. And that wasn't as bright as usual.

Marissa stilled. Something was off. She frowned in concentration.

Reality hit her like a brick through a window. Which was exactly what it looked like had happened to Grandma's Attic. The large pane of glass at the front of the store included a gaping hole.

Fear shot up Marissa's spine to the base of her neck in the

form of goosebumps. Anybody could have broken into Billie's shop…anybody from George's killer to a petty thief. And that person might still be inside.

Whether someone was there or not, it was likely the criminal had destroyed the surveillance system. Which meant Marissa was not on film. No records of her whereabouts were currently being created.

She shot into motion once again, doubling the speed of her baby steps and digging through her purse for her phone or keys or pepper spray. Her phone was about to die, so she should probably go for the pepper spray.

Her breath huffed in the air. Her pulse pounded even louder. But, thankfully, no footsteps echoed after hers.

She settled on grabbing her car keys and locking herself safely inside her Jeep. She wasn't going home now. Not if both the sheriff and Connor were only a couple of blocks away at the church. She gunned her motor and stepped on the gas.

Under a bright white steeple sat Griffin's police car next to Connor's truck. Sheriff Griffin stood outside Connor's driver side window.

Marissa slammed into park and charged from her vehicle. She wasn't sure who she was more excited to see. Griffin or Connor?

She'd start with Griffin since he was closer. She ran the best she could in the frozen parking lot and slid into the side of Connor's truck to stop herself the way she used to do at the roller-skating rink as a child.

Griffin shot her a withering look. "It's going to be hard to function in stealth mode with the whole Scooby-Doo Gang here."

"We're missing the dog," Tandy retorted from the cab before Marissa had even caught her breath.

Connor glanced at her without making eye contact. "I didn't know you were coming, Marissa."

She gripped Griffin's arm, but only partly to get his attention. The other part was for balance. "There's been a break-in."

Tandy's face appeared next to Connor's. "At Caffeine Conundrum?"

Connor twisted to get a better look at her now, eyebrows drawn. "Are you okay?"

"No." Marissa closed her eyes and shook her head. She wasn't explaining this well. She took a deep breath to focus. "I mean, yes, I'm fine, but no, nothing happened to our shop. It's Billie's."

Sheriff Griffin punched a fist into his palm. "They were going after the surveillance video."

Marissa had been afraid of that. "Didn't you already get the video footage from George's death?"

Griffin muttered under his breath for a moment before responding in comprehensible words. "Billie couldn't remember her password. She was waiting to hear back from her son who'd set up the system."

Marissa frowned. "Who would have known that?" She hadn't known that. Unless the thief had known that, a break-in would be pointless.

"The guys at the body shop would have known." Griffin hung his head. "I tried to use the knowledge that we were getting evidence of a murder to scare them into confessing."

"Well..." Connor did his best to break the awkward silence.

Marissa would help him out. "It doesn't matter now because you are going to catch the car thief red-handed." Though obviously it was a good thing she'd rushed over and was here to help. The sheriff always seemed to aim at his own foot when he fired off his mouth.

Tandy clicked her tongue. "Don't you think the FBI should be here for this arrest?"

Griffin lifted his chin and glared. "I'll let McNeil know when I have the perp behind bars. All I need is for you to lead me back the way you came, Connor." He marched toward his patrol car.

Marissa wasn't staying behind for this. She'd pull out her phone and film any action so that this time the authorities really would have evidence. If the battery didn't die.

Balancing against the truck with one hand, she clip-clopped around the front end to pull open the passenger door. She stepped one foot onto the running board and motioned for Tandy to scoot.

Tandy scooted the wrong direction as if they had time to rearrange for Marissa to sit in the middle.

Marissa blocked her path. "Get in the middle. Griffin's ready."

"I don't…"

The other woman might not be as skinny as Marissa, but this was no time to worry about discomfort. "Hurry so we can get your car back. Then you won't ever have to be in the middle again. Why are you making a big deal out of it?"

"I don't know." Tandy gingerly squeezed over on the bench seat, sitting straight with knees together and hands on her lap.

Marissa jumped in and slammed the heavy door.

Connor rolled up his window and pulled onto the street without a word.

"What did I miss?" Marissa leaned forward to see both their faces. "Tell me everything."

Neither Tandy or Connor answered. Maybe they were too intent on finding the right driveway.

Marissa peered farther down the road. It wound and curved through the trees with long driveways splitting off here and there. "How far do we have to go?"

Connor cleared his throat. "Maybe half a mile."

Marissa nodded. She was glad she'd come. Now she'd get to see justice prevail. "Did you get a good look at the guy's face? Did you recognize him?"

"No." Connor's short answer told her he was definitely concentrating. The guy usually preferred to joke and kid.

"Me neither." Tandy bit at her fingernails. Such a bad nervous habit. Marissa would have to get her a bottle of nail polish with a nasty flavor to break her of it. "I don't think I've heard his voice before either."

Marissa gasped. "You talked to him? What did you do? Go knock on his door and pretend to sell Girl Scout cookies?"

Tandy sat up straighter. "Not exactly."

"There it is." Connor swerved to the side of the road in front of a gravel driveway. He motioned for Sheriff Griffin to turn.

Marissa unbuckled her seatbelt to reposition herself toward the passenger window to get a better look. She had a front row seat for the show. The last time she'd seen someone get arrested, she wasn't nearly so safe.

She grabbed her phone to film the action, but the blank screen told her it had indeed died. "Tandy, can I borrow your charger?"

Tandy pointed to the house under surveillance. "If you want to go get it out of my Bug."

Hard pass. "Can I borrow your phone then?"

Tandy handed the device over without her standard lecture, and the darkness hid any disapproving looks she might have tried to include in the exchange.

"I'll get a portable charger soon. I promise." Marissa

clicked on the camera icon. "I hope Griffin doesn't bungle this one." She pressed record and zoomed in to watch the sheriff knock on the door. Someone answered, and the lawman went inside. "What if he comes running out? Or we hear gunfire? Or Tandy's slug bug bursts through the garage door to make a quick getaway."

"Nobody is going to drive my car through a garage door."

Tandy was probably right. Marissa smiled over her shoulder in a show of support.

Connor held up his phone. "I've got Agent McNeil on my speed dial."

They waited. Finally, Griffin led a man out of the house in handcuffs.

Marissa deflated into her seat. She was glad Tandy's car hadn't been damaged any more, but there hadn't been much to see. Oh well.

Flipping the phone camera to selfie mode and hitting the flash button, she held it up to capture her friends behind her. "Smile, guys."

Tandy chewed on a fingernail. Connor's grin looked more disgruntled than anything. "Are you disappointed too?" she asked. "Hoping for a little more drama like me?"

"Nah." Connor slid his eyes Tandy's direction. "I'm good without drama."

"Yeah." Tandy smiled brightly. Not a natural look on her. "No drama for me either."

"Wow." Marissa widened her eyes at her own reflection. "You two are boring. It's a good thing I joined you tonight. I can't imagine what you would have done out here without me."

Chapter Five

"I KISSED CONNOR LAST NIGHT."

Cocoa, Tandy's Pomeranian, barked at Greg from between her feet. Ever so loyal. At least if Greg left her, she'd still have one male in her life.

Greg lowered the bouquet he'd been holding out, fully revealing the gray suit and wool overcoat. His everyday attire. If he'd only worn a fedora, he'd be a regular Cary Grant. Did a woman ever cheat on Cary Grant? Tandy doubted it.

"I…did not see that coming," Greg said, and he wasn't talking about her dog. Cocoa always yipped.

She scooped Cocoa into her arms to calm him down, though she'd expected Greg to be the one who needed calming. Instead, he responded to Tandy's confession in his debonair way. How did he remain debonair in the face of a six a.m. ambush at her front door? Tandy had better explain quickly to keep him there.

"I didn't want to kiss Connor. He was giving me a ride home when we saw someone driving my car. We followed, and when the thief found us parked outside his house, that was the best cover we could come up with. I was afraid he'd kill us the way he killed George."

Greg's head tilted. His eyes softened. "That would have been good information to start with when pleading your case." He was at least going to give her a hearing.

"Is it too late to plead innocent?"

"The term is 'not guilty.' And I'm the guilty one. Had I

been a better boyfriend, this would never have happened." Greg extended the coffee mug flower arrangement once again. "I'm sorry I wasn't there for you yesterday. I didn't even look at my phone until after midnight, so I didn't realize what was going on. Are you okay?"

Tandy reached for the mug with one hand and inhaled its summery scent. Not quite as nice a smell as the scent of coffee. But she wouldn't complain.

Greg was taking responsibility because he was a responsible person. What made him a good boyfriend was what also made him so good at his job. She couldn't have *all* his attention, or it wouldn't be worth having. "Thank you. And yes, I'm okay."

She sat the bouquet on the entry table, adjusted her wiggly pup in her arms, and arranged a few of the short stems to get a better look at the mug. It read *Coffee is my Valentine*. So sweet of him to be willing to share her affections with coffee. Not sweet that it had her thinking about the tea she'd tried the day before.

Coffee was her thing. Which was the real reason she adored this arrangement. The flowers would die, but coffee was forever.

Greg reached past her for the hook with her scarf and jacket. He looped the scarf around her neck and pulled her close enough to read her eyes. "Will you be kissing Connor anymore?"

"No. Only you." She smiled, awaiting their first kiss.

Cocoa's tongue licked her cheek.

"And Cocoa."

"Good." He scratched Cocoa's head then reached past her to grab her jacket. "That would have made competing against Connor and Marissa in The Dating Game rather uncomfortable."

Competing against the other couple was still going to be uncomfortable when the other man was the only man on stage who Tandy had kissed. Rather than make a big deal out of it, she turned around to slide her arms into her coat while juggling her dog. Perhaps Greg was waiting to make their first kiss as memorable as possible. At least she could breathe again now that she wasn't holding in a secret.

Greg was even able to joke about the kiss. Plus, he apologized for being so busy at work. Things were going to work out for them.

Greg offered his arm, and she looped her hand in the crook of his elbow so he could escort her and Cocoa down the stairs of her apartment to his waiting luxury sedan for a ride to work. "Tell me more about George's murder. Do you really think the man who stole your car also killed him?"

Tandy slid her eyes sideways. He was talking like an attorney again. "George's half-brother, Derrick Snodgrass, stole my car."   Greg wouldn't consider representing the criminal in court, would he? "I hope he's guilty of George's murder. If not, then there's still a killer on the loose."

"My dad did not kill anyone."

Marissa scooped tea leaves into an infuser and poured hot water over the top to make a drink order for George's niece, Susan Snodgrass. She never would have expected Susan to be a tea-drinker with her tattoos, pink hair, and nose piercing, but she did have a sweet side, and the large plastic glasses frames hinted at intellect.

The young woman had come to Grace Springs to plan George's memorial, but, surprise, her dad was arrested for his murder. Poor thing.

"Here." Marissa slid the chocolate tea across the coffee shop counter. It was the only way she knew how to help. Though her parents had their own issues, they'd never killed anyone. That she knew of.

Susan didn't even touch the mug. "Uncle George gave my dad a job here after he got out of prison. They both used to boost cars together, and yeah, maybe Dad went back to his old ways, but he would never kill anybody. Especially not his brother who was trying to help him."

Marissa didn't know what to say. Definitely not the quote about there being no honor among thieves. Nor was she going to pose the question as to who else might have committed such a crime. That's what had sent her off on her own investigation last year and had almost gotten her killed.

The bell over the door chimed to announce Tandy's arrival. About time.

"Tandy, meet Susan Snodgrass."

Cocoa bared his teeth and growled as if he understood the connection and wanted to protect Tandy…or get his car seat back from Susan's father who stole it. Or it could have been the college student's cotton candy hair that made him wary.

Tandy's eyes widened. "Snodgrass. As in—?"

Marissa made the slashing motion across her throat as subtly as possible. "As in George Knibb's niece."

Susan had enough to deal with already without the realization that her dad stole Tandy's car. The young woman adjusted her glasses. "Uncle George's memorial is at three o'clock if you want to come. His body won't be cremated until after an autopsy, but I want the community to pay their respects before anyone brands him a criminal."

Tandy pinched Cocoa's muzzle closed and took him to his fenced off puppy corner. Though she probably felt like growling herself. "I'll be at your uncle's memorial. I'm sorry about his death."

"Me too." Susan looked down. "I'm even sorrier the cops are accusing my dad of killing him."

Tandy left Cocoa so she could hang her jacket on a wall hook. She eyed Marissa as she passed, her look speaking of frustration and disbelief.

Greg didn't seem to be as disbelieving. He planted himself next to Susan's seat. "You think your dad's innocent?"

Susan's spine shot straight. "I *know* he's innocent. Dad loved my uncle more than anyone. Now he can't even attend his brother's funeral because he's in jail for his murder."

"Half-brother," Tandy corrected.

Marissa shrugged at Tandy. For starters, the half-sibling thing didn't really matter. Plus, it could be possible that there was another killer. She didn't want it to be Derrick Snodgrass anymore—for Susan's sake.

Tandy grimaced before turning to wash her hands and get to work.

Greg propped an elbow on the counter to face Susan. "Does your father have an alibi for the time of the murder?"

Susan slouched back into her depressed state. "He was working at the garage. None of the other employees were there yet, so they can't vouch for him."

Tandy leaned a hip against the counter while she dried her hands, a sure indicator of coming sarcasm. "Does he have an excuse for stealing my car too?"

So much for Marissa helping Susan.

The young woman's forehead lined as she turned toward Tandy. She had beautiful skin, and Marissa hated to see her getting wrinkles. "That was your car? I didn't know. Dad said he was going to pay my college tuition. I guess he resorted to grand theft auto to make the payments."

Tandy glanced at Susan's mug with a smirk as if her tea preference alone made her an unreliable witness. "You don't think George caught him trying to steal the Corvette too?"

Randon strode through the door like he had super hearing and was just waiting for his car to be mentioned so he could show up and annoy people.

Susan didn't even react to the bell as her gaze hardened at Tandy. "Even if Dad stole the Corvette, he would have turned himself in before turning on family."

Randon stopped in his tracks. Apparently, he hadn't been summoned by discussion of his vehicle and wasn't expecting to run into relatives of the thief on his coffee break. He leaned forward to get a better look at Princess Bubblegum. "Your dad stole my car? Is it in police possession? Is it damaged?"

Susan spun in her seat. "My dad claims he *didn't* steal your car. I'm only saying, even if he had, he wouldn't have killed his own brother over it."

"Your dad was George's brother?" Randon crossed his arms. "He got caught with Tandy's car, which makes him a thief. Though a stupid thief. Not only did he get arrested, but he chose to steal a car worth so much less than mine." He held up a hand as if that would smooth things over. "No offense, Tandy."

"No, you're right, Randon. The Corvette is worth a lot more than my Bug. It's worth enough that someone thought it was worth killing for." Tandy scooped beans into the grinder, then waved the scoop in the air. "Susan, you said your dad wouldn't kill your uncle, but what if he didn't realize who he was hitting over the head with a rock? Or maybe he did know who he was hitting, but he didn't intend to kill him, just knock him out so he could finish stealing the Corvette without getting caught? If it's not him, then you're saying there's another car thief out there."

Randon stepped forward, sandwiching Susan between him and Tandy. "Do you actually think this other criminal randomly happened to steal my car on the same day Tandy's was stolen in a tiny town where car theft has never been a problem?"

Susan's head swiveled back and forth like she was watching a tennis game, except instead of watching a ball, it was her father getting slammed. Her lips quivered, and her eyes filled with tears.

"I don't *think* so." Tandy lifted a finger and pressed down on the button of the grinder like a judge pounding a gavel, except her action sent the earthy scent of coffee beans buzzing through the air.

Marissa still wasn't a fan of the smell, but she did desire the energy coffee offered. If she could, she would use it now to rescue the poor college girl who'd come into her tea house for respite. She tugged on Tandy's scarf to pull her toward the doorway.

Tandy gripped the counter and held herself in place.

"Tandy." Marissa spoke sweetly through gritted teeth. "I need your help in the kitchen." She made eye contact with Greg and tilted her head Randon's direction, urging him to intervene on the other end.

Greg gave a slight nod, already in action. He stood and angled his shoulder to block Susan from the angry car owner. "Randon, you're smart enough to know that in America everyone is innocent until proven guilty."

Randon huffed. "I'm also smart enough to know the judicial system doesn't always work. And I want my car back."

Susan stood to face him, her simmering pain heating up

into a boiling rage. Perhaps her pink hair came from being a hot-tempered redhead who'd tried to bleach the color out. "All right, smarty. Don't you think if my dad took your car, the police would have found it by now?"

Greg pulled out a business card. He could probably help Susan more than a cup of tea could. "Your father might have a good case. I'm a defense attorney, if he needs representation."

Tandy finally let go of the counter and let Marissa drag her out of the room. She must not have had any more snappy responses to Susan's argument.

Marissa lowered her voice to keep from being overheard. "Just because you're mad at Susan's dad doesn't give you the right to try to drive off our customers."

Tandy plucked one of Marissa's cranberry scones off a cooling rack and stuffed half of it in her mouth. "She wasn't one of *my* customers. And Cocoa didn't like her, so she's probably a criminal too." Her tone lightened. "By the way, what kind of tea did she order?"

Marissa pulled a Valentine's platter from the shelf to use for displaying her pastries as well as rescuing them from Tandy's stomach. "It's the new chocolate tea I'm featuring this week. Chocolate is known to release endorphins, so I thought it might help her feel better."

Tandy spoke around the chunk in her cheek. "You made her feel good enough to defend a killer." She glanced toward the storefront. "Is that the kind of tea you fixed Connor yesterday?"

Marissa paused, thinking back. "No, I made him what Latinos call *té con leche*. But why are we talking about that?"

Tandy reached for another scone.

Marissa hit her hand away.

"Because I'd rather talk shop than discuss the fact that

my boyfriend is out there, offering to represent the man who stole my car and probably killed his brother. It's like his job is more important than me."

"You really think so?"

"Sometimes it feels that way." Tandy unwrapped her scarf from around her neck. "But that doesn't mean you can beat us in The Dating Game. We've never broken up before the way you and Connor have, so we're still a stronger couple."

Marissa waved away the ridiculous claim. Nobody could beat her and Connor. They had no secrets from each other.

"I meant, do you really think Susan's dad is a killer?" Marissa set the tray down and twisted to get a better look at the hurting young woman out front. She was now flanked by both Greg and Randon, who seemed to be offering an apology. That had to be a first. "And do you think Greg believes he's innocent?"

"It's not like he needs the work." Tandy swiped another scone. "I'm going to find the facts to prove Derrick Snodgrass guilty and get Greg to change his mind about defending him in court. I can't imagine Greg would want to defend a murderer if he knew the truth. Then he'll have more time for me."

Marissa reached for a scone of her own and chewed in contemplation. Her pastry was the perfect combination of tangy and sweet. She only needed something warm to wash it down. "If your investigation ensures George's killer goes to jail, then I'll help."

"Good." Tandy headed toward the front of the shop. "You can handle business for me while I run over to Billie's and find out what's happening with the break-in."

Not what Marissa had in mind, but at least the rest of her scones would be safe. "Fine."

Tandy disappeared then returned with her jacket. "You do know how to work the espresso machine, right?"

"I do, but nobody is going to be drinking espressos." Nobody except Marissa. She needed the energy to handle what was gearing up to become another emotional day.

Tandy swept past Greg and retrieved her pup for the walk to Grandma's Attic. Her boyfriend didn't even seem to notice. So much for their reconnection.

Cocoa's warm tongue licked her cheek in a reminder of who really loved her. She kissed the top of his tiny head and strode toward the exit.

Connor pulled the door open from the outside then waited for Tandy to join him on the sidewalk. "Did you tell Marissa you kissed me? Did she kick you out?"

Tandy snuggled Cocoa into the front of her jacket and zipped it up to both their necks to keep warm. The kiss was the least of her worries. Should it bother her that Greg didn't care more? "No. Though Greg's in there, and he knows."

Connor remained outside with her and let the door fall closed.

"I'm headed to Billie's to ask about the break-in. George's brother is claiming he didn't kill George. I want to find out if Griffin's been able to pin the break-in on him. If so, then he has to be the murderer. Otherwise, why would he try to destroy evidence of the crime?"

"Makes sense." Connor reached for the doorknob once again and peered apprehensively through the window.

Tandy took a step toward Billie's then paused. "Hey, if you want to switch drinks again, ask Marissa to make you the *té con leche.*"

Connor glanced over his shoulder at her with a not-happening face. "Sorry, I'm headed straight upstairs to avoid the guy who knows his girlfriend kissed me."

Tandy gave him a small smile. She could tell Connor that he was worrying over nothing, but she didn't want to admit how little Greg seemed to care. She crossed the street and entered the antique store to find glass workers repairing the front window and Griffin listening in as the FBI agent questioned Billie. Did Agent McNeil also doubt the perp Griffin had in custody was George's killer? Griffin wouldn't be too happy about that.

Billie gave her a brave smile. "I guess a security camera isn't enough. I need an actual alarm system."

Tandy glanced from the woman to the law enforcement officers. "Without an alarm system, you don't know what time the store was actually broken into, do you?"

Billie shook her head.

Agent McNeil barely glanced at her before focusing on Billie once again.

Griffin, however, approached her. Maybe hoping she could help him solve the case. She *had* been the one who'd called him after tracking down her car thief.

He scrolled through the notes on his phone. "I've questioned the surrounding businesses, and it seems the break-in didn't happen until most shop owners went home for the evening. That puts the crime between five and seven p.m. when Marissa noticed the broken window."

Tandy nodded. Nothing surprising there. "Then it's possible that after you went to the body shop, Derrick Snodgrass overheard your claim that Billie had a security camera. Could he have taken off in my Bug, stopped here to destroy the evidence, then continued on to where Connor and I saw him?"

Griffin peeked at the FBI agent as if to make sure there hadn't been any sudden revelations to contradict her assertion. "I'd say that's the most likely scenario."

Tandy scanned the room. Nothing appeared broken or stolen. "Any other scenarios you are considering?" Certainly not a robbery. It had to have been about the camera.

Griffin leaned forward like he was about to tell secrets.

"Sheriff." McNeil stopped him without even looking over. "None of this is public information."

Billie motioned toward her. "Tandy isn't the public. She's a victim. The stolen Volkswagen belonged to her."

The agent flipped through a pad of paper. He'd probably been doing his job so long that he'd started before smartphones were a thing. "I'm aware of that."

Tandy arched her eyebrows at the man's response. He'd be handsome except for his arrogant indifference.

She leaned in toward Griffin. They could tell secrets if they wanted to. "Is Agent McNeil irked that you arrested the suspect without him?"

Griffin didn't answer, but his chest puffed up a little bigger.

Tandy faced the big city agent again. Funny she should think of him as an outsider when she'd moved from a big city only a few months ago. "Besides being a victim, my boyfriend's also offering to represent your suspect in court. The suspect's daughter is across the street at my coffee shop, telling everyone he's not guilty."

That got McNeil's attention. It came in the form of a scornful stare.

"Why?" Griffin held his hands wide as if addressing the question to heaven. "Why would Greg do this to me?"

"Don't worry about it." McNeil strode toward the door, pausing to pat Griffin on the back. "You did good work last night, and this case is going to be airtight."

Tandy eyed the agent suspiciously. He seemed a little too buddy-buddy after having his case solved for him. "Why are you here then, McNeil?"

McNeil stopped and sized her up. "If it makes you feel better, Miss Brandt, you can tell your boyfriend I received a tip from one of my informants that someone from the body shop had been illegally ordering keys from car manufacturers. I had my eye on Derrick Snodgrass since he has a recent history of grand theft auto."

This helped Tandy's case more than Greg's. "So you were already here investigating when George was killed?"

McNeil continued like she hadn't even asked a question. "Snodgrass couldn't keep his hand out of the cookie jar and decided to start with Randon's collector car, but he got stuck in the snow. He likely took off for the shop to use a tow truck, but George saw the Corvette first and assumed Randon was the one who'd abandoned it. Unfortunately, George must have caught his brother trying to steal it again."

That's exactly what she'd suspected. "Susan doesn't think her dad would kill his brother over a car, but I told her that it could have been an accident."

McNeil's drab blue eyes glinted with a trace of respect. "Or it could have been an act of rage."

Tandy nodded slowly. She'd seen the rage in Derrick's daughter. Who was to say that wasn't a family trait? "You suspected Derrick Snodgrass all along?"

"I only needed solid evidence." McNeil chomped his gum. "I'd expected that evidence to come from the security camera here at Grandma's Attic, but luckily you saw Snodgrass driving your car last night. Thanks to you, Miss Brandt, I get to wrap up the case and head home."

Case closed. Tandy would tell Greg about the electronic

keys Derrick had ordered illegally, and Greg would drop his client. Tandy sighed in relief.

Griffin echoed the sigh.

Though McNeil should be the one sighing. How nice that he got to go home when the rest of them were heading to George's memorial.

Tandy stayed behind as the law enforcement officers packed up and took off. She wanted to see how the other victimized business owner was doing.

Billie sliced up an apple, put the pieces on a vintage Asian rice bowl, and lowered it to the floor for Cocoa who wiggled against Tandy's chest at the sight. Tandy unzipped her jacket to release the hound. She didn't mind the treat as it cleaned Cocoa's teeth and freshened his breath. She didn't agree that he should be served on such a costly and fragile dish, but Billie spoiled everyone she met.

As if on cue, Billie looked up at her. "Apple cider?"

Tandy smiled. "You know that stuff is too sweet for me." Plus she had to save room for *té con leche*. "I came over to see how you're feeling after the break-in?"

Billie hugged herself. "I bought the security camera so things like this wouldn't happen. At least nobody else was hurt."

Tandy nodded. "We're getting a security camera too. Are you going to George's funeral?"

"Yes." Billie looked at her vintage diamond watch. "Joseph is picking me up soon."

"Oh good." Tandy let her eyes wander around the store at the ornate furniture, delicate dishes, and shelves of costume jewelry. It was nice seeing an older woman finding new love, and she hoped she and Greg were still together at that age.

"Are you going with Greg?" Billie asked as though she

could read Tandy's thoughts.

Tandy blinked to get rid of any expressions that might be giving her away. "Yes."

Billie reached out and caressed her arm in a grandmotherly fashion. "Does he know how you feel about him representing the man who stole your car?"

Tandy shrugged off her discomfort with the idea, not Billie's touch. "It's his job."

Billie rubbed up her arm until she was giving Tandy a backrub despite how her tiny frame barely reached Tandy's shoulders. "I'm sure your feelings are more important than his job."

Tandy folded her arms against the helplessness Billie's gentleness released. "I don't want to be selfish."

Billie tilted her head. "It's not selfish to be honest."

Tandy twisted her lips to one side to consider the wording for her emotions. "If you can tell that I'm uncomfortable with him representing the guy who stole my car, he should be able to as well."

"Hmm…" Billie's hand slipped down Tandy's back then she stepped in front to face Tandy. "What you're saying is that you feel like a lower priority, and you're afraid to tell him that because he might not prove you wrong."

Tandy focused on the peacock blue and rust colored interlocking designs of the oriental rug. Why did Billie have to see through her so clearly? "Yes."

"So instead of being vulnerable and telling him how you feel, you're going to run around gathering evidence against his client in hopes that it will convince him to change his mind."

Tandy peeked up. "Maybe. But you make it sound way worse than it is."

Billie met her gaze and gave her hand a firm squeeze.

"It's simple. The first key to communication is to be vulnerable."

Isn't that what Tandy had done that morning while telling him about kissing Connor? That's more than Connor and Marissa had done. So she could be worse off.

As for talk about Greg's work, he'd apologized but then went right back to prioritizing clients over her. If he never changed, was she supposed to keep asking for attention and getting rejected? Or could she learn to deal? AKA manipulate. That didn't sound good either. The term "help" sounded better. She was helping Greg make good decisions for his business. There.

Billie meant well, but the idea of vulnerability could be as outdated as her antiques. These days, a woman had to be tough, independent, and resourceful.

Tandy would help her career man by protecting him from taking on a guilty client. This would be finding justice for George, as well. There was nothing wrong with that.

Marissa flipped the shop sign from open to closed even though it was the middle of the afternoon, but the whole town was pretty much closing down for George's memorial. She pulled on her dress coat with the flared skirt that was too fancy to have pockets and waited for Connor to join her. Her lace dress itched, but it was the only black dress she owned besides the one with the skinny belt and full, knee-length skirt that Tandy had borrowed.

Her friend didn't own a dress and refused to wear lace. Most likely she would pair it with a motorcycle jacket and biker boots. She'd run home to change since she had to take Cocoa back before the service anyway.

Connor descended the stairs, looking like he'd stepped out of a men's catalog rather than pulling a quick-change in the bathroom. She'd barely seen him that day with as hard as he'd been working in the loft, but he was worth the wait. The last time he'd worn a suit and tie was on New Year's Eve when they'd decided to start dating again.

Though this wasn't as festive an occasion, she was glad to have Connor by her side. Focusing on the loss of a life made her more appreciative of the people she still had around.

She pulled on her fur-lined gloves. "I'm so glad I have you."

Connor stopped in front of her at the door, and she lifted her chin for the expected kiss. Instead he tilted his head and studied her. "There's something I need to tell you."

Uh-oh. That didn't sound good. In fact, it sounded like he might want to break up. But how could that be? Everything had been going so well. They were even competing in The Dating Game in a couple days.

Marissa steeled her heart. She was the one who did the breaking up, not the one who got broken up with. "What's that?"

"Last night…" He looked down.

What about last night? It had been a crazy night. He'd been planning to make her spaghetti then ended up tracking down Derrick Snodgrass instead. And she'd discovered Billie's break-in.

Had he been worried about her? Felt bad he didn't make her the spaghetti he'd promised? They hadn't had much alone time lately, but they could make up for it. Life could be worse. "It's okay," she said.

He looked up. A crease formed between his eyebrows.

Tandy burst through the door, full skirt swishing

underneath her leather jacket. "Come on. You guys can ride with us."

Connor blinked wide eyes. "You and…Greg?" he asked.

Marissa bumped him with her shoulder as she turned toward the door. "Who else would she be with? Let's go." She climbed into the backseat and let the seat warmers comfort her like a hug. Tandy climbed in after her, giving Connor the extra leg room of the front seat.

Connor took his spot and tugged at his tie. "How are you, Greg?"

Greg stepped on the gas. "I've been better."

"Oh, yeah?" Did Connor's voice crack? That was weird.

"Yeah. It's weird going to a memorial for the victim your client has been accused of murdering."

Connor nodded for a long moment. "I bet."

Tandy tilted sideways to whisper to Marissa under the smooth jazz playing on the radio. "Greg doesn't believe the FBI that Derrick is the only guilty party."

So that's why Tandy wanted her there. She was supposed to help keep Greg from poking around and investigating at the somber event.

"I feel bad for Susan," Marissa offered aloud as a peace offering. "It would be hard to attend a funeral where everybody believes your dad is the man's killer."

"Especially when you know your dad is innocent," Greg added, turning onto the side street.

Connor shifted a couple of times in his seat. "Everybody thinks their loved ones are innocent."

Greg pulled into the parking lot. "She says that her dad wouldn't have risked stealing Randon's car because it was so rare. He stole cars to sell parts, and the risk of putting stolen parts from a one-of-a-kind Corvette out on the market was not worth the money he could make off it."

Marissa tapped her chin. This was new information to her. "If Randon's car was really that rare, who would steal it and how would they expect to get away with it?"

Tandy narrowed her eyes at the indication Marissa was considering Derrick's claim. But she didn't speak, so she must not have had an answer to Marissa's very valid question.

Greg pulled to a stop and parked before twisting around to look at her. "That is a great question, Marissa."

Tandy lifted a finger. "If it's a collector's car, then maybe a collector wanted it. They could have known about Derrick's criminal history and offered him money to steal the car. We should ask Randon if he's had any offers or if he beat out someone in an auction for the vehicle."

Greg shot Tandy a measuring glance. Was he measuring the plausibility of her suggestion or the motive behind it? "We should definitely talk to Randon. Because one of those collectors could also have hired a different thief or stolen the car themselves."

Marissa tapped her chin and looked at Tandy. She understood Tandy's reasoning for wanting to see Derrick Snodgrass behind bars for the theft of her own vehicle, but was she doing justice a disservice by not considering all angles? And more importantly, could her attempt at single-handedly trying to fix her relationship with Greg be doing more damage than good?

Tandy smiled tightly. "Let's go talk to Randon."

Chapter Six

Tandy spotted Randon at the front of the full church, though it was kind of hard to miss him sitting in the front pew next to the girl with pink hair. How did that happen?

She followed Greg down their row then turned to nudge Marissa. "I thought Randon was mad at Susan for defending the man who stole his car."

Marissa glanced the direction she pointed like it was no big deal. "Oh, yeah. Well after you left for Billie's, Susan had a little breakdown, and Randon ended up comforting her."

Tandy narrowed her eyes as she sat on the hard, wooden pew. First of all, she didn't know Randon was capable of caring about anybody's feelings other than his own. Secondly, if he was capable, why did it have to be Susan's feelings he cared about? It might cause him to tune out his inner conspiracy theorist.

Marissa beamed like she'd set them up herself. And maybe she had. She was a sucker for the color pink. "I think they are kind of adorable together."

Tandy gritted her teeth and focused on the funeral program. There was a photo of George, grinning up at her in his coveralls. Her jaw released with grief. Had it only been the day before when she'd served him coffee?

Organ music hushed the crowd into silence. She'd been to funerals before but always for elderly folks who'd lived long lives. Like Opal the organist, who was living longer than anyone expected her to, though she didn't seem happy about it.

Pastor Meade stepped to the podium. "Thank you all for coming today. George was a dear friend of mine, and not only because he saved me a lot of money on church van repairs."

The crowd chuckled, and Greg reached for her hand. Tandy took a deep breath and forced herself to relax. She'd wanted more time with her boyfriend, right? It was just a shame an innocent man had to die for her to get it.

The Pastor cleared emotion from his throat. "George came to me a decade ago after getting out of prison. He wanted to confess his sins. I told him he didn't need me to do that."

Tandy glanced toward Susan. Would the talk of confession make her feel guilty?

Pastor Meade continued. "I explained that God is always available for communication with us. All we have to do is talk, listen, and value that time together as a gift because God values us."

The word "value" plucked at one of Tandy's heartstrings, and her attention turned from Randon and his walking Valentine to the minister who was speaking to her soul. Value was what she wanted from Greg, wasn't it? And it was exactly what she was afraid to ask for. As if she didn't think she was worth valuing.

She clutched his hand and shifted closer. Could he sense that she felt this way?

"After that..." Pastor Meade pressed his lips together for a moment before continuing. "He taught me about prayer. He came here on the morning he died as he joined me every Wednesday morning at six a.m. I've never heard anyone so vulnerable when they talked to God."

Vulnerable? Like Billie suggested was the key to communicating with people? Why would one need to be vulnerable with God if He already knew everything?

Tandy glanced over her shoulder to find Billie, but the woman had her head down with eyes closed as if in prayer.

"George didn't only listen, but he would search for understanding in everything. He would quote Proverbs 25:2, saying, 'It is the glory of God to conceal a matter; to search out a matter is the glory of kings.'" Pastor Meade shook his head. "He drew closer to God to really see things from God's perspective. And that, my friend, is how I believe you define a man after God's own heart."

Tandy shifted at the idea. Was she more after a man's heart than God's heart?

"The George we know went straight from prison jumpsuits to mechanic jumpsuits, but he lived the end of his life like King David. And right now…" The pastor pointed to heaven. "I believe he's got a crown on his head that he's about to go cast at the feet of Jesus. Because God didn't just have value in his life. God gave him value."

Whoa. What a visual. Made the value gotten out of stealing a car seem kind of silly.

Marissa leaned closer. "How is anyone supposed to follow that?"

A few people tried. Two employees, his butcher—apparently he ate a lot of meat, his barber—which was funny because he *didn't* have a lot of hair, and then Susan stood up.

Tandy sat at attention. Was Susan even doubtful of her dad at all? How would it affect her if she found out he was a murderer?

Susan adjusted the microphone then tucked a pink strand of hair behind her ear. "My first memory of Uncle George was when he came to visit and brought me a Power Wheels. Most kids had bikes, but I had my little pink Barbie Convertible."

That still didn't justify the pink hair.

"I'd come visit him here in the summers."

Tandy could relate to that. Grace Springs had been her happy place as a child.

"And when my dad went to jail." Susan looked down.

Tandy's heart melted a little, and she rolled her eyes at herself. She wanted Derrick to be guilty because that would make her life easier, but the more Susan spoke, the more she didn't want Susan to have to go through any more pain. No wonder Greg fell for this sob story.

Susan shared memories of George teaching her how to drive, and how she'd driven his Fiat through a garage door, not to mention that time she'd worked in his body shop and accidentally wrote down the order for him to paint a car blue instead of black. They tugged at Tandy's heartstrings until the point she was beginning to hope the girl's father wasn't guilty of killing her hero.

They finished by singing Amazing Grace, which was pretty much the anthem for Grace Springs, despite the overwhelming judgement that always came from the organist, Opal. As the music faded, they headed down the aisle to the vestibule where they waited to discreetly question Randon.

Marissa leaned close. "You still think her dad did it?"

Tandy gave a relenting lip twist. "It still makes the most sense, and he still needs to go to jail for stealing my car, but..."

Greg lifted his eyebrows with excited approval. "But?"

Dang, he'd overheard. "For Susan's sake, I hope he's innocent."

Connor stuffed his hands in his pockets and rocked back and forth from his heels to his toes with a guilty glance toward Greg. "It's good to have an open mind. Like the pastor said in there, we need to try to see things from other people's perspectives."

Marissa tilted her head. "I think he was talking about God's perspective, not other people's."

Connor shrugged. "Well, we want good communication with other people too."

Tandy arched an eyebrow. He was one to talk. He couldn't even tell Marissa about their kiss. Though maybe that's what he was hinting at here. A message for Marissa to try to see things from his point of view and not only her own so he didn't have to worry about being vulnerable. Hey, those two things kind of went together. Vulnerability and understanding.

Randon and Susan exited the arched doorways together, though she was surrounded by little old ladies offering to bake her casseroles while he was not.

"Hey, Randon." Greg motioned him over.

Randon checked on his Pretty-in-Pink Barbie before joining them. "Thanks for coming, you guys. It means a lot to Susan to have the support of the community."

Tandy pinched her lips shut rather than say, *Yo, dude, her dad probably stole your car, remember?* Because while Tandy wanted to protect Susan now, it was weird for Randon to want to protect her. He was too in love with his own reflection in the mirror.

"It's a Valentine's miracle," Marissa whispered, obviously doing better at the open mind thing than she was.

Greg planted a hand on Randon's shoulder. "I am Susan's dad's attorney now, so naturally I'll support her. I simply want to ask you a couple questions that might help support her even more."

"Sure. Shoot." Randon shrugged. All of a sudden, a decent human being.

Greg released his hold on Randon so he could

gesticulate. Part of his courtroom dramatics that often leaked into their personal lives. "I was wondering if there was anyone else interested in your Corvette when you bought it. Maybe a collector who would do anything to get the car back in his…or her…possession." How very PC of him to not disqualify a woman from killing a giant tough guy with a rock.

"Oh, yeah." Randon glanced over his shoulder at Pinkie Pie. "I actually told all this to the police, but I can tell you too."

Tandy frowned. "Did they investigate this suspect?"

"Probably. But I don't really consider him a suspect."

No other words could have made Tandy more suspicious. "Why's that?"

"Meh." A very Randon word. "He's as anti-theft as you can get. Specifically, that's his job. He works for a car company and creates technology to prevent theft."

Warning bells rang in Tandy's head and vibrated her heart. Though Randon couldn't possibly be talking about the person she knew in this field. Even if the person she knew had always wanted a Corvette and recently landed a huge signing bonus when moving to Toledo, the chances had to be slim. There were lots of car companies in the area.

Greg chuckled. "In my mind that makes him the perfect criminal. I want to look him up. What's his name?"

Tandy held her breath. She wouldn't breathe again until Randon gave them a name other than the one she was thinking. Any name but Vic Whitaker would do. She wouldn't be picky.

"Vic Whitaker."

She had to have heard wrong. She was dreaming. No, she was nightmaring.

"Vic Whitaker?" Greg typed the name into his phone.

She could see it spelled out in black and white.

He Googled. Her boyfriend was investigating her ex right there in front of her. And she'd thought telling him about kissing Connor had been awkward.

Her lungs burned, and the edges of her vision turned hazy. It was either breathe or pass out *then* breathe, because consciousness was kind of required for holding one's breath. She gave in and gasped for air, drawing attention from all eyes around.

The words burst out before Tandy could stop them. "Derrick did it. And I'm going to prove it."

Marissa left Greg and Tandy to work on their investigation or relationship issues—or whatever weird thing was going on between them—and headed into her shop. George's reception had lasted longer than expected, so she was free to keep the shop closed for the day, but she wanted to prep for the morning.

She flipped on the light switch, illuminating the space gold against the gray haze of twilight and locked the door behind her. The place had come a long way since they'd bought it, but she couldn't ever change the fact that her very first customer would no longer return. He'd never even tried her crumpet.

Marissa gave a wistful smile at all the tough guy stories people had shared after the memorial. George preferred messy foods like chicken wings, he'd held season tickets for the Cleveland Cavaliers, and, as they all knew, he only wore coveralls.

Jumpsuit George. She still had his jumpsuit, didn't she? Dropping her purse and coat on a table, she made her way behind the counter to where she'd last stashed it. Correction, she'd *hidden* it because she didn't want anyone to know she'd agreed to try it on.

She'd try it on now. In George's honor.

With reverence, Marissa lifted the stiff material and headed toward the bathroom. After all, she had to take off her dress in order to put on the coveralls. She made the switch and looked in the mirror.

Not attractive at all. So ugly, in fact, that it made her smile. Give her a wrench and wipe a smear of grease on her cheek, and nobody would ever recognize her. She twisted side to side, striking several tough-girl poses. Arms crossed. Hands on hips. No, guys didn't do that. She shoved her hands in the giant front pockets of the coveralls instead. Her right fingers slid over something smooth and rectangular. Like a phone. Had George left his cell phone behind?

She pulled the device out. It didn't have a screen. It was more like a box with little colored bumps on one end that looked as if they lit up green and red when a switch was flipped.

It was an electronic gadget of some kind. Like the microphone transmitters used for headsets during beauty pageants. George certainly wouldn't have been using it for such a purpose. What could this box be transmitting? And where would it send the signal? She flipped the tiny black switch. Her pocket vibrated.

Marissa reached inside the jumpsuit pocket once again and pulled out another smaller device with an extendable antenna. A set? Surely, George hadn't known he'd given this to her. Or had he done it on purpose? Did he realize he was in danger, and he'd hidden this in the jumpsuit for safe keeping?

She bit her lip, and her heartbeat thudded louder. If she

was holding evidence, she needed to turn it over to the police.

She looked around suspiciously as if George's murderer was watching her, waiting for his opportunity to pounce. Since she was still in the bathroom alone, the only movement was that of her own reflection.

She widened her eyes at herself. "What do I do?"

The sooner she got this to the sheriff, the better. She rushed out to grab her purse, still in the jumpsuit. Should she change so that her shoes matched her outfit, or should she wear the heels anyway? Oh, there. The snow boots Connor brought her that she'd also stashed behind the counter without intent to ever wear.

She set the mystery device on the bar and scrambled for the boots. They were truly hideous. All brown and rubbery. Who in the world designed those things? UPS employees?

She grabbed her key fob to start her Jeep and warm it up while putting on the most practical shoes she'd ever owned. The fob beeped, her tail lights flashed outside, and right there on the counter, the mystery device light flashed from red to green.

She froze. And stared.

Green meant go. What triggered the device to be ready to go? All she'd done was push the key fob.

Her stomach churned in dread. George had been a car thief in his former life, a car thief had likely killed him, and if she wasn't jumping to conclusions, she was in possession of a device that would help people steal cars.

Unfortunately, she had a history of jumping to conclusions. Like the time she suspected Tandy of murder.

She could be fearful over nothing. There was only one way to find out.

Marissa shoved her bare feet into ugly—but warm—boots, left her car keys and the device with the antennae on the counter, and marched outside with the other half. She stopped in front of the door to her car and waited. Nothing happened.

She shook the box and turned it around to see if she was missing anything. Her chest heaved in relief. This wasn't a car-theft tool.

She switched it off and took a step backwards. Her clunky sole caught on the curb. She tipped sideways but her boots with the chunky traction *didn't* slip, and she was able to lunge wide and catch herself.

Whew. That was a close one. So close she could never tell Connor. He might try to get her to wear these ugly boots all the time. As it was, she hoped nobody in town had seen her wearing them at all, especially while in the brown jumpsuit, which was a fitting color for the pretzel she'd had to twist herself into to prevent a fall.

Laughing at what she must look like, she shifted her weight and pushed herself upright. Her thumb bumped the button on the box in her hands. The light flashed green again, and the lock inside her car door popped up. Her laughter died.

Marissa blinked at the box in her hands. She'd broken into her own car. That wasn't good for George, and it wasn't good for her. She had to get this thing to Sheriff Griffin before she found herself in more trouble.

Chapter Seven

TANDY WAITED IN GREG'S OFFICE FOR her ride home. He'd said he only needed to stop by for a minute, but that had been fifteen minutes ago. Was he in his office, trying to dig up more dirt on Vic? She might be better off asking Marissa for a ride, if her business partner was still at work.

Strolling to the window, Tandy peered down the street toward their shop. There was Marissa's Jeep. And there was Marissa, blonde hair flying. She must have slipped.

Naturally, an attractive African-American man appeared from nearby to catch her. Though he didn't seem to be as gentle as Connor. And with the way Marissa tried to push him away, she apparently assumed he was making a pass at her. Pshaw. Beauty queens.

The trunk lid of a blue sedan in front of Marissa rose high. Tandy squinted to get a better look at what was going on because from this angle it appeared the man was shoving Marissa inside.

The trunk slammed closed. Marissa was gone.

Tandy jolted in shock. She'd just witnessed a kidnapping.

"Greg, call the police," she shouted before bursting into the frigid air, determined to save her friend. Marissa would thank her later for wearing biker boots with the dress instead of the high heels she'd offered.

The man had already climbed behind his steering wheel.

She charged. He stepped on the gas and rolled out of reach.

Tandy's stomach lurched. Her feet pounded pavement.

She squinted at the license plate.

It started with an SWM. Skinny White Mocha. She could remember that. But she couldn't catch the rest of the plate number before they were too small to see.

Skinny white mocha. Skinny white mocha, she silently chanted in case he got away and that was all police had to go off of in their manhunt. Though she wasn't going to give up that easily.

Tandy raced down the block. Of all the times for her car to be impounded. Was she going to lose her partner because of this?

Her legs threatened to trip over themselves in haste. Her lungs burned. Her breath scratched at the air. She pushed faster.

The kidnapper had to slow for the corner ahead. Maybe she could catch him.

If not, it looked like he'd be heading past the police station. She wouldn't stop until she got there. Officer Griffin could jump in his police cruiser and put out an APB. Hopefully Greg would already have gotten ahold of him, and he'd be ready for action.

If not, Tandy might never see Marissa again.

In the dark, confined space, Marissa pressed against the trunk lid with her palms. She would not panic. Though it may feel like she'd been buried alive, she was not underground. She wasn't tied up either. She could escape.

The car slowed. It hadn't gone very far. Was the kidnapper having second thoughts?

The car turned, rolling her sideways and cramming her head against the hard, side panel.

So much for second thoughts. If they were turning on the street that it felt like they were turning on, it wouldn't be long before they were speeding up and heading out of town. Her heart thumped louder than the bass coming from the speakers.

She needed to move fast. Before they were on the highway and it was too dangerous to dive out of the vehicle. Or before she passed out from hyperventilation.

She'd find the trunk release latch. Newer cars should have those. Where would it be?

She twisted and turned, running her fingers along the edges of what very well could be her coffin. There. Something sharp caught her pinkie. She pinched fingertips together to grip the metal prong. Now what? Pull? Twist? No response. Nothing. Had the lever been broken off?

Her previous surge of hope erupted into desperation. She pounded the lid with the side of her fists. "Let me out!"

Would anyone hear? Or was she only making the kidnapper angry? She didn't care. She'd be *angrier*. She had the right to be.

She kicked like a ninja. The thick metal didn't budge even for her stomping boots, but reverberations from the impact jammed her hip. That wasn't going to work…unless she kicked something less solid. Something like the taillight.

Yes. She'd seen that in a movie once.

She angled her body toward the end of the car, her neck cranked at an awkward angle against the seat back. If this didn't work, she'd claw at the seat next.

"Marissa!" Tandy's frantic cry between gulps of air would be hard to understand. But she'd try anyway. With the car's pause at the corner ahead of her, she was gaining on them. "Open the trunk!"

The car turned and disappeared past the barber shop. *Skinny white mocha, skinny white mocha...* Was there a number two on the license plate, or was she only thinking two because it was a Chrysler 200?

Tandy cut the corner and pumped her arms to pick up more speed. She was almost to the police station. One more block...

The car slowed ahead of her. Did he run out of gas? Or was Marissa making such a racket that he couldn't take it anymore, and he was going to kill her right there?

He wouldn't get away with it. Not only would Tandy fight him, but Sheriff Griffin would be available as backup.

The driver pulled to the curb. Either he was the stupidest criminal on the planet, or he was turning himself in. She'd go with the criminal theory and not let up until the man was arrested.

She continued her pursuit, angling herself forward like an arrow to make her body aerodynamic.

The driver opened his door. He climbed out and circled toward the trunk. Tandy was not going to let him even look at her friend again.

Lowering one shoulder the way she'd seen football players do, Tandy rammed into the man's side.

He staggered. Pivoted. Held up his palms in defense.

She barreled forward to push him farther back.

His hands caught her before she could connect. "Tandy?"

She bunched her fists, pulled them up between the two of them, and stared into the dark, laughing eyes of her ex-boyfriend. The fight drained to her toes.

Vic Whitaker was on the suspect list. He was in town. And he'd kidnapped her best friend.

She fought for breath, and not only because she'd been in a full out sprint only a moment before. "Vic?"

One cheek dimpled. "I know you were upset that I broke up with you, but I didn't realize you were *this* upset. And you dressed up for me. That's a first."

She stepped away, smoothing her stupid skirt, and looking for solid footing on which to have this bizarre conversation. She willed her pulse to slow down as well. "You kidnapped my business partner."

Vic crossed his arms. "You do business with car thieves?"

"What? No. She sells tea. As bad as that may be, it's hardly criminal."

Metal smashed, glass cracked, and a taillight burst from the corner of the vehicle. An ugly brown boot took its place.

"Tandy?" The muffled voice sounded like Marissa's, but that couldn't be her foot in the ugly brown boot.

"Oh fantastic." Vic pointed the direction of the mess. "I caught her trying to steal a Jeep. I made a citizen's arrest to help the police. I didn't realize she'd damage my car."

What had Vic expected? He certainly couldn't expect her to believe his excuse. "She *owns* a Jeep. Maybe she got locked out and had to break in." Tandy raised her voice so Marissa could hear. "Marissa, did you lock your keys in the Jeep again?"

The boot disappeared, and part of Marissa's face filled the hole. "No!" Her response came with enough force that Tandy was a little scared of releasing her from the trunk.

Tandy shook her head at Vic. "There has to be a logical explanation for why she was breaking into a Jeep. You should have at least asked her what was going on rather than resort to kidnapping. That's not how you make a citizen's arrest."

"Police lock criminals in the back of their cars. I was doing the same." Vic lifted a shoulder, as if no responsibility rested there. "As soon as I let her out, you'll see that she wasn't using a coat hanger to get into her own vehicle. She has what's known as a Relay Attack Unit designed to unlock cars without a key. Only a car thief would own such a thing."

Now he was overtly lying. And Tandy would be able to prove it. Good thing he'd broken up with her last year. Otherwise she'd be dating a liar.

Sheriff Griffin sauntered from the police department. "What's going on here, Tandy? Why did you have Greg call me?"

Marissa banged against the inside of the trunk in response. "Griffin, get me out of here!"

Griffin's hand rose to his holster.

Vic sidestepped farther behind his car as if he might need to duck from bullets.

Griffin pointed with his free hand at Marissa's face in the hole. "Is someone in your trunk, sir?"

"It's me. Marissa."

Griffin's eyes narrowed in suspicion. "Let her out right now."

The trunk opened, and fresh air stung Marissa's skin like the glorious first dip of one's toes into Lake Erie. She gasped for breath, struggled ungracefully over the edge of the trunk and landed firmly on solid ground.

Standing tall, she faced her captor. A bald, black man with a goatee around his blinding white smile. Why was he smiling?

Tandy's gaze remained on her, as well. "Marissa? Why are you dressed like that?"

Marissa threw her hands in the air. Why did it matter

what she was wearing? This wasn't a beauty pageant or anything. "I like to dress for the occasion, and wearing a jumpsuit is a lot more comfortable than a lace dress when you're *crammed in a trunk*." She jabbed a finger the direction they should all be looking—at her kidnapper. "Arrest him."

Tandy blew out her breath but then stepped closer as if joining her side. "Vic claims he was making a citizen's arrest because you were stealing cars. Show him you don't have a device for stealing cars with you."

"That's preposterous. I..." Oh, wait. She'd been trying out the contraption when she'd been abducted. But that wasn't the issue. The issue was that she'd been abducted.

Her abductor leaned forward and pointed inside the trunk. "It's right there."

Not cool.

Tandy blinked in surprise. "How do we know that's not yours, Vic?"

Vic guffawed. "It will have her fingerprints on it, Tandy."

Ugh. It would.

Griffin waved them all away from the vehicle and pressed the button on the radio transmitter attached to his collar. "Griffin to Kristin. I need an evidence bag out front. Over."

Evidence against her?

Marissa huffed. "Okay. It's going to have my fingerprints on it. I found the thing in the pocket of this jumpsuit George gave me. I was trying it out on my car to see if it really was what I thought it was. Then I was kidnapped. *Kidnapped.* Have we forgotten that part, people?"

Griffin released the tentative grip on his weapon and stroked his chin. "You're confirming this gentleman's claims that he saw you breaking into a vehicle?"

"No. Well, yes." Marissa jutted her chin. "But he's a

kidnapper, and I don't think this is his first kidnapping. The safety release lever in his trunk had been removed. Otherwise I could have escaped without kicking out the taillight."

"You didn't have to kick out the light. I'd already stopped."

Marissa glared.

The sheriff's face swiveled the kidnapper's way.

The man's dimples flashed a couple times as if he was fighting a smile. Marissa had never hated dimples so much.

Even Tandy narrowed her eyes. Poor girl. From the conversation Marissa could make out through the trunk, she'd barely escaped a toxic relationship with this criminal.

The perp held up his right hand. "Confession: I kidnapped my buddy for a bachelor party last weekend. That's why I disconnected the trunk release—so he couldn't escape. But also why I thought the trunk would be the safest way to get this car thief to the police station."

Tandy tilted her head. "Which buddy is getting married?"

"DeShawn."

"He finally proposed, huh? I'm happy for Shanice."

Marissa stomped her foot. "Excuse me. We should be talking about handcuffs, not wedding rings."

Griffin cleared his throat. "I won't arrest you for tampering with evidence, Marissa, but I'm going to need the jumpsuit you're wearing along with this mystery device. You should have turned it in when you were giving your statement about George's murder."

Marissa had trouble focusing on anything Griffin had said after the part about claiming she tampered with evidence. She was the victim here. "You could arrest *me*?" her voice squeaked.

Tandy's ex nodded. "He could. If you'd been

forthcoming with the evidence, I never would have mistaken you for a thief."

Marissa held out her hands in disbelief. "It's not my fault you turned to a life of crime."

A corner of Tandy's lips curved up. "Vic works as an automotive engineer. Car theft prevention is his specialty. He's kind of passionate about it."

Marissa wanted to show him how passionate she was against kidnapping. And murder. Because if this guy had such knowledge about car theft, he could have been the one to steal Randon's Corvette and kill George.

Wait. "Did you say his name is Vic? As in Vic Whitaker, the auto collector who was also interested in buying the Corvette?"

Tandy's smile slipped. She nodded.

Vic's gaze ricocheted between them. "What 'Vette?"

Like he didn't know. Marissa pressed her lips together to gain composure before exploding. So *this* was why Tandy was set on pinning the crime on Derrick Snodgrass. Either she still had a thing for her ex and didn't believe he was guilty, or she couldn't stand him and didn't want him around for the investigation. "Isn't that convenient? A guy who wanted Randon's car and knows all about car theft turns up at the exact same time as an FBI investigation."

All eyes focused on the criminal. Finally.

Griffin's hand returned to his weapon. "Sir, what exactly are you doing in town today?"

The guy lifted his palms. The perfect position for handcuffing. "I did want the 'Vette. When I lost it to Randon Evans, I looked him up on the internet to find out more about what kinds of cars he collects, and that's when I saw that article about Tandy solving a murder case here in Grace Springs. I came here to see her."

Tandy's eyebrows arched. "Why?"

His hands dropped to his sides. "I miss you more than that 'Vette."

Tandy's mind buzzed with static. She'd once longed for this day. But Vic's timing couldn't be worse.

Marissa stuck her hands on her hips. "You're too late. She's dating an attorney now. And as part of his job defending his client, he's going to prove you guilty, dude."

Vic's eyes softened in a way that told Tandy he was more worried about losing her than going to jail. Or about Marissa calling him dude.

Tandy's thoughts whirled as Kristin brought out the evidence bag and Griffin pulled out his phone to take pictures of the trunk before retrieving the troublesome electronic device. "I'm going to need you all to come in and give your statements. Kristin, get Agent McNeil on the phone and tell him the car theft ring is more advanced than we thought."

Tandy didn't move, didn't take her eyes off Vic. "You live in Toledo now. I live here. I don't see how a relationship would ever work."

Vic shoved his hands in his pockets. "The company is letting me go remote. I could work from Grace Springs."

Tandy's cheeks burned. Was she going to get to have her coffee and drink it too? Ironic that lately she'd preferred tea.

"No." Marissa pointed a condemning finger. "No. Absolutely not."

Vic rubbed a hand over his mouth to try smothering a chuckle at her theatrics and their absurd situation. He'd always had a great sense of humor. And a magnetic smile.

"Stop smiling." Marissa must have felt it too. "Don't look

at his smile, Tandy. Look away. Do not look directly at him."

Tandy smiled back. She couldn't help it. "Even if you move here and prove yourself innocent of theft, Vic, there's still the problem that you kidnapped my best friend."

Marissa dropped her hand. Her wrath melted into awe as she turned toward Tandy. "I'm your best friend?"

"Of course you're my best friend. I chased down this car on foot to rescue you."

"You did, didn't you?" Marissa sighed and stepped forward into an embrace.

Tandy smiled over her friend's shoulder at Vic. What did he think of her having a close female friend? She hadn't had one when she was with him. In fact, she hadn't had one since Mom had left. It felt good. It felt like family.

Marissa didn't hang on for long. She whirled to face Vic once again. "Friends don't let friends date kidnappers."

Vic leaned a hand on the hood of his car and crossed one ankle over the other, obviously not perturbed in the least. "You can pick your friends and you can pick your boyfriend, but you can't pick your friend's boyfriend."

Okay, Tandy's heart trilled just a little at that. He wanted to be her boyfriend again. He'd once been everything she'd thought she wanted. Was she stupid for being intrigued at the idea? Would getting back together with someone who'd once left her only be setting herself up for another heartbreak?

Marissa stepped in front of Tandy, blocking Tandy's view, and allowing Vic's image to be replaced with Greg's. Tandy's current boyfriend may not have kissed her yet, but he was her other best friend. He was the boyfriend who'd never abandoned her. What kind of person would she be if she abandoned him?

Chapter Eight

TANDY HAD ONCE THOUGHT ONLY FLIRTS like Marissa got themselves into love triangles. She'd always had long dry spells between boyfriends, and she'd kind of prided herself on it. She was an independent woman. Or she *had* been. But now she was so distracted with men that she couldn't even focus on the idea of a car heist ring or Vic being a suspect in a murder investigation.

She was trying though. And for that reason, she picked a seat on the opposite side of the tiny police station from Vic to wait to give her statement. The only problem was that with Vic across from her, she couldn't avoid his searching eye contact. Or contagious grin.

Shoot, she was grinning at him again. The front door opened. Greg was going to catch her grinning at Vic.

Tandy straightened and wiped the smile off her face before turning to face her boyfriend.

But instead of Superman in a 3-piece-suit, she found a rugged looking mountain man in a toolbelt.

She sank deeper in her seat with relief. "Oh, Connor. Hi."

Connor scanned the room, noticed Marissa through the window of the back office and lowered himself into the seat next to Tandy. "Is she all right?"

Tandy turned sideways and lifted a hand to hide her mouth from Vic as she spoke. "Marissa's fine, but I'm struggling with this whole love triangle thing."

Connor stiffened. His brows drew together. "Tandy, I thought you agreed that there was nothing between us."

Between the two of them? Oh yeah, they'd kissed the day before. That morning she'd felt guilty for kissing Connor, but the experience was nothing compared to eye contact with Vic. She was a horrible girlfriend, wasn't she? "Of course not," she agreed.

Connor peered closer. "Are you worried because I haven't told Marissa about the kiss yet? I was going to do it tonight, but then she got kidnapped, so I'm thinking she might not be in the best place for that conversation, emotionally speaking."

Was Marissa ever in a good place, emotionally speaking? "Probably wise." Tandy tilted her head slightly toward Vic. "The bigger problem is that her kidnapper is my ex-boyfriend. He's here because he says he wants to get back together with me."

Connor's head jerked up and he glared at her ex.

Good night, she hadn't realized he cared so much about who she dated. She hadn't even mentioned that he was the car collector interested in Randon's Corvette.

"Did he kidnap the wrong woman?" Connor spoke quietly to her though he continued to glare at Vic. "Why isn't he behind bars?"

Right. Connor wasn't worried about Tandy's love triangle. He was worried about Marissa's alleged abduction.

"He isn't really a kidnapper," she explained.

A tapping sound came from the office window. Marissa peered at them from the other side then motioned like a maniac for Connor to join her.

Connor rose. "What in the world is she wearing?"

"George's jumpsuit."

"Your answers to my questions get weirder and weirder." Connor strode toward the office. "Maybe Marissa will make more sense."

"I doubt it," Tandy called after him.

The door closed, leaving her alone with Vic again.

He caught her eye. "Is that your attorney boyfriend?"

Tandy couldn't help laughing at the idea. "No. Connor is Marissa's boyfriend."

Vic smirked. "That's gotta be a record. My first day in town and I've already given two men a reason to hate me."

Tandy quirked her lips. "It could be worse. My first day in town, a woman died right in front of me." The cold breeze blowing from the front door distracted her with the realization that her boyfriend might really have arrived this time. "Imagine being new to town and a murder suspect…" Her voice trailed off at the sight of Greg.

He even had his Clark Kent glasses on today. Could he use his x-ray vision and see how fast her heart was beating?

Greg wasn't looking at her though. His eyes narrowed as he studied Vic even though he didn't know their connection yet. "You're Vic Whitaker, a suspect in the murder of George Knibbs?"

Vic remained in his relaxed posture with forearms resting on thighs. "I don't know anything about a George Knibbs. I came to Grace Springs because I made the mistake of breaking up with Tandy a few months ago, and I want to see if she'll give me another chance."

Greg rocked back on his heels then turned to face her slowly. "You dated him?"

"Yeah, I probably should have mentioned that." Tandy stood to make her case. "In my defense, I told Vic I'm dating you."

"Actually." Vic tilted his head in that puppy dog way of his. "Your friend is the one who said you were dating someone else. You only said you couldn't date me because I kidnapped her."

Tandy bugged her eyes at Vic. He obviously wanted to put her in a difficult situation, never mind that his words were true.

Greg crossed his arms. "Tandy and I will talk about who she wants to date later. What I want to know from you now is where you were on February 11th at six in the morning."

Tandy arched her eyebrows. If Vic was guilty of murder, that could potentially solve all their problems. Greg would win his case, and she'd get more time with him without having to worry about this stupid love triangle anymore. Although the reason she'd defended him earlier was that she knew the only thing Vic was guilty of involved a killer smile.

Marissa tossed her hair triumphantly as she marched out of Griffin's office. Tandy's ex may get off without a kidnapping charge, but Marissa had made quite a case to Griffin about why Vic Whitaker had to be involved in the theft of Randon's car and the murder of George Knibbs.

Connor had been no help at all after he'd found out she tried to use the mystery device on her own car rather than contact authorities. Couldn't he cool it with the safety tips? She was, after all, wearing the snow boots he'd given her. He followed her into the main lobby, freeing the interrogation room for another statement.

"Tandy, you're up," she announced.

Tandy's eyes widened as if trying to send her a message. Marissa couldn't read the message, but she could read the rest of the room. Greg and Tandy's ex were in some kind of standoff where Greg was the only one standing. The Vic dude chilled in a row of chairs facing them from the far wall.

Tandy rubbed Greg's arm before heading into the office.

"I'll be back."

Was Tandy worried her boyfriend would leave without her? She should know better. Greg was like a Golden Retriever—loyal despite being easily distracted.

Marissa would make sure Vic knew this, as well. He did not deserve a second chance with Tandy.

The door clicked shut.

Marissa led Connor toward the seats next to Greg, though she didn't sit. Three against one. "Hi, Greg."

"Hi." Greg sent her a perfunctory glance then scanned her up and down with a frown. "What are you wearing?"

Connor plopped onto a chair. "She's wearing the snow boots I bought her. About time, too."

Marissa nudged Connor's boot with hers. They had bigger issues to deal with than the chance she might slip on ice.

Greg's gaze travelled to her feet. "Nice. They even have pockets. Very practical."

"Yep." She actually hadn't noticed the pockets because they were so hideous that she tried to avoid looking at them. But their ugly practicality completed her ensemble perfectly. She sashayed past him and performed a little turn as if on a catwalk. "And in case you didn't notice, I'm also wearing the jumpsuit George gave me right before he died."

Vic nodded even though she hadn't been talking to him. "Would this be George Knibbs?"

Marissa spun to face him. "What do you know about George Knibbs?"

Greg stepped next to her as if preparing to play a game of Red Rover. "I was asking him the same thing."

"Y'all are crazy." Vic leaned against the wall.

Marissa did feel kind of crazy in the jumpsuit and boots. She was, for the first time in her life, completely uninhibited.

She didn't have to worry about wobbling on high heels or slipping in snow. She didn't have to sit like a lady and cross her legs at the ankles as if she was in a skirt. She didn't have to suck in her tummy the way she did when wearing a stretchy sweater. She had the freedom to tromp and flail all over the place. No matter how she acted, she couldn't possibly make herself look any more ridiculous than she already did.

"We'd be crazy *not* to suspect you," Marissa pointed out.

Vic stared her down, the dimples he flashed for Tandy nowhere to be seen. "You really think that if I was guilty of stealing cars and killing a local that I would draw attention to myself by coming to the police department with another local in my trunk along with evidence from the investigation?"

Marissa huffed. "It's a super way to throw suspicion off yourself."

Vic shrugged. "There wasn't any suspicion to throw."

"There is now." Greg stood poised as if presenting his case to a jury, not fighting over a girl.

If Marissa had ever mastered that kind of poise, she would have been the reigning Miss Ohio…and she'd be missing out on the freedom of wearing coveralls twice her size.

Greg cleared his throat. "You still haven't answered my question. Where were you the morning of February 11th?"

Vic stood. He sauntered over until the men were face to face. He grinned the kind of grin that could get him almost any girl he wanted. *Almost* being the operative word. "I was at my apartment in Toledo, packing to drive out here and reconnect with my ex. You may think stealing Tandy makes me a thief, but, sorry, you can't arrest me for it."

The office door swung open. Tandy stopped and eyed the men in front of her.

Sheriff Griffin propelled her forward through the doorway. "Mr. Whitaker, come in please."

Vic lifted his chin as if to say he was done with Greg. He smoothly pivoted toward the door and headed that way until he reached Tandy. He faced her, smiled a smile that could put Cupid out of business, and stooped his head like they were having a private conversation. Then he spoke loud enough for all to hear. "After you have that talk with the attorney you're dating, give me a call to let me know the verdict."

Tandy didn't have a comeback, which was telling in itself. But maybe she was only experiencing momentary speechlessness. Marissa had warned her not to look directly at Vic's smile. It had even struck *her* silent. She covered her mouth, cheeks burning for her friend.

Griffin broke the silence by ushering Vic into his office then stepping into the front room with them and closing the door behind him with a *thunk*. "You are all free to go. Marissa, you're going to bring me the jumpsuit and the other half of the device tonight?"

"Yes." She wouldn't argue. Though she had kinda been hoping to sleep in the jumpsuit. It was even more comfortable than pajamas.

"If any of you find something else suspicious, bring it directly to me. Due to this new evidence, I'm going to reopen the case."

Greg focused on Griffin, his purposeful avoidance of eye contact with Tandy making Marissa squirm. "Are you saying my client, Derrick Snodgrass, might not be prosecuted for murder, after all?"

Griffin huffed. "What I'm saying is that you all should take extra precaution to make sure your vehicles are safe. Lock your car doors. Park them in the garage. And if you have remote start, keep your key fobs in your freezer at home so a device like the one Marissa found can't access the code and turn on your engine."

Marissa tapped her chin. If Vic had only been after the Corvette, and he was the criminal, then why did they have to worry about other cars getting stolen? Was it because of the device she found?

Tandy let Greg open the car door for her. Even though he wouldn't look her in the eye, he was still being a gentleman.

She sank into the chilly leather interior and shivered. Greg's heart seemed to have turned every bit as cold toward her. Hopefully once she explained, it would warm as quickly as his seat warmers.

He opened the door and slid in beside her, starting the vehicle and adjusting the knobs for radio and heat so she could hear him over the volume. They needed to talk.

"You don't think he did it?" Greg asked.

Tandy assumed "he" meant Vic and "it" meant murder, but then, she also would have assumed Greg would ask about her relationship with Vic before discussing the case. "Is it too hard to believe that he's only here because he wants me back?"

Greg shifted into drive and pulled into the street, headed toward her apartment. "If he killed George, the whole story about trying to win you back could be an excuse for coming to town. It's really too much of a coincidence."

Tandy nodded in mock agreement. "So, you're not jealous."

Greg shrugged. "Do I have anything to be jealous about? Have you been talking to him or texting him? Are you planning to date him?"

"No to all of the above." There. Hopefully that would make him—and her—feel better. Despite Vic's spectacular smile, she'd already determined she wasn't going to go out with him. She was already in a relationship.

She'd simply refuse to think about how Vic had driven hours to see her whereas Greg worked across the street and hadn't even stopped in for coffee on her opening day. Instead, she'd remind herself that Vic's leaving was the whole reason she was so insecure in her relationship with Greg.

Greg nodded. "Even if you do plan to date him, you should wait until the real killer is arrested. To be safe."

Tandy swallowed an icy bite of air, coating her guts in a cold frost. "I just told you I don't plan to date him. Don't you believe me?"

Greg didn't answer until he'd turned into the apartment parking lot and pulled into a spot below her unit window. "I want to believe you, but..." He shook his head. "Yesterday you kissed Connor. Today you have an ex-boyfriend show up. Do you know how awkward it is to be in a room where every man there has kissed your girlfriend except you?"

His words punched Tandy in her frozen guts. They shattered within like an icicle, leaving her cold and empty. "I'm sorry you had to be in that position. It was awkward for me too."

Greg twisted to face her and ran a hand through his hair. "Is that why you didn't say anything? Why you didn't tell Vic right there that you were done with him?"

She should have, huh? That might have been better than trying to pretend everything was normal.

Of course, she also wanted to believe that Vic was truly in town for her, in which case, she didn't want to hurt his feelings. But the excuse Greg gave her sounded better. "Yes."

He studied her. "Is there anything else I should know?

Perhaps why you and Vic broke up in the first place?"

She thought she'd told him already. Though there wasn't much to tell. She shrugged. "He moved to Toledo for a job."

Greg reached across the seat and brushed a strand of hair from her face. "You didn't want to do long distance?"

Tandy gave a dry laugh at the memory. "*He* didn't want to. And I'm glad. Because then I wouldn't have ended up here."

His fingers grazed her cheek, and she wasn't cold anymore. She rested her face in his palm. Leaned forward.

Greg tilted his nose to the side of hers. His breath brushed her skin, sending chills down her spine. "Tandy?"

Her eyelids grew heavy. She let them drift downward, taking her closer to her dreams. "Yes?"

"Since you don't care about Vic anymore..." They were still talking about Vic? "Then you won't mind that I'm going to try to prove he's George's killer."

They were still talking about Vic.

Chapter Nine

Marissa leaned over the counter to kiss Connor good morning, though he didn't notice because he was too busy staring up at the loft and all the work he still needed to finish before the next night.

"Happy Valentine's Eve," she said to snag his attention. "I'm almost finished making your drink. You want the *té con leche* again?"

"Um...yeah. Thanks." He stepped to the side so she could help the patron behind him. "Is Tandy here?"

Pots and pans clanged from the back room in response. Either Marissa's business partner hadn't had her coffee yet that morning or she'd had a fight with Greg the night before. Marissa would have preferred to stay out of the way, but she needed help. "Tandy, I could use you out here," she called before focusing on her next customer, the stern organist from church. "What can I do for you this morning, Opal?"

Opal scowled—the only expression Marissa had ever seen on her face. "You can start by not yelling at people. This isn't Wall Street."

"Sorry." At least Marissa knew this woman would not be ordering coffee. She was already dressed for high tea with her Kate Middleton hat. "May I recommend the *té con leche* I'm making for Connor? It's how they drink tea in South America. It has part tea and part steamed milk—"

"No, you may not. I'm lactose intolerant." Opal got the intolerant part right. "If you want me to keep coming here, you need to know that I only drink Earl Grey, steeped for exactly four minutes."

"Yes, ma'am." Marissa rang up the sale on the cash register then got to work, turning her back to shield the fact that she was making Connor's drink at the same time.

Tandy joined her, grinding coffee for an espresso shot. With the way Marissa's morning was going, she could use the extra dose of caffeine too. Once Tandy went into the kitchen to create another racket, she'd pretend to prepare more espresso for a customer.

For now, Marissa poured tea into one of the special teacups she'd ordered for Valentine's with the red hearts painted on clear glass. She would have preferred to give the heart cup to Connor, but she couldn't risk one breaking upstairs, so he got the paper cup. One more day of renovations.

Tandy eyed the drinks. "Is that *té con leche*?"

Marissa poured and popped the lid on. "Yes. You want to try it?"

"No need."

"Afraid you might like it?"

"I already know how I feel about it."

Marissa shook her head. She'd let Miss Hyde drink her coffee so she could turn back into Barista Jekyll. "Well, Connor loves it." She lifted the warm cup and turned to hand it to him.

He accepted, his gray eyes flashing between her and Tandy. Apparently, he was a little scared of the barista too. "Thanks, hon. There's something I need to talk to you about when you get a chance."

"Oh yeah?" She smiled, excited for whatever surprise he had in store. Though a little crusty on the outside, Connor's heart was gooey for her on the inside. Kind of like a chocolate croissant. Her fave. She should make some of those for tomorrow's grand opening of the tea house.

The timer rang four minutes, and she retrieved Opal's Earl Grey. Usually Marissa would serve it still steeping, but she didn't want to mess up the discerning new customer's demands on her first visit. She removed the infuser and planted her feet firmly before picking up the delicate cup.

One hot pink suede calf boot slipped. Her belly fluttered, but she caught her balance before any tea sloshed over the side. She made sure to avoid Connor's gaze as she pivoted to serve Opal. She wouldn't give him the chance to suggest she wear snow boots inside, though it might not be such a bad idea. If only he'd bought her pink ones instead of brown.

Opal extended shaky, wrinkled hands to accept the drink.

Marissa scrunched her face, debating whether to offer to carry the drink to Opal's seat for her or not. The chance that she would spill it would probably be equal to that of Opal spilling, but at least if Marissa spilled on herself, there wouldn't be any lawsuit. "I can carry it for you. Where would you like to sit?"

Opal tucked her hands into her chest. "I'd like to sit in the tea room. This area of your shop is too industrial and primitive."

Tandy twisted to face Opal, her head tilted and eyes bulging as if to say, *Reallllly?*

Marissa balanced the cup in one hand to wave her business partner down with the other. "Drink your coffee, Tandy." She reset her smile before addressing Opal. "I'm sorry. The loft is where we will be serving high tea. It doesn't open until tomorrow."

Opal's thin lips practically disappeared when she pressed them together. "But I'm here now."

Marissa blinked rather than let her smile slip. "It's not

complete. Connor is finishing up renovations today."

Opal turned her scowl his direction. "It doesn't look like it to me."

Marissa's favorite contractor didn't move from his position, leaning against the counter, cup in hand. He wasn't a lazy person, but it might look like it from Opal's perspective. "Go ahead, Connor. I'll come up and talk when I get a break."

He pushed to his full height with a grimace. Maybe the surprise he had for her wasn't a good surprise after all. She squinted at him curiously before leading Opal to the table in the farthest corner.

Finally. Tandy had been afraid Opal would never leave. Or more importantly that Marissa would never turn away.

Tandy breezed past Connor, exchanging cups and continuing to the chalkboard by the front door to rewrite the part of their drink specials that had somehow been smeared. Though none of the drinks listed could compare with this drink in her hand.

She lifted the cup to her lips and sipped at the rich creamy tea inside. It filled her internal emptiness with hope. And peace.

So what if Greg wanted to try to pin George's murder on Vic? That had nothing to do with her. She'd probably never see Vic again anyway.

The front door swung open. Vic entered, dimples on display. "I thought I might find you here."

She tilted her head back farther, turning her sip into a guzzle. Gulp after gulp, she wished on all the tea in China that Vic would disappear before she had to face him again.

The warm liquid sloshed down her throat and heated her from the inside out until there was nothing left in the cup. Slowly, she lowered it to find amusement sparkling in Vic's dark eyes.

Marissa appeared beside her. "She needs her morning coffee to deal with you."

Usually Tandy hid behind her own snarky remarks, but with Vic, she'd let Marissa make them for her. If Tandy wasn't the one defending herself, then there was less chance her ex could penetrate her defenses.

Vic smirked. "Is that any way to treat a new customer?"

"Only new customers who have a history of stuffing me in the trunk of their car," Marissa retorted.

Opal gasped from the corner. Her cup clattered. The eavesdropper.

"Marissa, you didn't give me a napkin." Opal's harsh tone came out a little more wobbly than usual. Was she afraid of sticky fingers or was she worried that the business owners associated with a kidnapper?

Marissa shot the suspected criminal one last glare before turning to help the older woman.

Tandy would have to stand on her own. "What can I get you, Vic?"

"I'd like a kiss."

Well, that was honest. Or was it? Could Greg be right that he was using her as an excuse for being in town when the truth was that he was only there to steal cars? Had he not hurt her enough?

She tossed her cup in the recycling bin and planted her hands on her hips. "You can't dump me and not talk to me for months then reappear and demand we start again where we left off. That is the most arrogant—"

"Yes. That would be arrogant." Vic pointed towards her

feet where the giant chalkboard easel displayed half their menu. The chocolate part of "Chocolate Kiss Coffee" had been smudged into a white streak. "I'm just trying to order a drink. What would your boyfriend say if he knew you were thinking about kissing me?"

Tandy lifted her chin. The triumphant glint in Vic's eyes told her he'd set a trap for her, and she'd fallen right in. She could do better than that.

"I might believe you if you ever drank anything other than sweet tea."

Vic's grin grew.

Marissa reappeared, eyelashes fluttering. "You drink tea?" When she decided to turn on the charm, there was no artificial sweetener needed for her drinks.

"I drink tea." Vic turned his big ol' personality toward the dog dancing inside the fence with excitement. "But I don't love it as much as I love Cocoa!"

Tandy stepped between Vic and the gate. "You don't get to pick back up with me *or* Cocoa."

"Aw, don't be like that." Vic stepped closer. "Cocoa and I have a connection. You even named him after me."

"He is not named after you." Either she would have to let him pass to see her dog, or she'd have to be okay with him invading her personal space. Being close enough to smell his mossy scent was already a little too personal. She stepped aside.

Vic pumped the air in triumph then bent over to scratch her dog behind the ears. "Yes, he is. He's named after my skin color."

Marissa watched with wide eyes.

Tandy shook her head at the ludicrous claim, so her friend didn't get the wrong idea. Cocoa was already traitorous enough with his over eagerness and his licking.

How dare he lick Vic. "He's named after his fur color."

Vic held his hand still against Cocoa's fur. "We do match." He stood up with a grin. "It's like we're family."

"You're a customer." Tandy rolled her eyes toward Marissa. "Why don't you seat him with Opal, and they can have a tea party?"

Vic looked past the women toward Opal in the corner. "Is this the Opal you're talking about?"

Opal scowled his direction—like a supervillain pitted against his heroic smile.

"Yes," Tandy confirmed. "And she's more likely to give you that kiss you asked for than me."

His dark eyes lit with the challenge. "Don't get jealous now."

"What?" Tandy's voice squeaked.

Vic didn't answer but sauntered toward the angry granny. "Opal, is it? You certainly look as precious as the gemstone."

"Precious?" Marissa choked on the word.

Vic pulled out the chair across from Opal. "I heard you also drink tea. Would you mind if I join you? I'm new to the area and haven't had much success at making friends."

"Good night," Tandy muttered." He thinks Opal will fall victim to his charms."

Marissa's frustration heated the air around her like steamed milk. Thankfully, she'd been able to stay angry at the charmer. "I was his real victim when he kidnapped me"

Tandy wrapped her fingers around Marissa's wrist to hold her in place so they could watch the show together. If anybody could deflate Vic's ego, it would be Opal. "Wait for it…"

Opal pointed at Vic, poised to give a lecture.

Vic reached for her hand then bent over and kissed it.

Opal's pinched lips parted. The wrinkles around her eyes smoothed. Her cheeks brightened from their oatmeal pallor to a grapefruit glow. She nodded for Vic to take a seat.

Tandy guffawed.

Vic winked.

Opal sent her a scowl.

Tandy's heart lurched. If the man could even woo Opal, how was she ever going to escape his pursuit?

She and Marissa scurried toward their counter for safety.

Marissa opened the refrigerator and pulled out a pitcher of sweet tea. "You gonna go bang some more pots and pans around now?"

"Yes." Tandy gritted her teeth and imagined smacking Vic in his happy face with a frying pan.

Marissa grabbed a glass. "I can't believe you ever dated a tea drinker."

Tandy peeked over her shoulder to find Vic deep in conversation with a woman who might have looked like Opal, had she not been laughing. Who knew Opal could laugh? "He's the reason I hate tea so much."

Marissa turned to face her, mouth wide. "It all makes sense now. You don't really hate tea itself. You hate the—"

"Pretension." Which had seemed to fit Marissa when they'd first met. But now Tandy's partner was free to romp around in jumpsuits and snow boots like a crazy woman. And she'd always been too klutzy to become a beauty queen. Hey, maybe Marissa would trip and spill Vic's tea all over him. That was the revenge fantasy most likely to happen.

The phone trilled. A much-needed distraction. Tandy reached to answer. "I'll get it."

Marissa lifted Vic's glass of sweet tea toward her chest and took cautious, baby steps. Darn. "After I deliver this, I'm going to head upstairs to talk to Connor. He said he needs to tell me something."

Tandy nodded automatically before the weight of Marissa's words landed with full impact. If Connor wanted to talk to Marissa, it was probably to tell her that they'd kissed on their little stakeout earlier that week. As if having her ex in the coffee shop wasn't enough conflict for one day, her co-owner was about to come at Tandy like a coffee grinder.

She grimaced before lifting the phone receiver to her ear. "You've reached Caffeine Conundrum. This is Tandy. How may I help you?"

"Tandy!" A voice screeched from the other end. "Is Connor there? I can't get ahold of him. This is his mom, and I need to talk to him about my Porsche."

"Yes, I'll get him." Tandy stood straighter, looking toward the loft floor overhead. With the agitation in Mrs. Thomas's voice, she wasn't calling to discuss an oil change. Oh no. Tandy gritted her teeth to ask the first question that popped into her mind. "Was your Porsche stolen?"

"No. Worse."

Tandy wrinkled her forehead in contemplation of what might be worse than having a car stolen. "Did you get in an accident? Are you okay?"

"I'm fine. The car's fine. It's just…"

Tandy shook her head and held a hand wide despite the fact that the other woman couldn't see her. "What?"

"I was trying to be cautious like the sheriff warned y'all last night, so I chained my front bumper to the fence post. When I went to get it this morning, the *back* bumper was chained to the fence post."

Tandy's mouth fell open, but she held back her laughter. The scenario would only be funny if it was a joke. "Are you sure you remembered correctly?"

"I'm positive. I aligned the car in a way that I could back

out without hitting the barn again."

Again? Tandy pressed her lips together to keep from blurting the word aloud. "Um…" There had to be a logical explanation. "Do you think Connor was playing a trick on you?" That didn't sound like him, though it would be pretty funny.

Mrs. Thomas calmed. Her tone turned teachery. "I considered all those options. Then I found a note on the front windshield."

A weight settled on Tandy's chest. The invisible kind that made it hard to breathe. "What did the note say?"

Mrs. Thomas groaned. "It said, 'We'll take your car whenever we want it.'"

Chapter Ten

Marissa shielded her eyes from the sunrise as Connor drove under the timber sign that welcomed guests to The Farmstead. She'd left the shop with Tandy so she could support her boyfriend and his distraught mother when police showed up on the property that should have been their family's safe haven.

"It must have happened when I was asleep." Connor rubbed his jaw, part playing detective and part blaming himself. "Otherwise, I would have heard the car engine and checked to see where Mom was going."

Marissa had hoped his reasoning would be that Abigail was mistaken. "Who would come onto your farm in the middle of the night? I want to blame Vic, but I have the feeling that if he were to mess with anyone's car, it would have been Greg's."

"Yeah." They rounded the shop where Connor stayed in the upstairs apartment and found a gathering of people all staring at a light blue Porsche. "I'd like to think it was kids playing a harmless prank, but kids wouldn't know how to break into a high-performance vehicle."

"That means real car thieves came onto your property, but rather than steal a car, they used their skills to simply freak your mom out. Why would they do that? Unless..." Unless their goal was to throw suspicion off George's brother, Derrick. And who had more motive to do that than Derrick's daughter, Susan? If she didn't already know how to steal a car, her dad could give her directions.

Connor passed the Porsche and parked closer to the historic farmhouse where icicles glistened from the roof of the wraparound porch. "Unless what?"

"Susan," she said.

Connor shut off the ignition and faced her, though with the way his eyes rolled in thought, he was focused elsewhere. "That actually makes sense."

Marissa didn't want to suspect the girl, but she hadn't wanted George to be guilty either. At least nobody had died in this crime. "Let's go see if Griffin has any clues."

Connor sighed. "For Mom's peace of mind, I hope he's already planning to arrest someone."

Marissa popped the truck door open and held onto the handle while jumping down into the snow. She hoped the case had been solved already too. Not only for Abigail but also for her business. If Connor was here at the farm all day, he wouldn't have time to finish her shop. She hadn't even gotten to join him in the loft before they'd been called away. She still had no idea what surprise he had planned.

She grabbed his hand and swung her door closed, then waited for Connor to walk around so she could grab his arm for balance. "Before we join your mom, do you want to tell me your surprise?"

Connor crunched forward, and she trailed after. It took a moment for him to respond. "Surprise?" Obviously, his thoughts had jumped ahead of them to the crime scene, and he was having trouble reeling them back.

"Yeah, that thing you wanted to talk about in the loft."

"Oh. Uh…" He scratched his head and shot her a fleeting glance. "I don't think this is the time."

Probably not. Being that the next day was Valentine's, it was probably something romantic. And this was definitely not the place for romance. Especially not if he was going to…

She stopped. Was he planning to propose again?

Connor tugged her to continue forward. When she didn't move, he stopped and glanced back. "You okay?"

She covered her mouth to keep from revealing that she'd figured out his plan, but she also looked at him with the eyes of enlightenment. An engagement would be different this time around. Now she knew they could work through difficult times.

This was the man she was going to spend the rest of her life with. This caring son. This hard-working contractor. This handsome hunk. The golden glint of sunrise highlighted each piece of stubble on his square jaw, making him appear manlier.

"Yes!" The word tumbled out of her mouth as if answering the actual question of would she marry him rather than a question of concern.

Connor's eyebrow quirked. He didn't even know how adorable he was, did he?

She loved everything about him, from his oversized truck to the fact that he still lived on his parents' farm. Completely impractical on one hand but realistic on the other.

When they married, he could move in with her. He'd pretty much renovated her house by himself.

"Okay then." He tilted his head toward the crowd in front of them. "Are you coming with me, or do you need to run into the house and use the bathroom? I know you drank a bunch of tea."

So sweet and so off base. In more ways than one. "I'm coming." She squeezed his hand tighter and tromped through the snow to keep up, wondering if he'd gotten her a ring this time. She really liked oval cut diamonds on rose gold.

Connor let go of her to embrace Abigail. "Mom, are you okay?"

Abigail didn't say anything, just let him comfort her in the way a mother usually comforted her child. Connor would make a good parent. How many children would they have?

The rumble of tires against gravel and packed snow announced the arrival of another vehicle. McNeil sat behind the wheel of a black Suburban in agent mode.

"Oh man." Griffin groaned. "Here we go again."

McNeil joined the group, and was it Marissa's imagination, or did he look at every single one of them like a suspect? Griffin, Connor, Connor's parents, a few employees, and her. Her belly fluttered a little, and not only from the excitement of an engagement.

The FBI wouldn't really think she did it, would they? She couldn't even break into her own car without getting caught.

Agent McNeil's jaw worked overtime on his gum. He'd be a handsome man if not for all that chomping. "Give me the rundown, Griffin."

Griffin would know Marissa didn't do it. He'd know she was working to get into the good graces of her future mother-in-law.

The Sheriff cleared his throat. "Mrs. Thomas turned on her vehicle remotely at 7 a.m. to warm it up. When she came out to her car approximately ten minutes later, she found it parked backwards despite it having been chained to the fence. There was also a note. The note's been sent to the lab, the interior of her vehicle is also being checked for DNA, and I'm currently questioning everyone with access to the property."

McNeil narrowed his eyes at Connor's mom like he thought she might be making this up. "Was the gate to your property open or closed last night?"

Abigail uncurled from Connor's embrace and wiped a damp eye. "We only shut it after hours in October to keep out guests that don't realize our pumpkin patch and corn maze are closed."

The man's jaw hardened. "But you thought you needed to chain your vehicle to a fence? Why not lock the gate or even park in the garage?"

Mr. Thomas stepped forward. "That's my fault. I'm working on my motorcycle in the garage. As for the gate, we didn't want to lock our son out. He lives on the property and has been coming home well after dark lately."

Connor straightened. "I'll start locking it when I come home from now on. I didn't realize we were in danger. I never imagined someone would—"

"Why were you out so late last night?" McNeil interrupted.

Connor rocked back on his heels. "I was comforting my girlfriend. You know she got stuffed in a trunk yesterday, don't you?"

McNeil turned his judgement on Marissa. "I heard you were withholding evidence, young lady."

Marissa's mouth fell open. "Not at all. I hid the jumpsuit George gave me because I didn't want anybody to see me put it on. When I found the device inside, I wasn't sure what it was, and I didn't want to make a big deal out of it if it wasn't a big deal."

"Yes, you seem the type who tries to avoid drama."

The sarcasm. Marissa jutted her chin forward and motioned for Connor to stand up for her.

He gave a small shrug.

She wrinkled her nose at the man she intended to marry. She'd have to teach him to do better when they were husband and wife.

She stood up taller to face McNeil herself. "How do I know if I'd turned it in on that first day that you wouldn't have lost it like you lost the recording from Billie's shop? I'm not the only one making mistakes here."

McNeil cranked the heat on his laser-like gaze. "How do *I* know you aren't the one who broke into Grandma's Attic and destroyed it?"

"What?" They'd already pinned that on Derrick Snodgrass. Though the allegation depended on him being the one to murder George.

"You were in the area at the time." The lines in McNeil's forehead creased deeper when he lifted his eyebrows.

Griffin shifted his weight to focus closer on her, as well. "That's true."

"Seriously?" She stepped forward, blessedly without a wobble. "Since I'm the one finding all the clues, let me suggest a theory for you."

McNeil motioned for her to continue.

"George suspected his brother of stealing Randon's car but didn't want to turn him in until after they spoke. As insurance, he planted the device he'd found in Randon's car in the jumpsuit before giving it to me. Derrick broke into Grandma's Attic to destroy the evidence, as you already suspected. Derrick was caught, thanks to my fiancé...I mean boyfriend." Oops. She'd gotten carried away in the heat of the moment. Back to her theory in hopes Connor hadn't noticed. "Enter Derrick's daughter who claims her dad is innocent. She doesn't want to steal a car, but she wants you all to think there are more thieves out there so her dad can be ruled not guilty and get out of jail. Hence, this insane little stunt."

Abigail's shoulders sagged in relief at the idea. "That makes sense. And it's not as scary. I mean, a girl trying to help her dad isn't as much of a threat as a murderous car thief."

Agent McNeil looked away as if not wanting to give

Marissa any credit. "I'll question her. But I'm also going to question the rest of you, starting with your farm hands."

Six of them gathered together in front of McNeil. Marissa knew most of them. Three had been there since she was a little girl and had to be rescued from the corn maze. One was the son of the first farm hand. The last two were new and barely spoke English.

"Do you think any of them could have done it?" Marissa whispered to Connor.

Though what exactly were they looking for? A prankster who'd found another one of the relay attack units Derrick Snodgrass had left lying around? She could see the younger employee being guilty of something that benign. But if this little stunt was in some way related to the theft of Randon's Corvette, it was very possible that Connor's parents employed the murderer.

Connor studied the men. "It's not Bert, Russ, or Carl. They are possibly more loyal to my parents than I am. And it's not Carl's son. The kid is headed to seminary next year."

Marissa studied the scrawny, bowlegged kid. There could have been a slim possibility that he was boosting cars to cover the cost of seminary—she'd known pastors to do worse things. But with the dazed look on his freckled face, he didn't even know what was going on.

"What about the new guys?" she asked.

McNeil focused on them, as well. She listened for his questions. Only he spoke to them in Spanish. That was impressive.

Connor shrugged. "I don't know enough about them to say. They don't speak English."

Marissa studied them more closely. They were dressed for work and for winter in lined flannels and boots much like the ones Connor had bought her. They listened raptly to whatever McNeil was saying, and their intent faces reflected concern. "Well, then it couldn't have been them because the note your mom found was written in English."

"That's a good point." Griffin joined her and Connor. Probably because he didn't speak Spanish either. "Your theory about Susan makes the most sense, Marissa. Except for one thing. We searched Derrick Snodgrass's property and never found Randon's car."

Greg sat on a bar stool across from Tandy and sipped his coffee. "If Derrick is the killer, and his daughter is only trying to make him look innocent with the stunt at Connor's parents' house, then why hasn't the Sheriff found Randon's car yet?"

Tandy looked into her mug with disdain. She didn't have her usual appetite for espresso, and it wasn't only because she'd filled up on tea earlier. "Who do you think did it then?"

"Your ex is the obvious suspect."

She'd figured that was where Greg was headed. "Griffin already questioned him."

"What does Griffin know?"

Tandy shrugged. "Not as much as me."

Greg set his mug on the counter. Yes, he'd stopped by the shop on his lunch hour today, but he was still talking about work. It would be nice if he pursued her the way Vic was doing. Unlike Vic, if he asked for a kiss, she would give him one, but he hadn't asked.

He lifted his chin. "How so?"

Tandy dropped into the seat next to him so as not to have to face off. "I meant that I know Vic better than Griffin does."

Greg turned his seat to face hers. "And you don't believe he's the one who turned Mrs. Thomas's car around?"

Tandy fiddled with the messy knot on top of her head. "I think he could. He's got the skills to break into a car and start the ignition without getting caught. But his whole life is about preventing car theft. Even if you thought he stole the Corvette because he wanted it, where's the motive here?"

"I'll present two motives to make my case." You could take the lawyer out of court, but you couldn't take the court out of a lawyer. "One, perhaps his job is in trouble or he has some new anti-theft device he wants to sell. This could be a scare tactic to get car theft back in the news so his employers see his role as more valuable."

While an interesting concept, Vic's career was more important than ever. Theft prevention had to stay on the cutting edge of technology to remain relevant. "What's the second motive?"

Greg studied her with somber, dark eyes. "Maybe he is after you."

Tandy shook her head. Now Greg was talking like a gossip columnist. "Last night you suggested his interest in our former relationship was only a cover for illegal activities. Now you're suggesting he's breaking the law to win me back?"

"He's setting himself up to look like a hero, and if it's not for his job, then it has to be to get your attention." Greg's expression was that of pity. "The whole thing with stuffing Marissa in his trunk literally had you chasing after him."

Tandy quirked her lips "If Vic wants someone's attention, all he has to do is smile."

Greg crossed his arms. "Really?"

"Yes." Tandy blew out her breath and stood. As much as she'd wanted more time with Greg, this wasn't the Greg she knew. "He even charmed Opal with it this morning."

"He was here this morning?" Greg spun his stool to

watch her as she walked around him and behind the counter. "See? He's trying to get your attention."

Tandy stopped and chose to face off this time. "Well then, how about I give it to him?"

Greg's mouth opened but nothing came out, which had to be a first for him. It felt kinda nice to be the one who left him speechless. Wait until he heard what else she had to say…

"I'll go out with him and look for evidence that he's the perp." She leaned forward, as if joining him as a conspirator. "I could look through his stuff for the rock that killed George."

Greg shook his head slowly and reached over to cover her hand with his. "I didn't mean it that way. I don't want you going out with him even to help me prove my case. I would never put you in danger."

He looked so sincere while making such a ridiculous statement that Tandy couldn't keep one corner of her lips from curving up. "That's probably the most romantic thing you've ever said to me."

"Hey." He gave a derisive chuckle. "I bought you flowers yesterday."

She smiled her forgiveness. "And a coffee mug."

He squeezed her hand and stood. "On that note, my coffee break is over. I gotta get back to work."

Tandy slid her hand away. Of course, he had to get back to work. But so did she. And hopefully Marissa and Connor would return soon too. She needed Marissa's help to prepare for the after-school crowd and for Connor to hopefully finish the tea room upstairs. "Okay, I'll see you tomorrow."

Greg nodded then paused. "Do we have plans tomorrow?"

She bet Vic knew tomorrow was Valentine's. If he truly

had come back to town for her, that might have even been his motivation. "Valentine's Day?"

"Oh, right. The Dating Game."

They didn't have a chance, did they? "Yep." Maybe one day they'd actually get to go on a date again.

Greg saluted, grabbed his briefcase, and headed toward the door. "I'll see you tomorrow."

Tandy saluted his retreating back. Not her usual sassy response, but the sass had been missing lately. Could it be due to her recent tea drinking?

The front door opened before Greg reached it, ushering in Connor and Marissa. Undoubtedly, Connor would be switching drinks with Tandy before he returned upstairs. Her mouth watered at the thought, and she mentally agreed to succumb to a few more hours of sasslessness in order to soothe her insides. At least until Vic left and she could be herself with Greg again.

Greg spun to follow Connor and Marissa who walked toward her. Did he really have more time for them than her? Or were his relationships only based on what could bolster his career? Tandy pressed her lips together to keep the sassy comment from spilling out.

Tea. She needed tea.

With a meaningful look Connor's direction, she grabbed a paper cup and moved toward the espresso machine. "Is your mom okay?"

Connor hooked his thumbs in his toolbelt. "Yeah. She's decided to believe the note was left by Susan Snodgrass. That scares her less than to think there was a killer at the farm."

Greg leaned a hand against the counter. "What do the police believe?"

Connor ran a hand through his hair and glanced up at

the loft, probably calculating how late he'd have to work to make the next day's deadline. "They are still questioning everyone."

"Who is everyone?" Greg asked.

Tandy gritted her teeth. The sooner she could drink a *té con leche* the better. "Hey, Marissa, are you going to make Connor some tea before he goes upstairs?"

Marissa shrugged out of her jacket, gazing dreamily into the distance. That seemed even more out of character than Tandy's lack of sass. "Yeah," she breathed.

Tandy popped the lid on her drink for Connor and leaned close to Marissa. "You okay?" Apparently Connor hadn't yet told his girlfriend about kissing Tandy.

Marissa retrieved a bin of loose-leaf tea and lowered her voice. "I think Connor is going to propose."

Tandy arched her eyebrows. For some reason she'd assumed that if Connor planned to pop the question, she'd be in on the plan. "Really?"

"You know about it, don't you?" Marissa swatted her. "You're such a bad actress."

Tandy blinked. "I'm not acting. I have no idea about this. What makes you think he's proposing?"

Marissa glanced over her shoulder toward the men then steamed milk with a smile. "He wants to talk to me in the loft."

Tandy knew what Connor planned to say in the loft, and it was more likely to result in a funeral toll than wedding bells for him. "That could mean anything."

Marissa mixed the milk with her brew, and Tandy inhaled the scent of creamy comfort. Marissa cut off the aroma by popping a plastic lid on the drink.

She turned to face Tandy, thankfully still so much in her

fantasy world that she didn't notice the drool in the corner of Tandy's lips. "Tomorrow is Valentine's. The tea loft is my dream come true. What could possibly be more romantic than proposing in my tea loft on Valentine's Eve?"

Tandy gripped Marissa's arm to keep her from returning to her boyfriend only to have her bubble burst. Connor had once ruined her previous dreams of a tea house, so it would be better this time if it came from Tandy. "Valentine's Eve is not a thing."

Marissa smirked. "We're going to make it our thing. Then we're going to kick your butts at The Dating Game tomorrow night because we won't only be dating anymore. We'll be engaged."

Tandy let go. Allowing Connor to crash and burn was probably her only chance to win The Dating Game.

Marissa sashayed past with the tea, which was quite a feat for her.

Tandy grabbed the espresso she'd brewed and chased after her partner. She wouldn't really let Marissa have her heart shattered. Though the importance of switching cups with Connor added extra incentive to prevent her partner's pain.

The men still discussed the local car thefts when Tandy reached them. "What did I miss?" she asked overenthusiastically. She really *wasn't* a good actress.

Greg looked at his watch. "It sounds like the FBI have two other suspects besides Susan and Vic. I've got to follow up on this lead. I'll see you all tomorrow."

Tandy tossed Greg a tight smile though he didn't even look up to catch it. Which bothered her more—how Connor had apparently told Greg something that implied there was still a murderer on the loose, or how Greg cared about it more than he cared about her?

Connor took his drink from Marissa. "What's going on between you two?" he asked Tandy. Apparently *he'd* noticed her expression. "Everything okay in the romance department?"

"No," she answered shortly, unsure whether she was referring to her own romance or his.

Chapter Eleven

TANDY LED THE WAY TOWARD THE stairs. "Come on, Connor. I'll catch you up while you work. And you can tell me what you told Greg."

Marissa followed, eyes bulging with unspoken meaning. "*I* was going to help Connor upstairs."

"I know." Tandy waved her away. "But I need a short break since I've been running this place all morning."

Marissa shrugged in surrender while gazing lovingly at Connor. "I'll come join you when Tandy's done with her break. In fact, I'll bring you up a surprise, since I know you have a surprise for me too."

Tandy climbed the stairs with a wince. She'd have to interrogate Connor for his news first before she told him Marissa was expecting him to propose. Otherwise, he'd probably go into shock, and she'd never find out about these other suspects besides Vic.

She paused at the top of the stairs to wait for Connor. He took the steps two at a time without spilling a drop of her precious tea. Maybe he *should* propose to Marissa. She needed his steadiness.

Checking to make sure they were out of Marissa's eyesight, Tandy reached for his cup to make the switch. They sipped in unison. Satisfaction had never tasted so smooth.

Connor set his cup down and grabbed a can of paint. The gold brocade wallpaper didn't need work, but Marissa wanted the iron fencing running along it to be painted white rather than match the "puppy corner" fence downstairs.

She'd make it look even more girly by decorating it with vines and flowers. As for all the gilded mirrors and paintings of English gardens that needed to be hung above the fence, they still rested haphazardly on the round glass tables, covered in sawdust.

Tandy casually brushed sawdust from the closest painting to reveal a portrait of her dog sitting on a chaise lounge. She was sure Cocoa had never sat on a chaise lounge before, but this was probably the only way Marissa would allow him in her loft. "Hey, it's Cocoa."

"You weren't supposed to see that." Connor squatted over a drop cloth and pried open a can of paint. The fresh scent held the promise of new beginnings. "Greg commissioned that piece from my mom to give to you on Valentine's Day. Can you pretend you've never seen it before?"

Greg had done this for her?

"Uh…yeah." Tandy had been doing a lot of pretending lately, so this should be no big deal. Except it was. This was how Greg pursued a woman.

He didn't just show up out of the blue and flirt. He planned. He worked. He went deeper than the surface. Because he really did care.

Connor glanced up from his position on the floor. "Are you crying?"

Tandy sniffed away her emotion. "No." Tea-drinking really was making her soft, wasn't it? "I didn't know your mom painted."

Connor's shoulders relaxed at her diversion tactic. "Like mother, like son." He slathered his first white strip along black metal. "Actually, painting is part of her whole mid-life crisis. Along with the Porsche."

The Porsche. That's why Tandy was here. The same

reason Greg had left so abruptly. Maybe she shouldn't be hurt by his hasty departure. He was doing what he did best, and he was doing it for his friends. "You said Susan isn't the only suspect. Who else does the FBI suspect?"

"Not the FBI so much as Griffin." Connor shrugged. "McNeil questioned our two new farmhands in Spanish and left, but since Griffin couldn't understand what was said, he is staying behind to use a translator app and interview them all over again."

A vision of Griffin trying to interrogate foreigners played in her mind like an old Chevy Chase comedy. "Do you think they are guilty?"

Connor returned to his work. "Farm hands usually don't know much about breaking into cars."

As much as Tandy didn't want to stereotype anyone, she had to admit the typical migrant worker didn't fit the profile of a high-tech car thief. "You think Griffin is being overly zealous in order to impress the Feds?"

"Our sheriff? Overzealous? Whaaat?"

Tandy gave a sad smirk. It would be funnier if not for the possibility of Griffin being right about there still being a murderer on the loose.

The door below burst open. Griffin strode in, eyes scanning the room. "Where's Vic Whitaker?"

Connor nodded toward the floor below. "Okay, he's overzealous."

Tandy would have loved to agree with him, but knowing Vic, her ex had done something to rile up the police. Either that or Greg had found new evidence to point Vic's way and turned it in.

She walked to the loft railing. "What's wrong, Griffin?"

The good sheriff stepped wide like he was ready to draw his weapon in a duel before looking up and meeting her gaze.

"He left his vehicle running out front with the doors unlocked. That is against the law in these parts."

Was he kidding? First of all, nobody said "in these parts" unless they were auditioning for a wild west film. Second, Vic would never leave his car unlocked. Third, that was the most preposterous crime she'd ever heard of.

It was like one of those silly laws shared as entertainment at a theater before the movie started: *In Juno, Alaska, it's illegal to take your pet flamingo into a barber shop.*

Even if flamingo-hating barbers had the power to create such laws, what kind of lawman would uphold them?

She was going to need her tea for this. She pivoted to grab the cup from the table, noticed Connor spattered in paint, and realized that if she went downstairs, Marissa could very well come up, expecting a wedding proposal and instead learn that her boyfriend had kissed her best friend. Even caffeinated, Tandy could only handle so much craziness in one day.

"I'm going to go deal with Sheriff Insano, but you should know that your girlfriend thinks you are going to propose."

Connor shot to his feet. "I am."

Tandy paused mid-sip. This was great news. Marissa would be thrilled. Except... "I thought you wanted her to come up here to tell her about kissing me."

"Should I?" Connor rubbed his jaw. "I've been trying to tell her, but stuff keeps getting in the way. And now I'm planning to propose tomorrow after our horse drawn carriage ride. I bought this teaspoon that says, 'Will you marry me?' and I thought that when we came back inside to warm up, you could serve us tea with the spoon inside. But if she's still seething over you kissing me, that could ruin the moment. And I want it to be perfect."

Tandy had thought her painting of a dog was romantic,

but to each their own. She smiled encouragingly. She didn't want to be responsible for destroying his big moment. "I'm sure tomorrow is going to be the best day of Marissa's life."

He rubbed his jaw. "I hope so."

Good night. Tandy was going to get to be a bridesmaid. Maybe Cocoa could even be the ring bearer. She held her cup in front of her like a bouquet and took the stairs regally while humming the wedding march. "Dum-dum-de-dum."

Vic swung the front door open before she could stop humming.

He stomped in. "Two questions. First, Tandy, did you finally figure out that I'm your Mr. Right?"

If her cup had really been a bouquet, she would have tossed it over her shoulder that moment. "No."

"Fine." Vic turned his focus to Griffin with even more passion than he'd sent Tandy's way. "Why is there a boot on my car?"

Tandy paused mid-processional. There went her hopes of Vic leaving town.

Griffin crossed his arms. "You left the keys in your ignition. Even if you're warming up your car, that's against the law. How am I supposed to maintain order in this town when citizens are tempting criminals into crimes of opportunity?"

Vic groaned. "I wasn't tempting them. I was baiting them."

Griffin's eyes narrowed. "Baiting? Like in a sting operation?"

Vic threw his arms up. "Exactly."

Griffin nodded slowly. "Not a bad idea..." His eyes narrowed. "...*If* you're a detective."

Tandy glanced toward heaven in disbelief. Griffin needed as much help as he could get, but he'd probably arrest her for saying as much. So, she'd help Vic instead. She descended the rest of the stairs with resolve. "Sheriff, obviously Vic had pure motives. No reason to punish him for fighting on your side. You should take the boot off his vehicle. Then he can head home before he gets too involved…"

Vic's unblinking gaze shifted her way. She felt its heat like an oven door being opened. "I'm already involved."

She'd never met a man so persistent. It would be an admirable quality if he'd had such commitment before they'd broken up. "Vic, we're *not* involved."

"Oh, I know that." He motioned with his head toward Greg's law firm across the street. "Your ex involved me in this investigation when he called my boss to ask if my job is in jeopardy."

Tandy clenched her jaw. She didn't want to believe it. "Why would he do that?"

Vic's smile started at low beam before turning on the brights. "It would seem that he thinks the only way you're not going to go out with me is if he puts me in jail for murder."

Marissa wrinkled her nose at Tandy's ex. Or was she wrinkling her nose at the realization that Tandy had to go out with Vic?

She still despised the man the way all women should, but for some reason, Greg felt threatened by him. The only solution was to get Vic arrested or cleared so he would leave town, and the best way to do that was with a spy. Tandy needed to go on a date to gather evidence one way or another.

Tandy pivoted on the worn heel of an ugly combat boot and headed toward the back room. "I'm not going out with you, Vic."

Marissa blocked her path. In this position, she was hidden from Vic by Tandy's body, so she had the freedom to whisper without worrying that the man could read her expression. "You have to go out with him."

Tandy scowled in an Opal-like fashion. "Did he sell you with his toothpaste commercial smile too?"

"No…" Marissa leaned forward. "If you go out with him, you can get him to let down his defenses and find out what's actually going on."

Tandy sidestepped and disappeared into the kitchen with a huff, leaving Marissa wide open for eye contact with Vic.

She smiled, fighting fire with fire. "Sweet tea, Vic?"

Vic hung a hand on the back of his neck and shot Griffin a glance. "Depends on how long I'm going to be here."

Griffin pulled out his pad of tickets. "Since you claim to have good intentions the way Tandy said, I'll take the boot off your car, but I'm still writing you up with a fine. If it happens again, I'll have to arrest you."

Vic's dimples flashed "If you hadn't interfered in my sting, sir, you might be arresting the real criminal right now."

Griffin glanced up from where he scribbled. "Do you want off with a fine or not?"

Vic held up his hands in surrender.

Grabbing a glass, Marissa poured sweet tea for Vic. That should keep him around long enough for her to talk Tandy into accepting a date and playing spy. She stood tall and sucked in her core muscles to help her balance the way her Pilates instructor had tried to train her. Then she carried the glass across the room with great care.

Connor watched from the loft above. Was he thinking about how much he loved her and wanted to marry her? She tossed her hair to look pretty and feminine for him—her future husband.

Unfortunately, the toss shifted her center of gravity. Her left heel wobbled, twisted, tipped. Her entire frame tilted sideways. She stomped her right foot across her body to catch her weight. With two more quick steps, she was able to keep from going down. She sighed in relief and reached one hand out to steady her weight on the table just to be sure.

The glass in her hand slid against the condensation on her fingers. She reached to keep it from crashing to the floor, but she only managed to juggle it for a second before pitching it directly at Vic.

Liquid darkened his khaki Henley and ice clattered to the ground. He stepped away in surprise. "What was that for?"

Marissa had been doing so well. But now, the one time when she wanted to keep Tandy's ex in her establishment, she had to go and do this. "I'll get you a towel. And more tea. On the house."

Vic wrung out the front of his shirt. "I should hope so. But make it hot tea this time. And I'll carry it myself."

Marissa shot Connor her best "oops" face before running underneath the loft to grab a towel from the kitchen. He'd better propose soon, or she was going to be so distracted that she might accidentally start a food fight.

Tandy stirred a bowl of pink frosting. "I'm making heart-shaped cookie bouquets."

Marissa grabbed a plaid towel then stopped to stare. She'd been the one to have the cookie bouquet idea while Tandy had considered it too frou-frou. The other woman preferred her hearts to be dark like chocolate. "Wouldn't you rather give Vic this towel so he can dry off from where I dumped tea on him?"

Tandy set the bowl down. "You dumped tea on him without me?"

"Sorry. I'm just so preoccupied by my excitement of Connor proposing." Her insides shivered in anticipation.

Tandy held out a hand. "Here. Give me the towel."

Marissa tossed the towel. "Can you make Vic a cup of hot tea too?"

"I'll pour him coffee."

"Tandy…"

"Fine. Tell me how to make *té con leche,* and I'll serve him that."

"Ooh, good choice." Marissa rambled off directions then darted out of the kitchen to find Connor.

Vic held his hands wide to display damp napkins as she passed. "I'm still dripping here."

"Tandy's bringing you a towel."

His eyebrows shot up with interest.

Maybe he wasn't that bad a guy, or maybe she was so overflowing with love and happiness that it splashed onto him like sweet tea. She giggled and was about to run up into the loft when the bell over the front door chimed.

Billie walked in. Marissa had been wanting to serve her orange spice tea, but not when Connor was upstairs, probably on bended knee with ring in hand.

She glanced up to find him watching her with a proud smile. Her belly warmed. He would wait for her. And at least she knew he wasn't doing it from a kneeling position.

She tilted her head toward the tiny Asian woman to let Connor know she'd be delayed a little bit longer, then she scrambled behind the counter to make the world's quickest cup of tea. "Hey, Billie. Want me to get you some orange spice tea? It has cinnamon in it like your apple cider."

Billie set her floral coin purse on the counter and smiled kindly. "That sounds enjoyable. Thank you."

Marissa sighed in satisfaction. In a moment she was going to be in Connor's arms with a ring on her finger. Billie would be okay by herself down here, wouldn't she?

Or better yet… "Is anyone joining you?"

Billie lowered her lashes, and her cheeks flushed. "Joseph is coming when he finishes up some business."

"He *is* a business man." Marissa tapped the order onto her computer screen. "You seem very happy together, though I never would have expected the match with as different as you are."

Billie snapped her tiny purse open and pulled out two dollar bills. "We are very different, but I believe that's what makes us work. If we both agreed on everything, one of us wouldn't be necessary."

Hmm. Marissa had never thought about it like that. "They do say opposites attract." She took Billie's cash and made change before turning to retrieve her tea kettle. Oh how she loved the tranquil sound of trickling water when poured into a mug.

"Yes, opposites attract. Though it also takes work. Since I don't always agree with Joseph, I have to try to see things from his perspective. That's the second key to communication—understanding."

"Second? Are you referring to the three ways Jumpsuit George communicated with God?" Billie had been at the funeral too.

Billie looked up and her lips pursed. "I suppose I was. We must listen to hear someone else's voice to get to know them better, not just to get what we want. In that same way, we should listen to God."

"I like it." Marissa scooped loose tea into a teaspoon

infuser and stirred. She especially liked it when she knew talking to someone would give her exactly what she wanted.

She served Billie then jogged up the stairs in time to the galloping of her pulse. This was really happening.

Connor looked up from his spot at the end of the iron fence, now painted white. It was perfect. Exactly how she'd imagined it. Only, for some reason, she'd thought he might have painted his marriage proposal on it like he had done on her kitchen wall when he'd proposed for the first time.

"It's beautiful," she breathed, then clasped her hands together in expectation of his standard response about how beautiful she was.

"Thanks." He peeked at her from the corner of his eye and cleared his throat. "I have to go buy more nails for the paintings."

That wasn't very romantic. "I thought you had a surprise for me."

He strode toward the stairs. "It can wait. Your loft can't."

Marissa peered at his reserved demeanor. Was he nervous? Was he getting cold feet? She'd be understanding like Billie had suggested. "I'll walk you out."

He looped his hammer in his belt. "Thanks."

She grabbed his calloused hand and escorted him down the stairs and through the coffee shop where Vic still waited for that towel Tandy was supposed to bring him. Apparently, he'd decided to pick up Cocoa and snuggle for warmth. That was going to go over real well with the dog's owner.

"Great service you've got around here," he called after them as they passed.

She sent him a chilly glare, though it had nothing on the temperature of the air when Connor pushed the door open and led the way out.

He squeezed her hand once before releasing it. "You

better get back in there where it's warm. I won't be long."

Marissa hugged herself against the frigid air as Connor hopped into the cab of his truck. She took a step backwards and almost ran into Griffin. The sheriff had squatted next to Vic's car to remove the boot.

He peered up crossly. "Watch out."

"Oops. Sorry." She sidestepped.

His phone trilled. He stood. "This is Griffin. Go ahead."

Marissa double-checked her surroundings to make sure there were no other crouching cops that she might stumble over before returning indoors.

"Calm down, Fred."

She grabbed the frozen doorknob and peeked through the window in case somebody inside the door might get smacked in the face if she entered. If it was Vic, she'd enter anyway.

"You're sure you didn't simply misplace the car keys?"

Car keys? Was there another stolen car? Marissa looked over her shoulder at Griffin, momentarily forgetting the way goosebumps polka-dotted her flesh.

"Oh man. Three sets of keys?"

Marissa frowned. Who had three cars besides Randon? Only a car dealership…

That was it. Fred owned Fairly Reliable Fred's.

Griffin caught her staring and turned his back. But as he walked away, she overheard him say, "Come on down to the department to file a report. There's a new guy in town I'm suspicious of, and I want to show you his picture to see if you recognize him."

New guy? That could mean Vic. And if Tandy didn't go out with him that night to keep an eye on him, he could get away with stealing more cars.

Chapter Twelve

Tandy handed Vic the towel on her way to make them both cups of *té con leche*. "You needed a cold shower anyway."

Vic smirked as he returned Cocoa to his Sherpa-lined dog bed where he belonged. Then he mopped up his shirt that had almost dried by the time Tandy had worked up the courage to talk to him. "Your heart is what's cold."

She turned to both pour his tea and hide her smile. "What did you expect when you decided to drive out here? That I'd be sad and alone on Valentine's?"

"Absolutely not." The stool behind her creaked. Though Vic could leave now that Griffin was taking the boot off his car, he'd followed her to the bar and was settling in instead.

She turned to face him with two cups. She placed his on the counter rather than hand it to him and risk the chance of brushing fingers.

Though their skin didn't touch, his gaze caught and held hers. "Based on the way you purchased a foreign car to spite me, I expected you to be spending Valentine's *angry* and alone."

She'd like to argue that he was way off base, but she had been angry when she'd relocated to Grace Springs. "I've moved on." At least there was that.

He sipped his tea. "And your new relationship seems to be working out for you as well as your impounded Volkswagen."

Tandy lifted her cup towards her lips but paused at his

remark. If not for the puppy portrait she'd seen upstairs, his remark would have hit a little too close to the bullseye. "You want more tea dumped on you?"

Vic laughed. "No, I..." He sobered. "You're drinking tea?"

The bells over the entrance chimed, announcing Marissa's return.

"Don't tell Marissa."

Vic wiggled his eyebrows as if the idea of blackmail delighted him.

Tandy tilted her cup in a menacing way.

"Don't tell me what?" Marissa slip-slided across the room in her fancy boots not designed for snow. "Never mind. I have something to tell you."

Tandy sighed in relief but snapped a lid on her cup to hide her beverage anyway.

"Fairly Reliable Fred's had car keys stolen."

Tandy shifted to catch up with the conversation. "They had keys stolen, but not cars?"

Marissa held up a finger. "Not yet."

Vic turned to look at Tandy, and Marissa's finger dipped down to point at him.

Tandy frowned. Did Marissa think Vic was responsible now too?

Vic followed the direction of her stare and found Marissa's accusing finger.

Marissa tried to cover the allegation by turning her finger and tapping her lips in mock thought, but she wasn't quick enough.

"Hey," Vic defended.

Marissa dropped the gesture. "I'm simply repeating what I heard Griffin say."

"The sheriff said my name? I thought I proved I'm on his

side by trying to catch the thieves."

Marissa bit her lip. "He didn't actually say your name. He said he's suspicious of 'a new guy' in town, and who else would that be?"

New guy? Tandy twisted her mouth in thought.

Vic held his hands wide. "What is it with small towns being so suspicious of newcomers?"

Tandy held up a hand. "Wait. Vic's not the only new guy. Connor said there are two new farmhands who work for his parents. He said Griffin was interrogating them when you left."

Marissa scrunched her nose. "Not very well."

Vic snapped. "That makes more sense. They were at the scene of that crime, and I bet they'll try to steal the cars from Unreliable Fred's tonight too. Whoever the thief is, he's going to want to strike before someone notices the stolen keys."

Marissa planted her hands on her hips and faced Vic. "If the cars do disappear tonight, how will we know it wasn't you who stole them?"

Vic shrugged. "What do I have to do to prove myself innocent? Catch the thieves in the act like I tried to do with my car earlier?"

Tandy shook her head. "No, that's—"

"Yes." Marissa set her chin. "Tandy will go with you."

Tandy couldn't believe she was alone with Vic. Granted, it wasn't a date, but sitting in the car for a "stakeout" was even dimmer and quieter than the first time Vic took her out. Of course, at Primavista they'd had views of the whole city and Italian food rather than their current view of a car dealership and the lingering, greasy scent of fast food hamburgers.

If only Tandy had been able to get ahold of Greg to let him know what she was doing. She'd tried calling and even stopped at his office, but he'd been in court, so she'd had to settle on voicemail. She'd made sure to explain how she'd tried to get Marissa to go with Vic, but the other shop owner wanted to be there when Connor returned in case he was planning to propose.

Tandy also made sure to explain that if Greg hadn't called Vic's boss, Vic wouldn't feel such a strong need to vindicate himself. She was doing this to help get her ex out of town sooner, which she assumed was what Greg wanted.

Hopefully, Vic wasn't the key thief with his whole objective being that of getting her alone in the dark.

"Here's my question." She crumpled her burger wrapper and licked tangy ketchup off her fingers. "If the car thief is so sophisticated, why did he have to steal the keys at all?"

Vic popped a fry in his mouth. "Maybe the only relay attack unit that the car thieves had was the one Marissa found in George's jumpsuit pocket."

Tandy frowned. "Stealing keys still seems risky. They are car thieves. Why not simply hotwire a car?"

Vic wiped his mouth with a napkin. Or was he hiding his smile? "That only works on older cars."

Tandy surveyed the make and models of the cars at Fairly Reliable Fred's. They seemed to be less than twenty years old. "Randon's car was older. They couldn't use the gadget on that one, could they?"

"Nope."

Tandy slid her eyes Vic's way, not wanting to seem suspicious. "Do you know how to hotwire a car?"

Vic shrugged. "Of course. Though if you know anything about cars, it's easy."

She studied him closer out of the corner of her eyes. If

anybody could get away with murder, Vic could. "How?" she challenged.

Vic huffed as if he knew she was testing him. "Well first, you'd wanna see if the car might start by putting a screwdriver in the ignition and turning it like a key. Marissa's boyfriend carries a screwdriver on his toolbelt, doesn't he? Maybe he's the bad guy, and we're going to catch him tonight."

Tandy gave her thinnest smile. "Connor was with us when George was killed, so he couldn't have done it."

"Okay." Vic shrugged. "But if it was him, and his screwdriver didn't start the car, he could use it to pop off the panels from the steering columns." He motioned to the area underneath the wheel.

Tandy leaned closer for a better look in the dim light.

Vic demonstrated the actions with his hands as he explained. "After that, he'd simply need to connect the wires that lead to the battery and the electrical system then touch them to the brown wire for the starter."

Tandy studied the dashboard. "That seems too simple."

Vic motioned to the gas pedal. "You'd probably need to give it a little gas to get the ignition to turn over."

Was this how the Corvette had been stolen, or had the thief made an extra key to drive it away in perfect condition the way they'd done with her Beetle? George had said he'd checked it out for Randon, so it had probably been in his shop at one time, which would have given Derrick access to his keys.

Vic met her gaze, and she realized how close she'd been leaning. "Let's talk about you," he said, breath warm on her cheek. "How did you meet Greg-the-Great?"

Tandy shifted back into her seat to create distance. She didn't want to answer, but she needed to convey her commitment to her boyfriend so Vic would back off.

"My parents used to have a summer house along the river when I was little, and Greg was my buddy back then."

"No kiddin'?" Vic popped another fry. "You knew him when we were together."

Tandy rolled her eyes. That made it sound like Vic had been her first choice. "I hadn't seen him since we were thirteen. We reconnected when I moved here."

"What a fantastic surprise to find out he'd grown up to work for a law firm. He probably makes good money, huh?"

"Yes." She cloaked her words in sarcasm. "Can't you tell how materialistic I am by my Beetle and one-bedroom apartment? I'm obviously dating him because I'm shallow."

Headlights flashed in the distance. The tension shifted from hanging between them to a shared stiffness. Were they about to catch a car thief?

The SUV rolled past, and Tandy exhaled, sinking deeper into chilly leather.

Vic crumpled his bag and set it to the side. When the whites of his eyes flashed her direction, no trace of humor remained. "You're not the shallow one, Tandy. I am."

Tandy rolled the unexpected confession around in her brain. No matter from which angle she studied it, it didn't fit. How could Vic be shallow unless he really was a car thief, and this was his confession? But that didn't fit either. "What?"

"I broke up with you without telling you why. Without going deeper to work on the challenges of our relationship." No trademark grin took the edge off his solemn words.

Tandy didn't know how to deal with an earnest Vic. If he meant what he said, she needed to figure out what he was talking about. "Our challenge was that you had to move to another city. I knew that."

Vic looked down and tapped the gearshift. "I didn't have to move to Toledo. I've always been able to work remotely."

The impact of such a revelation jolted Tandy backwards against the door. If he hadn't had to leave Cincinnati, then he'd chosen to leave. What had she done to drive Vic away? Did she want to know?

He grimaced. "I didn't realize how much I would miss you, so I came here to be honest and see if we could have another chance. I didn't expect you to start dating someone else so quickly."

Okay. She needed to defuse these truth bombs. First, Vic used his relocation as an excuse to breakup with her. Second…second didn't matter yet. She couldn't focus on the fact that he missed her if she didn't know why he'd left in the first place.

"Why *did* you break up with me?" Her heart thrummed with the insignificance she'd felt ever since Mom left.

She'd been angry that Vic had chosen the job over her, like she'd been angry that Greg was choosing his job over her, but now it sounded like Vic had chosen *nothing* over her. He'd rather have been single than be with her. Unless he wasn't single…

She swallowed. "Was there someone else?"

Vic grunted.

Tandy closed her eyes and leaned against her headrest. With the way blood roared in her ears, a whole motorcycle gang could ride into the car dealership and take off with every car in the parking lot, and she wouldn't have even noticed.

"I wanted there to be someone else," he finally said.

Well, that didn't help. Tandy opened her eyes to scowl. "You didn't cheat on me, but you wanted to?"

"No, no." Vic's pleading tone softened the walls around

her heart. "I'm messing this all up."

Vic never messed up his words. They were always confident and joyful like his smile.

"I'm better with cars. Remember when I drove a Dodge Challenger?"

He was comparing her to a Challenger? "Yeah, and you loved it. Except when you found out that it was in the top ten most dangerous cars, you sold it for a Chrysler."

"Yeah. I didn't want to take the risk."

Tandy shook her head. "How am I a risk?" Sure, she had an edgy side, but she'd also almost cried over that portrait of Cocoa.

Vic stilled, his eyes meeting hers in the dim light. "You're white."

Was he racist? Could a black man be racist? "I thought that didn't matter to you."

He started to reach for her but then pulled away. He dropped his hand into his lap. "It didn't. But it mattered to my sisters."

Her spine jerked upright. Her arms flailed. "Your sisters? I thought your sisters loved me."

"They do." He grimaced. "Just not as my wife. They hate it when successful black men marry white women because it feels like a slap in the face to them. Like black women are not good enough."

Tandy knew the feeling of not being good enough. She ran her fingers into her hair and pressed her palms against her scalp, though that wasn't going to keep her mind from being blown. Had Vic really wanted to marry her? Was marrying someone of another race that much different from dating them? If Vic's sisters loved her, why couldn't they accept that Vic did too? And why should this matter now? The two of them weren't even dating anymore. "Why are you telling me this?"

"Because I should have told you a long time ago. I thought I was doing the sacrificial thing by protecting you and any possible children from discrimination and—"

"You *should* have told me." For the first time since Vic had arrived in Grace Springs, they agreed on something.

But what would have happened if he'd told her? How would she have reacted to in-laws who didn't want to be related? And if her children had brown skin, they'd be dealing with racism in a way Tandy had never experienced. Like Brittney, the little girl in her first-grade class who'd cried when a thoughtless boy told her that her skin looked like poop. At the time, Tandy had argued Brittney's skin looked like chocolate then licked her arm to prove it. For some reason that hadn't helped.

If Tandy and Vic had married and had kids together, their children would surely get judged by both races. And all this time, Tandy thought *she'd* had abandonment issues.

"I'm sorry, Tandy."

She stared at Vic's handsome face in a new light. What would she have done if Vic had been honest in the beginning? Had he truly been protecting her by not making her face her own prejudice? Was she glad she didn't have to make that choice now?

"I. Can't. Breathe." She sucked at the stale air and grabbed the door handle.

His hand caught her arm. "Wait."

She pushed against his chest. She was a fighter.

With that knowledge came the answer to the question she'd been afraid to ask herself. She *was* a fighter. "Vic, if you'd told me this when we were still together, I would have married you."

He stilled, except for his lungs, which rose and fell

underneath her palms.

So she continued. "If you'd been honest from the beginning, we could have worked through this. It's not the color of our skin that kept us from being on the same team." She pushed away and straightened, separating herself from her ex in a new way. "I know it wouldn't have been easy, but I would have fought for us the same way I'm going to fight for my relationship with Greg. I'm going to be vulnerable with him even if it means he might reject me the way I felt you did."

Yes. She would. And she needed to start right now. She grabbed for the door handle again.

Vic caught her hand. He didn't pull this time, only held on firmly and respectfully. "Thank you for telling me, but that's not why I tried to stop you a moment ago."

Tandy studied the features she could make out in the dark. He didn't seem to be looking at her. "Why then?"

He didn't answer, but she followed the direction of his gaze to see for herself. A hooded figure snuck from car to car across the street.

Chapter Thirteen

TANDY FUMBLED FOR HER PHONE TO call Griffin. A sense of déjà vu brought back the memory of how she and Connor had found her Slug Bug. At least this time she hadn't kissed anyone.

Better yet, she'd found closure on an old relationship. But that wasn't what made her heart hammer against her chest.

She hit the contact icon for Griffin and held the cell phone to her ear, willing the sheriff to answer right away.

Vic pulled his cell out, as well, only he used his to film the burglary taking place in the car lot. "I don't think this is a farmhand from Connor's ranch."

The phone rang unanswered across the line. Tandy peered through the night at the figure unlocking a door of a convertible Mustang. "Why not?"

"Look how small the thief is. It has to be a woman."

"Susan Snodgrass?" Greg wasn't going to like this one bit. He may even like it less than he liked Tandy being alone with Vic. Was that good or bad?

Vic swiped his fingers across his screen to zoom in. "Besides Susan, the only other female in town who we know can steal a car is Marissa."

Still no answer over the phone. "You're not thinking of making another citizen's arrest, are you?"

Vic's teeth flashed as his grin returned. "We can't let her get away with this."

Tandy narrowed her eyes. "I will not be an accomplice to kidnapping."

"Tandy?" Griffin growled. "Who are you kidnapping?"

Tandy grimaced. The sheriff always answered at the worst times. "Nobody. I'm with Vic at Fairly Reliable Fred's, and we found your car thief."

"I'm on my way." Something clattered, and Griffin's breathing puffed louder in her ear. "Don't let Vic stuff them in his trunk this time, but also don't let them get away."

An engine rumbled from across the street. Headlights flashed.

Tandy's pulse gunned it. "The thief started a car. What do we do?"

"Block the exit," Griffin barked loud enough to be heard from the driver's seat.

Vic cranked on his ignition in response.

Tandy lowered the phone and leaned toward Vic, desperation coloring her view of possible outcomes. "What if she's armed? What if she's actually the one who killed George?"

"She?" Griffin's voice echoed from a distance.

Vic flashed on his headlights, lighting their way and hopefully blinding the enemy. "Then we'll block her exit like Griffin said and climb out the passenger door to escape bullets."

Adrenaline sputtered through Tandy's limbs. She held her breath and gripped the door handle, ready to make a hasty retreat.

Vic shifted into drive and stepped on the gas. The car jerked forward, straight toward the Mustang in the parking lot. The convertible grew larger, racing them toward the exit.

"You're supposed to block her way out, not play chicken," Tandy screamed.

"Oh, I'm gonna block it all right." Vic spun the steering wheel, turning the car sideways and screeching into place between the curbs.

The Mustang didn't slow.

"Vic!" Tandy let go of the door and reached to pull her ex away from the driver's side.

The car rocked on impact, giving her the full sensation of a mosh pit at an actual rock concert. Metal screeched like only heavy metal could. An airbag caught Tandy the way the floor had caught her that one time she'd tried bodysurfing. This show was not something she'd paid for. Though, unfortunately, Vic might have to pay.

Tandy waited for the spinning in her head to stop so she could reorient herself. The car shimmied to a halt, engines whined quietly, powder from the airbags floated eerily in the beam of headlights, and the scent of burning rubber singed her nose hairs.

Vic moaned from his bucket seat compacted into hers. At least he was alive. "I can't believe Susan hit us."

Tandy unsnapped her seatbelt from across tender ribs and twisted to face Vic. "Are you okay? What hurts?"

Vic leaned away from the warped car frame that now shared his seat then reached across his body to hold his left arm close. "I'm fine. She didn't get away, did she?"

Tandy glanced through the shattered window into the windshield of the Mustang. All she could see of the hooded felon was a mouth hanging open. "She looks as shocked as we are."

"Yeah, hard to get away when you destroy your getaway car." Vic grunted then gingerly twisted his head to get a look for himself.

As if the heat of Vic's gaze melted the perp's frozen state, the car thief shoved the car door open and scrambled out.

Sirens blared. Blue and red lights flashed, coloring their surroundings like a disco ball.

The thief ran, zig-zagging through lines of cars like a football quarterback. Griffin's vehicle raced to the other side of the lot. The sheriff slammed on his brakes and jumped out.

The perp scampered, lighter on her feet than Griffin, but not as powerful.

Griffin circled a MINI Cooper and made the sack.

Tandy sank into her seat and let out a deep breath. Their little car crash hadn't been for nothing. Though what a night. Not to mention Vic's confession of how he'd given her up like his Challenger because they were both too much of a risk. A laugh bubbled out. She couldn't help it.

Vic grimaced. "What?" He was likely in pain, but it could have been worse.

She motioned to his side of the car. "Good thing you traded in your Challenger for this safer vehicle."

His eyes crinkled at the sides. He might not be able to laugh about it yet, but someday he would. And just like he was better off without his muscle car, he'd also be able to look back at their relationship as an exciting ride that he'd given up. If they learned something from their communication failure, they could both do better for themselves.

She grabbed her door handle and opened it this time. Once she climbed out, she turned to help Vic follow. Her limbs moved stiffly, but she wouldn't be as sore as Vic.

He remained in his spot, watching through the windshield. "Look," he said.

She glanced toward the spot where Griffin had tackled the thief. The sheriff pulled the perp to her feet and tugged the sweatshirt hood back.

The thief hadn't been Susan Snodgrass after all. The thief wasn't even a woman.

The face Tandy stared at couldn't be the mastermind of a high-tech crime ring, and he certainly couldn't be George's killer.

Her lips parted in shock. "It's a kid."

Marissa had loved making Valentine's treats ever since she was a kid, but it wasn't the same when her boyfriend had taken off on Valentine's Eve. They should be celebrating their engagement.

She scooped sugary scented pink frosting into a piping bag with a sigh. Maybe it would help if she made Connor a special cookie bouquet. She'd have it ready by the time he returned with nails from the hardware store.

She printed words across the frosted cookies to make them look like conversation hearts.

BE MINE

XOXO

SOUL MATE

KISS ME

What she really wanted to write was MARRY ME. Isn't that what Connor wanted too? Or had she been wrong about that?

What a depressing thought. Made her want to stuff all the cookies in her mouth.

At least Tandy could relate to her with relationship issues. She was out trying to prove her ex-boyfriend innocent of a crime so he would leave town and she could move forward with her current boyfriend.

Hmm…Tandy was out. Marissa peeked from the kitchen through the front of her closed shop to make sure her partner wasn't returning to fill Marissa in on the results of her stakeout before heading home.

Nope. Marissa still had the place to herself. Which meant

she could make herself a cup of espresso and pep right up from her funk.

Sneaking behind the counter—even though nobody was there to catch her—Marissa scooped beans into the grinder. The nutty scent was growing on her and made her feel more awake despite not having taken a drink yet.

Wow, she was turning into Tandy. What would Tandy do while waiting for the espresso machine to heat up?

Well, first, Tandy would have said "good night" instead of "wow." Second, if Tandy wasn't out there catching car thieves, she'd be here doing research about them on the internet. Marissa pulled her new phone from her apron pocket. It beeped the beep of a dying battery, so she retrieved a portable phone charger from the lost and found bucket. It had probably been Randon's. He had a million of them.

Now where did she start? She didn't know anything about car thieves.

She entered "Car Thieves" into the search engine and looked for the most recent date. February 12th popped up. Yesterday? Had George's death made the papers? Her stomach churned, but she clicked anyway.

A photo of multiple cars smashed to pieces appeared on her screen. She slid her fingers wider to enlarge the tiny print underneath.

Philippines President sends message to car smugglers by demolishing 29 luxury cars found shipped illegally to a Manila Port.

Marissa frowned. At one-point-two million dollars, that seemed like a waste. Though if the cars were stolen in a country like America, the original owners would have received insurance money, so the smugglers would be the only ones out any money. Besides the insurance companies though, what was the likelihood the cars could be returned to the original owners?

Marissa entered a second question into the search bar to find out where the cars were being smuggled from. Another list of articles popped up. Something about Canada being a haven for smuggling cars followed by an article on American smugglers. She clicked on the American story then sighed in relief to find her country was cracking down on smuggling rings. The border patrol had even ordered freighters that had left port to return when they suspected stolen vehicles were being shipped under the guise of used fitness equipment. Apparently, organized crime operations such as terrorist groups in third world countries would pay top dollar for luxury vehicles. Their United States counterparts were renting or financing cars such as Ferraris and Lamborghinis under fake names, or simply carjacking them, then they were all sent overseas to be sold on the black market.

That information definitely deserved a "Good night!"

Marissa shivered. At least such crimes were much bigger than what her small town was dealing with. No drug lord or kingpin living in the African desert was going to pay top dollar for Tandy's slug bug or something from the lot at Fairly Reliable Fred's. As for Randon's Corvette? It was old. More valuable to a hipster who wanted to impress his buddies at car shows than a sheik to use for racing against a camel. Now maybe Abigail's Porsche...but that one hadn't actually been stolen.

The bell over the front door chimed, jerking Marissa from her thoughts. She hadn't even gotten a chance to make an espresso. But that was okay. Connor was more important than coffee.

He carried a small plastic bag toward her, still hunching against the cold. The weather had colored his cheeks pink, though underneath the scruff of his five o'clock shadow, it only made him look manlier for having braved the elements. She adored him, and she needed to make her adoration clearer.

"Hey, hon. I made you something." Marissa set her phone down and scurried to the kitchen for the cookie bouquet.

Stuffing a small tin bucket with the florist foam, she arranged the cookies on sticks to look like a bunch of heart shaped flowers. She hid the foam under red crinkled paper strips and admired her masterpiece. Now to carry it out front without ruining it.

Marissa used the same technique employed when carrying teacups. She held the bouquet out in front of her, took baby steps, and kept her eyes fixed on it. After making it through the doorway and behind the counter, she looked up triumphantly.

Connor stood at the espresso machine, coffee cup in hand. "Tandy left this on so I made a cup to warm myself up. Then I turned it off for her."

Marissa tried not to look too longingly at his cup and kept the loss to herself. "Oh, okay."

Connor motioned toward the bouquet with his mug. "Is that for me?"

"Yes." She set it on the counter with a flourish. "I know you're working really hard on this project for me, and I appreciate everything you're doing."

Connor plucked a cookie. "I want to make tomorrow perfect for you."

"Really?" So tomorrow was the big day…

She stepped into his arms and gazed up into his cashmere gray eyes. He even smelled warm and cozy like cuddling in a cashmere blanket by the fire.

"How about I make you spaghetti tonight?"

Connor set the cookie down so he could wrap his arms around her. "I would love that. But I should probably tell you something first."

She studied his eyes. She wanted to believe he was going to propose, but he seemed too serious for romance.

She ran her fingers into the thick hair at the base of his neck and reminded herself of Billie's advice. The second key to communication was to understand. Whatever he had to say, she would understand. "What's that?"

His gaze caressed her. His mouth opened.

The bell over the front door rang. "You guys are not going to believe this."

Vic followed Tandy inside. "Y'all should lock the front door when your business is closed, you know. This town isn't safe."

"I know." Marissa deadpanned, wrinkling her nose in an apology to her boyfriend before turning to face their intruders.

Connor lifted a shoulder as if to say, *We should have expected this.*

Tandy unzipped her jacket as she crossed the floor. "Our car thief is a ten-year-old!"

Marissa must not have heard her right. "You think a ten-year-old killed George?" George was a big man. That couldn't be possible.

"No." Vic joined them, arm in a sling.

Marissa did a double take. Had this ten-year-old beat up Vic, as well?

Tandy sank onto a stool. "This kid heard in the news about how there was a car thief in town, so when he went with his mom to the car dealership today, and when his mom couldn't afford a car, he decided to steal one for her and blame it on the car thief."

Marissa held a hand to her mouth. "A ten-year-old swiped the keys?"

Connor crossed his arms. "Did the boy even know how to drive?"

Vic pointed to his bad arm. "He could go, but he couldn't stop."

Marissa widened her eyes in horror. "He ran you over?"

Vic sank down next to Tandy. "Nah. He totaled my car."

"Oh my goodness." Marissa had once tried to kick Vic's taillight out, but she never would have totaled his car. "Did you stick him in your trunk and take him to the police station?"

Vic gave her a look of mock admonishment. "No."

"Be nice, Marissa," Connor chided.

Marissa fluttered her eyelashes up at her boyfriend. Anything for him. She snagged a cookie pop from the bouquet and extended it Vic's way. "Sorry. Have a cookie."

Tandy nodded toward the frosting inscription. "Just don't mistake that for an invitation."

Marissa read the red words. KISS ME. She snatched the cookie away and returned it to the bouquet before he could accept, her cheeks burning.

Tandy plucked the XOXO cookie from the fancy arrangement and took a bite. "So now we're back to the drawing board. We have George's murder, which may or may not have been committed by his brother. We have a convicted felon behind bars for stealing my car. And we have the prank on Connor's mom, which could not have been pulled off by the man in jail. Then there's the device Marissa found in George's pocket, which could have been owned by George or anyone else. We don't know how these crimes are related, and our only suspects are George's niece, a couple of farmhands, and Vic."

Vic took the cookie away from Tandy. "You don't get this until you take me off your suspect list."

Tandy smiled at her ex in a relaxed kind of way. What had happened between those two on their stakeout?

The bell over the front door rang again. Marissa looked up to let the prospective customer know they were closed.

Greg strode across the room, eyes on Tandy and Vic. "What did I miss?"

Tandy shot to her feet and wiped crumbs off her face like she was caught with her hand in the cookie jar. "Did you get my voicemail?"

Greg leaned against the counter with one hand. "The one that said you were out with Vic?"

"We weren't *out* out," Vic tried to explain for her. A change of position from when he'd attempted to get between them at the police station.

Greg silenced him with a condescending stare.

Tandy stepped forward to separate the men. "We were staking out the car dealership like I said. I was trying to help you."

Greg shook his head and looked away. "I want to believe that, but I feel like I've heard this before. The other day you claimed you only kissed Connor because you were going to get caught by Derrick Snodgrass."

Marissa's eyes blinked wide. "You kissed Connor?"

Chapter Fourteen

Warning sirens rang in Tandy's ears. Which fire did she put out first?

If only Connor had told Marissa what happened right after it happened. Tandy would help him attach their figurative fire hose to the hydrant of honesty, so he could douse out his girlfriend's blazing temper, then she'd deal with her own barn burner.

She started by bugging her eyes Connor's direction, then she relaxed their expression to shoot a look of innocence Marissa's way. Her words, however, blurted out with the force of full water pressure. "We kissed because we were scared and thought it was a life or death thing. Don't worry. Next time I will choose death over kissing Connor." Then she flinched and ducked like one might do when expecting an explosion.

Marissa's surprise melted into what appeared to be mild amusement. But then she reached for Connor's coffee cup, giving away her true state of shock. She sipped like she thought she was drinking tea.

The rest of them stared.

"You've had quite the week, Tandy." Marissa smiled like she didn't have a care in the world. "You've been out with all three of these men in the past three days. That's messier than a love triangle. What is it? A love parallelogram?"

"With you here, Marissa, I think it makes a star," Vic countered. "A love star."

Tandy shook her head. "So helpful, Vic." Wasn't he

supposed to back off now?

"Sorry," Vic's mischievous smile betrayed the sincerity of an apology. "I just didn't know about…" He motioned toward Connor. "That's a fantastic excuse, by the way. Forced to kiss someone for survival. I'll have to try it sometime."

Connor ran a hand over his head. "Marissa, this is what I was going to tell you. I didn't want you to get the wrong idea. There's nothing between Tandy and me."

Marissa sipped again. "I know. I'm fine."

But was she? Tandy exhaled, extinguishing the spark of uncertainty in her intuition like a birthday candle. Connor would have to snuff out any remaining embers of emotion in Marissa.

She turned to face her own flame. "Greg, I don't blame you if you're mad at me, but I want you to know you're the only one I'm interested in."

Vic stood and joined her, shoulder to shoulder. "It's true, Greg. I tried my best to steal your girlfriend, but unlike her foreign car, she's equipped with some serious anti-theft devices."

Greg crossed his arms. "I knew you were a thief."

Vic shrugged. "Unfortunately, not a very good one."

Tandy spread her hands wide and glared at her ex. "Why are you still here?"

Vic's eyes lit as if reflecting the fire he'd fanned. "I want Greg to learn from my mistakes."

Greg didn't budge. "Sure you do."

Vic's chin lowered, making him look more sincere than cocky for a change. "I do because I want Tandy to be happy, and she wants a relationship with you."

Greg didn't have anything to say to that, but hopefully he listened.

Vic was a good guy. Simply not used to losing. "Thanks,

Vic."

"You're welcome." He turned his grin on her and shoved the hand from his good arm in his pocket like he could hang out all night.

Tandy gave him a pointed look. "Now go."

"Okay." He winked before sauntering out the door.

Greg studied her. Did he believe Vic? Did he believe her? Did he believe Connor?

She glanced over her shoulder to find Connor and Marissa heading into the kitchen. Marissa had handled the revelation a lot more calmly than Tandy would have expected, but maybe that's because Vic's reappearance in Tandy's life had taken Connor out of the hot seat.

Now that both men were gone, Tandy could focus on the kind of relationship she wanted to build with Greg. But what did he want? She turned to study him. "What are you thinking?"

Greg's dark eyes snagged hers, still filled with questions. "You didn't kiss Vic?"

She didn't know whether to be offended that he didn't trust her or flattered that he really did care. "No." She tilted her head to get a better angle for peering into his soul. "We ate burgers and talked about why we didn't get married, then we caught a ten-year-old stealing a car."

Greg blinked a couple times. "I'm gonna come back to the ten-year-old thing because my brain cannot compute it, and also because it might be connected to my case. But I need to know about the marriage part first."

Tandy smiled—both at his confusion and in her relief. She was more important than Greg's case. "We didn't get married because we didn't communicate the way we should have. And I don't want to make that same mistake with you."

"Okay…" Greg nodded slowly. "Well, if we're going to

improve our communication, I should tell you that I don't want to lose you. To a car thief. Or Connor. Or any more Taye Diggs lookalikes."

A laugh bubbled out at Greg's reference. "Vic kinda does look like Taye, doesn't he?"

Greg didn't laugh but the corners of his lips wiggled slightly. "Yes, which makes me glad you value communication over appearances."

The bunched muscles in Tandy's neck relaxed to let her shoulders sink away from her ears. Being with this side of Greg was as relaxing as drinking *té con leche*. "And I'm glad to know that you value me over your job."

Greg's eyebrows drew together. "You know I do."

Tandy quirked her lips to one side. "Maybe I was only insecure because I thought Taye, I mean Vic, chose his job over me."

"Oh, sweetie." Greg stepped closer and grasped her fingertips in his. How could such a gentle touch feel so secure? "My job is about creating stability. I want to get the bad guys off the street, but I also want to build a home and foundation for a family someday. Why didn't you tell me you felt this way?"

It had been a long time since Tandy had had a family. Her heart quivered. "I didn't want to be rejected."

Greg leaned even closer. He smelled of leather—probably from his jacket, but it made her think of his office chair and the big old books he studied. That might have bothered her before, but not now that she knew she didn't have to compete with his career.

"I'm not going to reject you." His eyes roamed down to her mouth then back up. "Is there anything else you need to tell me?"

She bit her tingling lower lip. She really wanted him to

kiss her, but she'd wanted that before, and he hadn't. Dare she ask? He'd said he wouldn't reject her, but she'd rather he'd want to pursue her on his own.

Cocoa yipped from the corner as if reminding her of the painting she'd seen upstairs. Greg did pursue. "I should tell you that I saw the painting you commissioned for me upstairs, and I love it."

The blue of Greg's eyes flicked navy for a moment. "I'm glad you loved it, though I'm going to have to sue Connor for not keeping it better hidden."

Tandy laughed, knowing he had absolutely no intention of ever suing anyone. Yes, she definitely desired this stable, committed man and his portrait of Cocoa over the way her ex used romance as his art form. Even the cookie Marissa had offered Vic had practically become a pickup line. Just because it said KISS ME…

Tandy smirked. "Oh, and there's one more thing I need to tell you." She reached toward the counter to retrieve the KISS ME cookie from the bouquet. She lifted it between them and spun the stick.

Greg's smile grew. His gaze connected with hers, still and warm.

Her breath compressed in her lungs as if it were frosting in a piping bag.

He took the cookie from her and set it down without looking away. His hand returned to cup her cheek, fingers strong yet gentle. "Tandy Brandt, I've wanted to kiss you since we were teens, which has put a lot of pressure on me to make our first kiss perfect."

She felt the pressure too. It fizzed inside like a shaken soda.

He released her fingers to cup her face with both hands. "If I'd thought of the KISS ME cookie idea, we would have kissed a long, long time ago."

She reached for his waist. This was finally happening. "Pretty sweet, huh?"

His lips brushed hers lightly. "Yes, you are."

She cut her smile short so he could come back for more. He deepened the kiss, and she wrapped her arms behind his back. This had been worth waiting for.

"Tandy," Marissa called from a distance.

Greg pulled away slightly to let her respond, but she gripped his jacket to keep him close. She'd waited a long time for this, after all.

"Tandy!" the distant voice grew louder.

Was Marissa watching them? Did seeing her kiss Greg give Marissa a visual of her kissing Connor, and now she was going to blow up?

Tandy released her grip and nuzzled Greg's nose once more before stepping away. Whoa. Kissing him had really messed with her balance. She clutched his arm to hold herself steady. Maybe this was why Marissa was such a klutz—she was always off-kilter from Connor's kisses.

Tandy's lips felt a little swollen too. She touched them curiously before facing Marissa. "What?" she asked, still in her haze.

"Agent McNeil is on the phone for you." Marissa avoided awkward eye contact by putting the KISS ME cookie back in its pail.

Hopefully nobody would eat the treat after it had been passed around so much. Marissa should use the whole cookie bouquet as a display for future sales instead of selling it. Though Tandy would prefer to take it home and display it next to the flowers and coffee mug Greg had given her. And keep it forever.

Goodness. Was she ever going to get her breathing under

control? Her lungs were even starting to burn a little. Greg had kissed the wind out of her.

Marissa nodded toward the phone. "The FBI has questions about the arrest Griffin made tonight. I get the impression McNeil is worried our sheriff is being a bit too enthusiastic about his job."

McNeil wasn't wrong about the enthusiasm. For example, Griffin had once arrested Tandy. But now that she'd become a resident, she kind of liked knowing their law enforcement cared so much. She'd defend him.

Tandy squeezed Greg's arm before letting go, but without his support, she had to grab onto the backs of chairs to get to the phone. If she wasn't completely giddy over Greg's kiss, she might be a little more concerned about her loss of balance and raspy breath and the way her tongue now felt thicker than usual. Kissing Connor certainly hadn't affected her this way.

She leaned against the counter for a moment so the room would stop spinning before she picked up the receiver. "Lello." Lello? She'd meant to say hello. What was wrong with her. She wiggled her tongue around in her mouth, though as swollen as it had become, it didn't have much room to move.

"What was that?" Asked the stern voice over the phone. "Tandy, are you there?"

She looked to Greg for an answer to that very question. Was he experiencing the same physical responses to their crazy good kiss?

Greg cocked his head, but he didn't seem to be having balance problems as he strode her way.

Marissa beat him to her side.

Tandy turned to face her friend, but the movement threw off her center of gravity. She stumbled.

Marissa caught her, then both she and Greg lowered Tandy slowly to the cold, wooden floor.

"Luth 'appenin?" Did her friends understand her question? Did they have any answers? She hadn't felt like this since her high school graduation trip when Dad took her to Maine and they'd eaten lobster.

McNeil's tinny voice continued to bark through the phone.

Marissa laid a palm on Tandy's forehead.

Greg gripped her shoulders from where he hovered above.

She stared at him in confusion, her throat constricting in panic. Could this be an allergic reaction? After her visit to a Maine hospital, Dad had bought her an EpiPen. She'd quit carrying it years ago in favor of simply avoiding shellfish. And she certainly hadn't had any shellfish today.

All she'd had recently was a bite of Marissa's cookie and the fast food Vic had bought her. He knew about her allergy, so he wouldn't have fed her any shellfish. Unless he'd wanted to hurt her…

She opened her mouth to express her revelation, but only a raspy cough came out.

Marissa tugged the phone from Tandy's grip, her pulse pounding in her ears at the memory of the last time she'd seen someone fall in this shop. The prior owner had been poisoned. And the woman hadn't survived.

Marissa pressed the phone to her ear. "Sir, Tandy is having trouble talking and breathing, and she stumbled to the ground. I'm going to call an ambulance."

"We're not waiting that long." Greg scooped his

girlfriend into his arms.

"I'll meet you at the hospital." McNeil ended their conversation.

Marissa pushed off the floor and set the phone in its cradle with shaky hands. Was the agent always this concerned over sick people, or did he think there was some kind of foul play involved? The question scratched at Marissa's concern like a lottery ticket revealing the losing numbers.

Connor peeked out from the kitchen. "What's going on?" His gaze traveled to Tandy in Greg's arms, but rather than wait for an answer, he grabbed his jacket and rushed to open the front door.

Marissa ignored the twinge of her heart at the visual of how much Connor cared about the other woman. She knew he would have done the same thing for anyone. And Marissa wanted him to. Especially for her friend. Even if the friend had betrayed her.

No. Tandy didn't betray her. She'd been in another scary situation. Marissa should have wanted Connor to kiss Tandy to save her life every bit as much as she wanted him to hold the door open for Greg to carry her outside.

Though the thought made Marissa feel like she was betraying herself.

She'd untangle her emotions later. Right now they had to get to the hospital. She raced out the door into the snow to catch up.

Greg spun toward her. "Get my keys out of my coat pocket."

Marissa glanced past him toward the street. His car was the closest, otherwise she would have pulled out her own keys. She stepped closer to him and stuck her hand in his cool, leather pocket.

Tandy lisped something else between gasps of air. Something about being "selfish"? Was she jealous of Marissa getting so close to Greg? It wasn't like she wanted to be.

Her fingers closed around the hard, jagged keys. She tugged the ring free and clicked the button on the fob. Connor stepped in front of her to pull open the passenger door.

Greg lowered Tandy in.

Tandy clutched at her throat and coughed.

Marissa's own throat tightened at the idea of not being able to breathe. The doctors wouldn't cut a hole in Tandy's neck for a tracheotomy, would they? Marissa needed to go with them to make sure her friend was all right, but she also needed to lock up.

Connor opened the back door of Greg's Mercedes and motioned for her to climb in. "You go. I'll close your shop."

Marissa nodded, thankful, yet unable to kiss Connor goodbye. The last person he'd kissed was Tandy, and she still hadn't come to terms with that fact. She'd kept her reaction in check earlier because she needed to be understanding. Though with the way her guts twisted, she didn't feel understanding. She ducked under Connor's arm and dove into the backseat. "Thank you."

He eyed her, knowingly. So knowingly that he might be staying behind on purpose.

Never mind that. Tandy was wheezing in the front seat.

Marissa snapped her door shut and leaned forward. "I'm going to ask yes or no questions. Nod or shake your head."

Greg climbed behind the wheel and started the engine in one motion. "Vic must have done something to her. I knew he couldn't have given up that easily."

Marissa shot him a wary glance as the car lurched away from the curb. "Poison?"

Tandy shook her head.

Not poison. Did Tandy know something? Marissa gripped her friend's hand. "Has this ever happened before?"

Tandy started to nod then leaned back and opened her mouth to suck harder at the air.

"Anaphylactic shock?" The words came out of Marissa's subconscious like her brain was repeating a Dr. Oz episode that she didn't remember. What did the term even mean?

Tandy grunted and squeezed her hand. Was she in pain or was she saying yes? Probably both. So much for nodding. "She's squeezing my hand. I think that means yes."

"It's an allergy then. I don't remember her being allergic to anything in childhood." Greg ran a stop sign. "Do you have an EpiPen, Tandy?"

Tandy loosened her grip.

Oh no. Either she was blacking out or answering in the negative. "She probably would have gotten it out by now if she did."

"True." Even when Greg was in fight or flight mode, he still reasoned like an attorney. "Vic would have known she had allergies. Did Vic put something in your burger, Tandy?"

Tandy jerked forward in a coughing fit, and Marissa couldn't tell if she was squeezing as an answer or out of fright.

"It's a good thing McNeil is coming." Greg turned the corner, stomping his brakes hard enough to make them screech. He stepped on the gas then spun the wheel to bump over the curb into the hospital parking lot. "Vic is going to get arrested, and I'm going to quit my job and become county prosecutor."

Chapter Fifteen

How often Tandy took her breath for granted. But now the simple act of inhaling was a fight, like when slurping up a berry stuck in the straw of a milkshake. Only not as delicious.

Had Vic really done this to her? Or could it be an accident? Her deluxe cheeseburger might have simply gotten too close to a popcorn shrimp basket when being prepared. Though strange it didn't affect her right away. Back in Maine that lobster had started her throat itching immediately. Then she'd begun gasping like she was currently doing.

Tiny puffs of oxygen clawed her throat. Her surroundings dimmed with every attempt to inhale. How much longer before her whole world went black?

The car jerked to a stop, and her door popped open to a gust of chilly air that would be welcome if she were capable of sucking it in to cool her burning lungs. Strong arms lifted her from her seat and she tried to curl into the comfort of Greg's chest, except coughing fits kept shaking her away. She clutched his neck to let him know she was grateful. And scared.

Marissa trailed behind without incident, momentarily the less clumsy one. She'd even been quick-thinking in the car there with the hand squeeze thing. If only she'd understood Tandy's explanation about the shellfish. But she was here, and that's what mattered.

Sliding doors whooshed open, and warmth enveloped her. Nurses rushed out from behind the counter before Greg even reached them. Tandy would have sighed in relief if she had any air to exhale.

"It's anaphylactic shock," Marissa called. "We think she has an allergy."

Tandy timed her small nod to the rhythm of her gasping.

A tubby woman in Valentine's scrubs stepped forward and popped the top of a clear plastic tube like she was Cupid, unsheathing an arrow. She took aim and shot.

Direct hit in Tandy's thigh. She barely noticed the sting as seconds later, the vice on her throat released its hold. She drank in a cleansing breath that washed away the terror. Then another. Until she was shivering in relief. A sob escaped, as well. Not an I'm-so-sad sob, but an I-cheated-death sob.

Greg laughed to let out his own tension and sank down in a chair, still holding her. She was finally able to curl into him while Marissa took care of admission paperwork and made a phone call. The fact that her phone hadn't died yet was almost as miraculous as Tandy's survival.

The sliding doors whooshed open to reveal Agent McNeil. He stood there with his hands on his hips like a superhero, and Tandy wouldn't have been surprised if he'd blown the doors open with Super Breath. He probably could have even blown her esophagus open with Super CPR.

He strode to their chair and planted his feet wide. "Are you okay, Miss Brandt?"

"I'm alive." In the midst of a murder investigation, that was better than okay.

"She went into anaphylactic shock. The nurse treated her with an EpiPen," Greg explained. "I suspect Vic Whitaker of feeding her something she's allergic to."

Tandy closed her eyes. She didn't want to think. She just wanted to breathe.

"I heard about their little sting operation at the car lot, which never should have happened. Taking the law into your own hands is dangerous. Even when your cohort isn't trying to kill you." McNeil paused. "So why do you think he was?"

Tandy especially didn't want to think about that. She'd had a heart to heart with Vic. He'd seemed so sincere. Could this be about the car thefts like Greg had suggested in the beginning? Someone was still responsible for turning Mrs. Thomas's Porsche around, if nothing else.

"He probably did it because she chose to be with me instead of him," Greg's tone dropped.

Tandy's eyes popped open. She forced herself to speak despite the way her throat had turned into the Sahara Desert. "That's not it. He bought the food before I told him I was committed to Greg." Something didn't fit here.

"Then it's connected to the car thefts." Greg studied her. "Either he came to town for Tandy and couldn't pass up stealing Randon's Corvette. Or Tandy is only an excuse for him to be here because he set up the whole car-theft ring. I suspect he wanted to create a scare to ensure his job stability, but it got out of hand with George's murder, so he stayed here to clean up the mess."

McNeil's eyes narrowed. "Interesting."

Marissa stepped forward. "You can ask him in a minute. I called to let him know about Tandy. I want him to come down here, so you can arrest him."

McNeil clenched his jaw. "I get it that you girls solved the last local murder, but this case is much more dangerous than a caffeine overdose. You can't keep hanging out with suspects and not get hurt."

Tandy twitched. Now that her lungs were comfortable, she was starting to realize the rest of her wasn't. And not only because she was crunched on Greg's lap between the arms of the chair. She slid her feet to the floor to face McNeil, though she didn't have the energy to stand yet. Greg supported her with his hands at her waist. "I don't believe Vic stole any cars. If he did this to me it was so he could be the one holding me right now. He must have thought my allergic reaction would kick in more quickly, and he'd be my hero."

"Ohhh…" Marissa's eyes grew wide. "I hadn't thought of that."

"I'll still question him." McNeil shook his head at the ridiculousness of their situation. "Does he know what you're allergic to?"

The front doors slid open as McNeil spoke. Vic strolled in, a grim expression hiding his dimples. Concern darkened his already dark eyes. "She's allergic to shellfish, and I'm glad to see she's okay. I was always very careful when we dated, and I didn't even eat shellfish in case it could affect her when we kissed."

Tandy felt Greg stiffen behind her. Here she was in the middle again. Though why did Greg have to let it bother him that she used to kiss Vic? She was kissing him now, and… Oh.

She gripped the arm of the chair and twisted to look at her boyfriend.

He flinched when her gaze met his. "I ate crab salad for dinner."

Marissa sank down across from Vic in the waiting room. Tandy and Greg had been ushered into an exam room so she could get checked out by a doctor. McNeil was outside on the phone with Griffin, and Connor was on his way to pick up Marissa. That left Vic as the only other person around.

She didn't quite trust him yet, but he *did* know a lot about car theft, and she wanted to know more.

"That was their first kiss," she said as an ice breaker.

One corner of Vic's mouth curved up. "Some kiss."

Marissa smiled sadly. Was it horrible that she wished if anybody's kiss was going to send Tandy to the hospital that it would have been Connor's? Drat. She needed to forget about it. Tandy was head over heels for Greg. Literally. "He'd been waiting to make their first kiss memorable."

Vic nodded. "Well, I'm glad to know he really cares about her, and their relationship is more than a rebound thing."

"It is." Maybe Vic wasn't such a bad guy after all. If Marissa could forgive her boyfriend kissing her best friend, then maybe she could forgive her best friend's ex for stuffing her in the trunk of his car. It was his passion for stopping car thieves that she wanted to talk to him about. "So, you know a lot about car theft?"

Vic rolled his eyes toward the fluorescent lights buzzing overhead. "I've been through this with your sheriff already."

He thought she was still suspicious of him? "I know he interrogated you, but has he asked you for help?"

Vic grunted. "Hardly."

Marissa shifted forward and leaned her forearms on her knees. "Well if he did, what would you say? Who is behind the prank on Connor's mom's car, and is it the same person who killed George?"

Vic took a moment to read her expression, his own reflecting cautious collaboration. "Only someone with knowledge about cars and a high-tech connection would both have the relay attack unit that you found in George's jumpsuit and also be able to break into a Porsche."

That made sense. Though who would this apply to besides George's brother and niece? "Do you know of any high-tech car theft rings in the area?"

Vic shook his head. "I don't, but I do know that with advanced technology, replacing parts like airbags and headlights are more expensive. That means the demand for cheaper parts through chop shops is on the rise, which is probably why George's brother got back into the game."

"Hm…" Marissa leaned back. "Could Susan Snodgrass be here to throw suspicion off her dad by doing things like turning Abigail's Porsche around."

"Possibly."

A chop shop made more sense for their area than what she'd been reading about in the newspaper. "Do you know about how car thieves are smuggling stolen cars out of U.S. ports to sell in foreign countries?"

Vic's eyebrows arched. "You've been doing your homework."

She didn't have time for his condescension. "Meaning you do know."

Vic huffed. "Yeah. It's about time the U.S. cracked down."

Marissa tapped her chin and mulled over the information. "Smuggling is going down, but chop shops are going up."

Vic shrugged his good shoulder. How could he be so nonchalant about this when he was supposed to be passionate about preventing car theft? "Yeah, smuggling doesn't really affect Ohio. Unless the smugglers could somehow figure out a way to smuggle cars first into Canada, they are pretty much stuck here."

There *had* been an article on how Canada was more lax on car smuggling. "How would they do that?"

Vic scratched his bald head. "Well, Canada is only on the other side of Lake Erie. If they were able to sneak cars across, they could then get shipped out through the St. Lawrence

Seaway."

Shipping cars from Ohio to the drug terrorists she'd read about in Africa seemed like a huge expense and big risk. Why would criminals go through that rather than buying a car legally? "How much did Randon pay for the Corvette?"

"Almost three-hundred thousand."

Marissa's mouth dropped open. Three hundred grand? Randon had more money than she realized, and so did Vic. "Where did you get that kind of money?"

Vic adjusted his sling. "Inheritance. I wanted to buy the 'Vette as an investment, but also to make myself feel better after Tandy and I broke up."

She stared. Did he truly feel three-hundred-thousand-dollars bad about the breakup? And whether he did or not, was it possible that his wealth came not from an inheritance but from smuggling cars?

Vic laughed. "If I were the car smuggler that you think I am, I would be able to sell Randon's car for two to three times that on the overseas black market."

Marissa kept her calculating to herself though obviously Vic knew what she was thinking. "I didn't say I think you are a smuggler."

Vic leaned forward, realized he couldn't rest his injured arm on his leg then leaned back again. "Then who do you think is?"

"It would have to be someone with access to a boat." Good thing she knew a guy with boats.

Billie's boyfriend, Joseph Cross, made his money from riverboat cruises, but could he possibly have the ability to ship cars? She'd find out tomorrow.

The line for coffee at their grand opening circled out the door and around the block. Tandy had been pouring heart shapes on the top of coffee for two hours straight and not even minding that she hadn't gotten a chance to drink her own. This grand opening was everything that she'd hoped it would be.

Not to mention the way Greg had kissed her the night before. It almost ended her life, but other than that, it had been grand.

Marissa wobbled away with Opal's tea, then strode back the best she could in red stilettos. "This stinks."

Tandy scooped a bag of the Valentine's Day popcorn she'd made to give out free for their first day. It wasn't regular popcorn but drizzled with white chocolate and tossed with sprinkles and conversation hearts. Conversation hearts were always good for word-of-mouth promos. "If your feet are hurting, Marissa, put your snow boots back on."

"With this skirt? Never." Marissa stepped behind the cash register to ring up orders as Tandy scooped. "It's not the shoes anyway. My feet went numb from abuse a long time ago. I've got a bunch of other stuff bothering me."

"Like what?" Tandy asked as nonchalantly as possible.

Her partner had no idea how her day would soon turn around with Connor's proposal. He was currently finishing up the loft for The Dating Game, though the couple would soon be well past dating.

Marissa huffed, answering between orders. "I was hoping to find time to track down Mr. Cross and ask him about the possibility of shipping things to Canada from here. I know he has riverboats, but as entrepreneurial as he is, I bet he has other boats too."

Tandy sprinkled a cinnamon heart through a stencil onto the top of a drink and handed it to a mom with three children who'd already finished half their bags of popcorn. "You really think someone is shipping Randon's Corvette across the border the way Vic suggested?"

"Vic knows his cars."

"Yes, he does." Vic's deep voice boomed from the other side of the counter.

Tandy looked up to see her ex, and amazingly enough, her stomach didn't churn at the sight. "Sweet tea?" she asked.

"Nah." Vic waved a hand. "I'm headed back to Toledo, and I don't want to risk y'all dumping tea on me again. I'd have to unpack my suitcase to change, and that's a lot of work with only one arm. I'm here to say goodbye." A glow of fondness gave his dark eyes a golden light and turned his grin from charming to endearing.

Tandy smiled. "Goodbye, Vic. Thanks for being real with me yesterday."

"You're welcome." He nodded. "Take care. And, you know, make sure you've got an EpiPen handy for the next time your new boyfriend tries to kill you."

"Sage advice."

Marissa pointed at Vic's chest. "Speaking of murder..."

Vic held his good arm wide as he stepped backwards. "If you track down any more evidence against me, Tandy knows where I live."

Tandy waved him away. She'd never *really* suspected him. "Goodbye, Vic."

A cute woman with tousled hair and a turned-up nose stepped toward the counter. "Y'all have sweet tea?" she asked in a southern drawl.

Vic stepped forward again. "Make that two sweet teas." He held out his hand to introduce himself to the cute stranger. "Hi, I'm Vic. Are you having a good Valentine's Day?"

Tandy rolled her eyes as she served drinks to her ex and the new woman in his love life. She wished him the best, she just didn't want to have to watch.

Marissa didn't take it as well. She pouted for some reason. "Connor's acting weird. I think that maybe he never planned to propose, and all his secretive stuff was about being afraid to tell me that he kissed you." Ah, *that* was the reason.

Tandy had thought the same thing at first, but now she knew his plan. Once business slowed down, Connor would invite Marissa to join him for one of the carriage rides his mom always offered downtown on Valentine's. That's when Pastor Meade would come in with his worship band to start playing love songs. Billie had even convinced Joseph Cross to get his new "publicity professional" to dress up like Cupid for the occasion.

Connor had gone all out, and Tandy hoped Marissa didn't let the news of their kiss ruin her day. "You know it didn't mean anything, right?"

Marissa handed her paper cups to make their next order for Officer Griffin and Agent McNeil. "Two black coffees. One with a shot of hazelnut."

The one with hazelnut had to be for Griffin. Tandy poured their drinks without comment, as she would rather avoid the possibility of her recent trip to the ER being made public news.

Marissa sent a grimace the direction of the loft, so her thoughts obviously weren't on the case either. "It's not about the kiss so much as it is about Connor not telling me. I'm trying to be understanding like Billie said, but he should also be more open."

Tandy pumped the squirt of hazelnut, popped lids on the cups, and handed them to the oddest couple in the shop before following Marissa's gaze up to where Connor worked. She couldn't explain that he had a good reason to keep his secret, but she could point Marissa in the direction of someone who was better with advice. "You should talk to Billie. She's here too."

"Oh, good." Marissa motioned their favorite antique store owner toward the counter. "Do you want Tandy's Mexican mocha or my orange spice tea, Billie? I know you've tried both, so now is the moment of truth."

Tandy slid sideways to be shoulder to shoulder with Marissa and give Billie a visual of her options. This was like the new Pepsi Challenge. She sweetened the offer. "Either one of our drinks is on the house for you today. You choose."

Billie opened her mouth, but hesitated, looking back and forth between them. "Joseph is joining me, so I'll take one of each."

Tandy passed a mug to Marissa then grabbed her own. "You are a very wise woman."

"In fact, you are exactly who I need to talk to, Billie." Marissa scooped tea into an infuser. "I'm trying to do what you said about being understanding, but I feel like Connor isn't being vulnerable. That got me thinking about how Pastor Meade explained that when George communicated with God, he valued that time. And I don't feel like Connor has been valuing me lately."

"Well." Billie spoke as slowly and thoughtfully as ever. "It's a little different in a human relationship than a relationship with God. With God, we get our value from Him, but in a relationship with humans, we are equals. It's not only about Connor valuing you, but also about you valuing him."

Tandy grabbed her cinnamon to sprinkle over the top. Billie made relationships seem so simple. "Communication key number three is to have equal value?" she guessed.

"Yeah. That's a good way to put it, and it's an important one." Billie nodded. "Because you could make yourself completely vulnerable, and you could be great at understanding the other person, but if they don't do the same for you, then it's a one-sided relationship."

That's how Tandy's relationship with Vic had ended. He'd tried to make Tandy's decision for her.

She slid the mocha across the counter as Marissa did the same with her tea. Billie circled a palm around each one as if using them to demonstrate equality. "To have healthy communication, we have to value ourselves enough to set boundaries. Not everybody gets access to our hearts. Only those who are also willing to be vulnerable and understanding."

That made sense. Like how both Tandy and Marissa had stepped back from interaction with their parents. "If you don't sent boundaries, the other person in the relationship could even take advantage of you. It's the same way Officer Griffin thought someone might not steal a car unless the keys were in it and doors unlocked. It would be a crime of opportunity."

Billie nodded and waved to Joseph who had just entered the front door. Oh no. He had a pink haired woman in a Cupid costume with him. Susan must have been hired as his new promotions manager. And she was early.

Tandy gritted her teeth and looked upstairs to see how Connor would react to this blunder. His eyes bulged, he shook his head, and he pointed from Susan to the front door repeatedly.

Marissa leaned forward. "Speaking of crime, I need to talk to Mr. Cross about the possibility of cars being smuggled on his boats." Her gaze found the man. She narrowed her eyes at his employee. "Is that Susan Snodgrass with him? Why is she dressed like an angel with a bow and arrow?"

Joseph waved back at Billie then lifted his attention toward the loft.

"Um..." Billie looked back and forth between Joseph and Connor. "She's working for him now doing marketing to raise money for her dad's bail. Today she's promoting a Valentine's sale on cruise packages."

Marissa's mouth hung open. "She's working for his shipping company?"

Susan made eye contact with Marissa. Susan ducked her head and spun. Then she turned to sneak out.

"Oh no. She's not getting away!" Marissa kicked off her heels and charged through the crowd, knocking customers and drinks right and left. "Stop her! Sheriff Griffin, stop Susan Snodgrass. She's involved in the car smuggling ring!"

Susan glanced over her shoulder, eyes panicked behind her plastic glasses, though neither the sheriff or the FBI agent joined in Marissa's chase. She turned toward the door.

Tandy covered her mouth in horror. No matter whether there was a real car smuggling ring or whether Susan was even involved, that wasn't why she was trying to get away from Marissa. The poor girl had thought she was going to be part of a proposal, and she'd been trying to sneak out to keep from ruining the surprise.

Marissa had other plans. She closed the space between them and reached to stop Susan from escaping. Her fingers closed around the bow and arrow and she tugged, sending Susan flying toward the center of the shop.

Marissa blocked the door with her body, feet wide, arrow aimed like a weapon despite the pointy end only being the bottom of a heart. Susan regained her balance and looked from Marissa to the crowd around her to Connor up above. He shook his head in disbelief. Or maybe defeat.

Susan pulled a brochure from her pouch. "Anybody want to buy a dinner cruise as a Valentine's gift?"

"Good try." Marissa stepped forward like a huntress. "I know the real reason you are working for Joseph Cross is so you can have access to his boats for smuggling cars. You're involved in your father's smuggling ring, and you're the one who turned the Porsche around at The Farmstead. Officers, arrest her."

The crowd gasped.

Tandy wasn't sure whether to laugh or cry. Hopefully Marissa would be able to laugh about this someday.

McNeil sipped his coffee. "Cupid's the villain, Sheriff. Case closed." He would be a handsome man if not for his sarcasm.

Griffin scratched his head then motioned for Marissa to lower the bow. "Put your weapon down, Marissa."

Marissa held her stance but focused her indignation on Griffin. "Didn't you hear what I said?"

The sheriff took a deep breath. "I did. And I also heard what Susan said when we questioned her. She was working for Cross the night of the Porsche incident. At a wedding show in Cleveland."

Marissa shot Tandy a beseeching look. Tandy shrugged. She didn't know what Marissa was thinking. This would be a prime example for a time when they could use more work in their communication.

Marissa tilted her head at Griffin. "Is that all the proof you have?"

"No." Joseph Cross raised his phone screen. "She did live

videos from the convention center. I've got them here if anybody wants to see. And, Marissa, I was also there, in case you're planning to accuse me of smuggling next."

Marissa lowered the bow and arrow and looked helplessly toward the loft. Connor had been right to worry about something going wrong on the big day.

Chapter Sixteen

"Done!" Connor clapped his hands together and tromped down the stairs in a valiant attempt to distract Marissa from the display she'd put on earlier.

Marissa glanced at her watch and blew out a deep breath. Would anybody return to the tea loft for The Dating Game, or would they all be scared of her?

Well, she was scared too. George's murder had wreaked havoc in all their lives. And for that same reason, Grace Springs needed this Valentine's event to bring them all together.

She and Connor needed something to bring them together, as well. Things had been off since she found out about him kissing Tandy. What a lousy Valentine's.

Horse hooves clopped outside the window. Marissa glanced out to see Abigail's carriage pull to the curb and let off a happy, young couple. That used to be her and Connor.

Since Connor was done with the loft, and the place had died down after she'd pulled a bow and arrow on Cupid, maybe the two of them could make time for a ride around the park. She'd finished all her dessert preparations, and nobody would arrive for the event for another two hours. She needed this.

Marissa stepped out from behind the counter, wrapped her arms around Connor's neck, and inhaled his cedar scent. "Thank you for remodeling the loft. I hope I didn't frighten all the customers away."

He rested his hands on her hips, though his eyes warmed

her more. They softened with relief at holding her again. "I'm sure you didn't. And I'm sorry about not telling you about the thing with Tandy."

He wisely did not mention the word kiss. Now that it was out in the open, they could brush it under the rug.

"Want to take me for a ride in the carriage?"

The corners of his lips curved up. His eyes flashed. "I've been wanting to go on a carriage ride with you all day."

He knew how to make her feel better. "Let me check with Tandy."

Tandy stuck her head out of the kitchen. "Check with me for what?"

Marissa pointed toward the empty carriage outside their front window. "I want to go for a ride around the park with Connor. Could you watch the place for a few minutes?"

"Sure." She glanced at Connor. "Should I have drinks waiting when you return?"

Marissa shivered. "Let's take drinks with us. I'll take one for your mom too, Connor."

Tandy did her little lips twist. "Mrs. Thomas might prefer to come in out of the cold for a bit. Why don't you ask her?"

Marissa grabbed two cups from the stack. "She could still come in but go ahead and make her a coffee while I make tea for Connor and me."

Tandy shrugged and ground beans for two cups, obviously needing one for herself. "You're missing out."

Marissa relaxed into their old pattern of rivalry. "I'm missing out because I don't drink coffee?" she challenged. "How so?"

"Coffee is like Sherlock Holmes. It solves everything."

Marissa tried to come up with an argument against coffee, but it was hard when she was wishing to reenergize with a sip of Tandy's bitter brew. She filled an infuser with tea leaves and steamed her milk. "Sherlock drank tea."

"No man is perfect."

Marissa smiled at the retort. She'd let the comment go. Her man drank tea, and that's what mattered. She combined the two liquids in her paper cups and snapped on the lids before handing one to Connor. "For you, my dear Watson."

Connor took her cup and smiled past her at Tandy. "The game is afoot."

If this was a game, they were two against one. "Let me grab my coat." Marissa spun to jog over to the hooks on the wall.

What her coat lacked in function, it made up for in cuteness. Maybe Tandy could take her picture with Connor as they rode together, holding their drinks. It could be used in advertising or promotion.

"Hey, Tandy." She glanced over her shoulder to find Tandy and Connor switching drinks.

Marissa paused and frowned. Were they doing a taste test like The Pepsi Challenge? Or was Tandy handing Connor the espresso she'd made for his mom?

Connor lifted the cup to sip, and as he tilted his head back, she came into his line of sight. His gaze snagged, and he jerked upright, choking on his drink. He wiped a sleeve across his mouth as if to destroy the evidence.

Marissa took a deep breath. She didn't want to overreact, but it appeared he was sneaking coffee. And perhaps this wasn't the first time.

Her mind rewound to the morning when she'd first tasted Tandy's coffee. She'd thought she'd been sipping his drink then after tasting it, determined it to be Billie's beverage. What if she'd been right the first time?

That meant Connor had been in cahoots with Tandy all along.

Her cheeks burned.

Because kissing Tandy was one thing, but drinking her coffee?

"Did you guys trade cups?"

Tandy turned her head to meet Marissa's gaze, and guilt widened Tandy's eyes to Zooey Deschanel size. That look told Marissa more than she wanted to know.

"We were only…" Connor motioned between the two cups, his voice trailing off because there was no excuse.

"How long have you been drinking coffee, Connor?"

He set the cup down on a nearby table. "Since you opened shop."

Marissa pasted on a smile, trying to keep her emotions at a low simmer. But they were about to boil over. She pinched her lips together and blinked rapidly to hold back the explosion.

Yeah, she was supposed to listen and understand, but there had to be situations where anger was justified. Like when her boyfriend didn't even try the special tea she'd made him. And he kept secrets with the other woman that he'd kissed. Not to mention how he lied to her about it.

In situations like that, one should be allowed to blow up without it being considered an overreaction. She imagined herself splashing his drink on him the way she'd done to Vic.

He held out a hand as if he could read her mind. He wanted to stop her before her thought turned into reality. "I didn't want to hurt your feelings."

"Oh. How considerate." She let her sarcasm splash all over him in place of his drink.

He stepped forward, reaching out. "Marissa…"

She stood her ground, giving him a look that halted his progress. "What?"

"It's not a big deal."

Did he not know her at all?

Marissa shot her business partner an incredulous look. Tandy was aware that it was a big deal, and she let him keep it a secret. Though, as far as Marissa knew, this could have all been Tandy's idea.

Tandy squirmed. "If it makes you feel better, I've been drinking the tea you make him. It's really good."

That did help a little. Though Marissa would never admit it, because this wasn't only about beverage preference. This was about vulnerability and understanding.

Connor motioned with a nod for Tandy to head into the kitchen. "That doesn't help *me*, Tandy."

Tandy took the hint and disappeared.

Marissa huffed and shook her head. "You only want Tandy's help when it comes to lying to me?"

Connor groaned. "I wasn't lying."

"Right. I know. You were protecting my feelings. Were you worried that I'd overreact and dump you again?"

Connor held out his hands as if offering her the chance. "Are you going to?"

Her heart tripped. How did they get here? She'd been expecting a proposal, and now he was expecting a breakup.

She'd been in his arms a moment ago. He'd finished construction on her loft as a Valentine's gift. They were supposed to go for a ride in the carriage. How did they return to that place? More importantly, did she want to return?

She took a deep breath, and her belly quivered as she met his gaze. "Connor, I don't want a bodyguard—someone who thinks he has to protect me from life's difficulties. That's what ruined Tandy's relationship with Vic. I want to be equals."

His jaw softened. He dropped his gaze. "I'm sorry, Marissa. I just don't want to mess this up."

In his attempt to protect their relationship, he may have

destroyed it. "Tandy and I don't enjoy the same drinks, but we have a good relationship." She sent a dark glance toward the kitchen. "Or we did."

"That's different. I figured you'd want your boyfriend on your side."

"Oh…" Marissa propped a hand on her hip and shifted her weight to point dramatically at the cup on the counter. "I *hate* that you like coffee. But as Billie said the other day, if the two of us agree on everything, then one of us is pointless. Our goal in communication shouldn't be agreement but to understand each other." That sounded good, but did she really believe it?

Connor stuffed his hands in his pockets. "Do you understand why I might have been afraid to tell you these things?"

Marissa didn't want to admit her failure, but that's why communication like this was important. Because they could point out each other's blind spots and grow. "Yes." Would he be open to seeing his blind spot? Could he become the man she needed him to be? "And do you understand why I don't feel like I can trust you right now?"

"In that case, I'll leave and give us some time apart." He strode out the door.

Greg arrived at the shop minutes before The Dating Game was scheduled to begin, but he still beat Connor. Tandy quirked her lips and glanced up at the loft to find Marissa taking turns seating patrons and checking for her boyfriend every time the bell over the front door rang.

Greg unzipped his jacket, hung it on a hook, then spun to grab Tandy's hands. "Happy Valentine's! I turned down the shrimp cocktail at lunch, so I could kiss you tonight."

"Much appreciated."

His lips brushed over Tandy's. Her toes curled in response. She'd kiss Greg hello even if it meant ending up in the ER again.

"I left in the middle of a meeting to get here for The Dating Game, and now that I'm here Connor and Marissa don't stand a chance." He tugged her toward the stairs.

Tandy tugged back. Greg returned like a yoyo, smiling down at her. "Did you want another kiss?"

"Later."

"What's wrong?"

"Connor's not here, and we don't know if he's coming."

"Is he okay? Did something else happen to his mom's Porsche?" Greg looked out the window as if looking for the real murderer to take his client's place in court.

"He's fine. Kinda."

Greg faced her, eyes focused to read between the lines. "Is Marissa still upset about him kissing you?"

"Well, that and…"

Greg tilted his head.

No way to sugar coat it. Not even creamer would help the taste of this truth. "I was sneaking him coffee."

Greg stilled. "Tandy…"

"I know. It's bad." She clicked her tongue. "It made me feel like a hero at first, and then I liked the taste of his tea when we traded, so I kept doing it."

Greg leaned forward like he thought he hadn't heard her correctly. "You liked the taste of tea? Did you tell Marissa? That might help soften the blow."

Tandy nodded glumly. "I thought it would help too, but there's the whole thing about dishonesty and secrets."

Greg tilted his head. "A lot of his secrets were involved

in today's proposal. I'd think Marissa would understand that."

Tandy quirked her lips. "He didn't propose."

"Oh." Greg dropped her hand and dug in his suit pocket. "The Dating Game is a chance for Connor to work on this relationship. I'll call him and tell him he needs to be here…"

The bell above the door rang. Connor breezed in. "I'm here." He took the steps two at a time, like a man with a mission.

Tandy watched then checked for Marissa. Sure enough, she was also watching, but Connor charged up the stairs and strode right past her, as well.

"I'm not sure if this is a good thing or a bad thing," Tandy muttered.

Marissa's breath caught. Connor was back. She didn't know if they were going to make it, but she really didn't want to lose him.

As for being contestants in The Dating Game, the timing could not be either better or worse. They were going to be forced to find out things about each other that they might not want to know so they could figure out if their relationship was going to work.

Connor ignored both her and all the guests, despite the effort he'd put into finishing the remodel and her effort at decorating each round table with tiny desserts on tiered trays and vintage teapots that had come from Grandmother's house. He strode to the temporary stage he'd designed that barely fit four chairs with a podium in the middle. He took his seat on one side and glanced at his watch pointedly.

All that work, and he wasn't even going to enjoy it. Well

then. Marissa leaned over the loft railing and waved for Tandy and Connor to come up. They climbed the stairs.

Joseph Cross nodded toward Marissa then stepped up to his place at the podium. They might have had their differences earlier, but he was a professional. It was probably because of his experience announcing Miss Ohio pageants in his seventy odd years that he'd donned a tux for the role. "I'd like to thank you all for attending this grand opening of the tea room at Caffeine Conundrum. And I'd like to thank the owners, Marissa Alexander and Tandy Brandt for inviting me to host such a lovely affair."

Polite applause as if they were at a golf tournament. Marissa nodded to the tables of guests ranging from Billie to Connor's parents. Her stomach flip-flopped at the pleased smiles they sent her way. Obviously, Connor hadn't told his parents that he'd been sneaking coffee and kissing Tandy.

She slid her gaze his direction to see how he felt about putting their struggling relationship on display for Valentine's Day. He kept his eyes fixed on a spot on the floor about two feet in front of him.

Mr. Cross placed a hand on the podium. "The shop owners came up with the idea for The Dating Game when Connor Thomas said he'd have the renovations finished by Valentine's Day. And didn't he do a wonderful job?"

More hand-clapping. As much as Marissa had always loved applause, it was beginning to grate at her nerves like Chinese water torture.

"The owners wanted a fun way to welcome you to their establishment and give you a chance to get to know them better. Without further ado, I now invite our contestants to come forward." Mr. Cross motioned to the stage where Connor currently slumped by himself.

Marissa followed behind Tandy and Greg, afraid the

tension humming between her and Connor would only increase in electricity the closer she got. Sure enough, the staticky feeling on her arms would have made for a super commercial about dryer sheets.

She sat primly and peeked sideways to see Connor's reaction. He continued to stare at that invisible spot on the hardwood.

Mr. Cross held his hands wide in typical gameshow host manner. "Let's meet our couples. First, we have our coffee connoisseur, Tandy Brandt, who recently moved to town and started dating her childhood sweetheart, Greg St. Claire. Greg is a criminal attorney, so he's probably used to this kind of pressure. What makes you think you two will win The Dating Game, Greg?"

Oh no. Mr. Cross was really going off script and hamming it up. Was he going to ask her and Connor that same question?

Connor moved, but only to rub a hand down his face.

Greg gave a winner's smile, and Marissa's heart sunk.

"Well, Joseph, Tandy and I may not have been dating as long as Connor and Marissa, and we've never been engaged before…" Ugh, he played dirty. "But we started out as young friends who looked forward to hanging out every summer when her family was on vacation. I know Tandy has my back because she took the 'Girls Only' sign off her tree fort when we met."

Tandy smiled. "I forgot about that."

The crowd chuckled.

Mr. Cross wiped a fake tear from his eye. "That treehouse story makes me feel a little sappy."

Marissa rolled her eyes. Though maybe if Mr. Cross told enough cheesy jokes, the crowd wouldn't notice the way Connor ignored her.

Mr. Cross turned to face them. "That brings us to Marissa who met Connor after college. How does the story go? You rode your bike off a bridge, Marissa, and Connor had to rescue you from the river?"

Marissa's lips pinched together. Not the kind of face she was taught to make during the interview portion of beauty pageants. She moistened her lips with the tip of her tongue. "I could have swum out of the river on my own, but Connor's always been…uh…protective."

Connor glanced her way at that. What? He didn't like it? She could have said *over*protective, but she wasn't trying to make him look bad.

Mr. Cross played it up. "Now tell me, Connor, how are you going to protect Marissa from losing to Greg and Tandy?"

Her spine stiffened. She forced herself to clasp her hands and smile his direction in what she hoped looked like an expression of anticipation rather than anxiety.

His gray eyes were granite. They held a challenge. The be-careful-what-you-ask-for kind of challenge. "I'm not going to protect her from anything. We'll be completely honest up here and see what happens."

Chapter Seventeen

MR. CROSS SMILED AT HIS AUDIENCE, chandelier light glinting off his pearly dentures. "For this first round, we are going to ask the gentlemen to go outside so our ladies can answer some questions. Once they've answered, we will bring you fellows in, and you will get a point for every answer you guess correctly. Good luck."

Connor stood in unison with Greg. Greg, however, bent over to kiss his girlfriend goodbye. Marissa pretended not to notice, pasting on a smile that was so fake, she might as well have been wearing dentures like their show host.

Connor led the way down the stairs, though Marissa's heart would have beat him to the first floor with how fast it sank.

Mr. Cross stepped from the podium to take Billie by the hand and pull her to her feet. "I'm inviting my lovely assistant to help me with this next part."

The crowd cheered politely. Except for Connor's parents. His mom watched him disappear out the front door below while his dad studied Marissa and rubbed his jaw in the same contemplative way Connor often did. Hopefully nobody else would catch on to the fact that besides playing The Dating Game, Marissa was also playing Charades.

Billie appeared in front of her, blocking her view. As it also blocked the audience's view of Marissa, she gave her cheeks a rest from the strain of smiling.

Billie handed her a stack of poster boards and a Sharpie. Concern softened her slanted eyes.

Marissa tried to look away.

Billie lifted an eyebrow above the frame of her red plastic glasses, signaling that she could see through Marissa's show.

Thankfully, Mr. Cross ushered Billie to his other side where Tandy waited for her supplies. "For each question I ask, our contestants will write their answer down. Are you ladies ready?"

Tandy checked on Marissa, her eyes wide with hope.

"We're ready," Marissa said for them both. Then she sent up a quick prayer. In her beauty pageant days, she always prayed to win. Today she prayed for survival.

"First question. How would you describe yourself in one word?"

Marissa stared at the blank page. She knew how Connor would describe her—Drama Queen. Thankfully that was two words. Also, he was supposed to answer how he thought *she* would describe *herself*.

She scribbled across the cardstock, her heart hammering. She'd never been this real on stage before.

The questions continued. Sweat beaded on her skin and trickled down her spine. She felt more heartsick with every answer. Could she claim to be ill and reschedule the event?

"It is now time for my lovely assistant to welcome the men back to our competition."

Billie must have descended the stairs while Marissa was writing because she was already opening the door below. Connor came in from the cold, hunched in his army green jacket, hands clenching his trusty toolbelt like a security blanket. How could Marissa be both angry at him and want to rescue him at the same time?

Greg patted him on the shoulder as they climbed the stairs. He probably knew what was going on now too. Was he being supportive or simply excited about winning.

Marissa turned to analyze Tandy who had dressed up for the event in black slacks, a black sweater over a white oxford shirt, and black flats. For a change, she almost looked like a good match for her professional boyfriend. Marissa, on the other hand, wore high heels, a full red skirt, and a t-shirt with sparkly kissy lips that didn't go with Connor's carpenter jeans and steel toed boots at all.

He sunk down in his seat, keeping his jacket on like he thought he might be planning to make a quick escape.

"Welcome back gentlemen. I hope you're ready to answer some tough questions."

Connor shrugged, and for the first time in her life, Marissa wished to fall off a stage like she had at the Miss Ohio pageant.

"We asked the girls how they would describe themselves in one word. Let's start with you, Greg. How do you think Tandy described herself?"

At least Connor didn't have to go first. While Greg took his sweet time, chuckling about how savvy and sassy he thought Tandy was, Connor looked Marissa up and down like he'd never seen her before? Really?

"I'm going to have to go with sassy, Joseph."

Tandy groaned and held up her sign saying savvy. "I haven't really been my sassy self lately."

Then Greg ogled over Tandy's beauty and brains a little more, which didn't help Marissa's nerves at all. Because, at the moment, Connor certainly didn't see Marissa in such a light.

Mr. Cross turned to face them. "If you can get this one right, Connor, you and Marissa will be in the lead. How would Marissa describe herself in one word?"

Connor met her eyes. He knew her better than anyone else, but because of that, now everybody else was going to know her a little better than she wanted them to. "Klutzy," he said.

Marissa held up her sign. KLUTZY.

The audience laughed. She lowered her eyelids, uncomfortable with the transparency. She peeked at Connor.

One corner of his lips curved up. It was nice to see him starting to enjoy himself, though his accuracy in this question didn't bode well for his honest answers to the next three. Winning this game could cost them their relationship.

"Great job, Connor. The score is one to nothing." Cross pivoted, turning his back toward them. "Now Greg, to get on the board, what is the most embarrassing thing that has ever happened to Tandy?"

Connor's eyes widened. He had a whole list of Marissa's embarrassing moments to scroll through. Her cheeks burned with the possibilities of what he could reveal.

Greg chuckled. "I'm going to have to go with the time her childhood crush—me—ended up being her defense attorney when she was wrongly arrested for murder."

"Wow," Mr. Cross exclaimed as if he hadn't known all about it. "Have you ever been embarrassed more than that, Tandy?"

Tandy shook her head then held up the poster board in front of her face to hide. Greg leaned behind it to kiss her.

So not fair. Even Tandy's embarrassing moments resulted in romance. Whereas—

"Connor, can Marissa top Tandy's embarrassing moment? And more importantly, can you guess what she would say it is?" Joseph's voice seemed to get deeper as the night went on. Or was he trying to hold back laughter at what he suspected might be coming.

"Well," Connor read her like a psychic pretended to read tea leaves. "Many of you have been witness to more than one of Marissa's embarrassing moments, including today's. And because of that, I'm going to say, her most embarrassing moment is this question. This moment. Right now."

Marissa didn't break eye contact as she held up her poster board. THIS.

The crowd roared with both laughter and applause. If only she and Connor weren't separated by a wall of distrust, then they could celebrate, as well. But even if she could tear down the wall, the next question was sure to build it back up.

"Impressive, Connor. Either you found out these questions ahead of time and are cheating or you know each other very well."

Connor's thin smile did not reach his eyes.

"Third question." Joseph drew the attention away from Marissa for the moment. She watched Connor to see how he would react to what Mr. Cross was about to say. "Greg, to even the score, you must answer this correctly: How would your girlfriend describe your last kiss?"

Connor stilled. His gaze bored into hers. If he was completely honest, he'd reveal to the whole room that he'd last kissed Tandy. And if he didn't, he'd be protecting Marissa with dishonesty. The very thing she'd blown up at him about.

"My last kiss?" Greg clapped his hands together. "I'm sure everybody noticed that we kissed behind the poster board, but what you may not know is that when I kissed her for the very first time yesterday, she had an allergic reaction to the shellfish I'd eaten and ended up in the ER."

The crowd gasped.

Connor huffed then lifted his chin in resolve. He was going to be honest.

But what if Marissa leaned over and kissed him right there? Then she'd be his last kiss. But he could very well define the kiss as manipulative.

"As I was very careful about what I ate today, I would define my last kiss as…" Greg wrapped an arm around Tandy's shoulders. "….safe."

Marissa wished her relationship was as safe.

Tandy shuffled the poster board to hold up the correct response. HOSPITAL FREE.

The audience tittered.

"Hmm…" Mr. Cross stroked his trimmed, white goatee. "Since you were referring to the same meaning, I will accept your answer. Tandy, I am indeed glad to hear that you were not seriously injured. And Greg, way to leave an impression."

More laughter. But that was sure to end once Connor answered the question.

Mr. Cross turned.

Marissa took a deep breath.

"For the lead, Connor. Tell us how you would describe your last kiss."

As if in slow motion, Marissa's eyes rose to meet her boyfriend's. She could almost hear the drip coffee downstairs, ticking off the seconds.

Connor's eyes flashed with the hint of an apology. Then he looked away and opened his mouth. "My last kiss was not safe. In fact, I'd call it dangerous. Because the last person I kissed was Tandy."

Stunned silence seeped into Marissa's pores like steam when pouring from her teapot. She glanced toward Connor's parents to see their reactions. Abigail held a hand to her heart. Mr. Thomas cleaned out an ear with his pinky finger as if he thought he'd heard wrong. Other people looked at her with pity or glared at Connor. Tandy and Greg seemed to take solace in whispering to each other.

"It's not how it sounds." Connor leaned back in his seat

as if thinking that perhaps the worst was over. "Marissa asked me to give Tandy a ride home since her car was stolen, and when we happened to see that very car race by, we followed it to Derrick Snodgrass's house. We were parked in the woods, about to call the sheriff when Derrick caught us. Scared that he might try to kill us, we pretended we'd only parked there to make out. He let us go, and we were able to lead the police to him."

Marissa watched indignance fade from the faces around, and she held up her poster board to join forces with Connor. RISKY.

Connor read the word then lifted both eyebrows high in surprise and perhaps appreciation.

"Yes," she said. "Kissing Tandy was a risk because their lives were in danger *and* because he knew I'd find out about it."

Lips bent upward. Eyes twinkled. Connor's parents relaxed into their seats.

Mr. Cross chuckled. "There's never a dull moment around here, is there? I will accept dangerous as a correct answer."

Connor gave her a nod of grudging acknowledgment. He might not feel the same way after the next question.

"Back to Tandy and Greg." Mr. Cross turned. "Being that you two shared your first kiss only this week, our last question may be a little premature, but our audience wants to know anyway."

Tandy wrinkled her nose. She had nothing to worry about since they were only dealing with hypotheticals.

Connor leaned forward, forearms on thighs. He probably assumed they had the win locked in now, though high score wasn't what Marissa was fighting for anymore.

"What is..." Cross paused for drama.

Marissa's heart clogged her throat.

"…the best way a guy could propose to her?"

Marissa tried to quiet her insides enough that she could pretend to listen for Greg's answer while really listening to hear Connor's every breath.

Greg crossed an angle over a knee as if this was a fun idea to consider. "I think Tandy would like something private and personal. Maybe like a coffee mug with a ring tied to the handle with a ribbon. Or that teaspoon one of her customers brought in for an upcoming proposal that says, 'Will you marry me?' on it."

Tandy grinned and flipped her poster board, but on Marissa's other side, a chair clattered sideways and toppled off the stage, distracting them all from Tandy's response. Had Connor seriously fallen out of his seat at the idea of proposing?

Marissa jerked around to find him standing in front of the platform, taking indecisive steps as if unsure whether he was going to stay or leave. His hands roamed in and out of his pockets, over his face, and through his hair.

"I'm sorry. I just…"

Marissa gripped the sides of her own seat for balance. She'd always been the one to overreact. What should she do when it was someone else making a scene?

Her eyes weren't the only ones glued to Connor. He looked around at them all, as if not confident in who he should address. "I've proposed to Marissa before," he said to the audience, though everybody already knew this. "We broke up, but then we got back together," he told Mr. Cross. His eyes finally met Marissa's, flashing from anger to disappointment to an apology then back. "And I was going to propose again today. After our carriage ride, and before this game."

Shock numbed her senses physically and emotionally.

Was he serious? If so, should she be happy or sad?

Tingles radiated from her sternum into her fingers and toes. "I wanted to marry you, but you've been keeping all kinds of secrets."

"Yeah. I have." He crossed his arms. "To pull off a surprise proposal you have to keep all kinds of secrets. My plan was to make this day perfect for you, and I didn't want anything to ruin it."

Oh no. Was that why he didn't tell her about kissing Tandy or drinking coffee? Because it didn't matter compared to the commitment of a lifetime? She covered her mouth, afraid to ask.

Connor dropped his hands to his sides. "Since we're being completely honest here, I'll tell you all the other stuff I've been hiding."

Could she handle any more?

"I know living above my parents' shop isn't manly, but it's helped me save up the money needed to buy my own house." He nodded toward his parents who clutched each other's hands as if in prayer. "In fact, when we finish shipping out this year's corn harvest to Canada, I'll have enough to pay for a house in cash. I'd been hoping that if you and I got married, I could pay off *your* home."

Marissa's covered her mouth as her whole body went numb. The thoughts in her brain turned to television static. "I had no idea."

His jawline softened. "You weren't supposed to. I wanted to make this the best day of your life. Which is also why I'd planned to be finished with your tea room today—Valentine's Day. This was no accident."

He'd done all of this for her?

She planted her stilettos and pushed to her feet. She

didn't know what to say or do, but she needed to be closer to him. Even if all these people were watching.

Gripping the edge of the podium, she lowered one foot from the stage to the floor with care. "Connor, I'm so sorry. I thought you were just trying to keep me from blowing up." With those words, her stiletto tipped sideways. She pitched forward, arms out to grip anything that would help her balance and prevent the sting under her ankle bone from becoming a serious injury.

Naturally, Connor caught her. That's what he did. His hands circled her waist like she was a mug of tea. She slid her palms up his chest to hook over his shoulders, so she could right her rolled ankle.

He faced her from only inches away, but the adoration that usually beamed through his expression was missing. "The thing is, Marissa, if you trusted me, then you wouldn't blow up. I went through all this trouble to make today perfect for you, and you still don't trust me."

Guilt pricked like Cupid's arrow. Here she was, in the arms of the man she loved, and she'd somehow found a way to destroy their relationship like she destroyed everything else that had the misfortune of getting in her way.

She bit her lip, absorbed confidence from his warm touch, and stared into the depths of his silvery eyes. "I want to trust you."

"But?" he asked, and she could almost feel the entire audience in the room lean closer to listen.

But what? But he'd been keeping secrets from her? Yeah, like how he planned to propose and how he would have enough money to pay cash for a house after they shipped their corn to Canada?

Wait. They shipped corn to Canada? The thought snagged her focus away like a shepherd's crook used to yank cartoon characters off stage. "Why do you ship corn to Canada?"

The corner of Connor's eyes wrinkled. "They make ethanol out of it since their government requires more ethanol to be used in gasoline than ours. Why?"

Her eyes roamed Connor's face as she connected the dots. If the car thieves were using the Thomas corn shipments as a way to smuggle cars, then they had a good reason to be on the farm and were likely the ones who turned Abigail's Porsche around.

"Connor…" she breathed.

An eyebrow dipped down in confusion. "Yeah?"

He had every right to be confused. She'd gone from the topic of wedding proposals to foreign fuel. She'd better explain. "I think stolen cars are being smuggled in your corn shipment to Canada."

Chapter Eighteen

Tandy had viewed Connor's confession like a soap opera until Marissa mentioned car smugglers. Then she switched the channels in her head to a crime drama--where she tuned in to Columbo.

Tandy stepped down from the stage. "Mr. Cross, you do the shipping for Thomas Farms, don't you?"

Joseph looked between Tandy and Connor. "I do."

Marissa directed her question toward Connor. "Where are you in the shipping process?" She happened to be still in his arms. Perhaps she was also picturing herself in a crime drama, but one with a romantic lead like Remington Steele.

Connor looked over his shoulder at his dad like the talk of smuggling was as irritating as a commercial break at a show's climax. Hopefully the couple worked everything out at the end of their episode, but Tandy didn't have the time to watch.

If Marissa was right about the smuggling, then Randon's car might be on Cross's boat right then. The FBI could impound it and maybe even get fingerprints from it to capture the entire smuggling ring as well as George's real killer.

Mr. Thomas stood. "We've got our second shipment loaded and ready for transport."

"It's leaving in the morning." Cross loosened his bowtie. "I'm part of the Trusted Trader Program with Canada, so I rarely get inspected, but the Thomas family and I have been doing this for a long time without any issues."

Tandy's nerve endings danced the Jitterbug. Either she'd drank too much caffeine, or she was onto something. "Mr. Cross, that would make you a prime candidate to be used in smuggling."

Greg stepped down beside her. He must be putting the pieces together, as well. Pieces that would get his client off with a not-guilty verdict. "We need to call the sheriff down to your dock right away, Joseph."

Connor dropped his hands from Marissa's waist, but not until after he'd sent her a look that said stay-tuned. Tandy could feel the heat of it from where she stood. "Should we go down there, Dad?"

Mr. Thomas shook his head in bewilderment. "I can't believe anyone could smuggle cars in with our corn, but I also didn't believe anyone could ever turn Abigail's Porsche around when she had it chained to a fence."

Cross didn't move. "Tandy, you know what it's like to be falsely accused. This could hurt my business. What reasons do you have for suspecting a smuggling ring?"

Tandy met the debonair man's intense eye contact. It said he didn't like to have his authority questioned, and this wasn't the first time she'd questioned it. "It's only going to hurt your business if there are stolen cars onboard your ship."

"It'll hurt my business to be investigated by the police."

Billie set her hand on Cross's arm. "Dear, there are worse things than hurting your business. These car smugglers could be the same ones who broke into my shop."

Cross's wrinkled brow smoothed slightly. "Fine. Call Griffin. But you're not going to find anything."

Tandy dialed the sheriff but didn't even wait for Griffin to answer before she grabbed her coat. She was going down there too. Greg didn't argue but led the way to his car. It was so great being on the same team again.

The crowd dispersed just as quickly. With Cross and the Thomas family all wanting to be at the dock for the investigation, there wasn't much of a gameshow left to watch.

Greg held the door open for Tandy as the patrons filed out of Caffeine Conundrum. This wasn't how she'd expected their grand opening to end, but hopefully it would be full tomorrow with everyone wanting to know if the car thief had been apprehended.

She sank into the passenger's seat as she finished her explanation to Griffin over the phone.

He muttered a few words under his breath before agreeing to meet them at the dock. "I suppose I should let McNeil know too."

Tandy smiled at his attitude. The poor guy kept having his cases taken care of for him. First by her and Marissa then by the Feds. And he tried so hard. "We'll see you there."

Greg snapped her door shut then walked around to the driver's side. "If the real murderer is caught tonight, then this is the best Valentine's gift you could have given me."

Tandy laughed. They may have had their challenges, but they were so meant to be together. "What? You didn't enjoy telling a room full of people all the secrets of our relationship?"

"I actually did enjoy that more than I expected to. But only because you were there." He started the ignition. "Do you think we won?"

The back door popped open as he spoke.

Tandy momentarily relived the competition. "Well, you didn't knock over your chair when asked about the possibility of proposing."

Marissa dropped into the rear, rocking the car slightly. "Did you two know Connor was planning to propose today?"

Tandy twisted to look her friend in the eye as she told the

truth. "Yes."

Greg's eyes widened, perhaps as he made the connection to Tandy's knowledge of Connor's proposal being connected to the teaspoon he'd mentioned. He shifted into drive without another word, and they headed back into the middle of Marissa's soap opera.

Tandy faced her friend. "Susan was supposed to be part of the proposal, but she showed up earlier than expected. As you know." Boy had that backfired. "Anyway...good job making the connection to the corn shipments."

Marissa pulled on her gloves and peered through the windshield at the taillights of the car up ahead. Big pickup truck. Probably Connor. Interesting that she wasn't riding with him.

"I do have experience spotting smugglers." She turned a pointed expression Tandy's direction which was spotlighted by a passing streetlight. "Coffee smugglers."

Tandy faced forward. She had other places to go rather than on a guilt trip. "You never smelled his coffee breath?"

"No. Perhaps I was *too* trusting. Like you were with Vic." Marissa pointed to the turn Connor took as if Greg needed her to navigate.

Tandy twisted around again despite the tug of gravity as Greg turned onto the side street that headed toward the river. "What?" she demanded. "How does Connor sneaking coffee have anything to do with Vic?"

"Well, Vic's probably the one in charge of this car smuggling ring," Marissa said. Likely out of spite. "Don't you think we'll find his fingerprints all over the shipping containers?"

"No." Tandy's tone could not have been more indignant. She quickly checked Greg to make sure she wasn't coming across too defensive of her ex.

Greg lifted a shoulder and sent her a quick glance in the dim light. "It's a possibility. I mean, the thing with Connor's mom's Porsche could have been to get back at Connor for kissing you."

"Greg, you're taking this attorney thing too far, building a case against an innocent man. Neither Vic nor Marissa knew I'd kissed Connor. So, according to the likeliness of your argument, Marissa is as much a suspect as Vic."

"Me?" Marissa squeaked. "You think *I* did it? I'm the one who made the connection with the shipping methods and the whole reason we're headed to the dock right now."

Tandy threw up her hands. "No, I don't think you did it. Just like I don't think Vic did it."

Marissa leaned forward between the seats. "Then who did?"

Tandy thought back to her stake-out with Vic where they'd seen the small thief and assumed it was Susan Snodgrass. Too bad the woman had an alibi for the Porsche incident.

"It's not Derrick Snodgrass," Greg defended his client.

Tandy didn't want to argue. "Probably nobody we've ever seen. I mean, this kind of crime usually happens in big cities. There's probably someone from the big city in town that we don't know about."

Greg slowed for the turnoff to Cross's dock. "From what I've seen, Griffin has been very, very thorough. Too thorough—giving Vic a ticket for not turning off his car and arresting a ten-year-old. I suspect that perhaps McNeil knows some stuff about this case that Griffin doesn't. I'm glad he's going to be here tonight."

Tandy was too. Kind of took the pressure off them to have to solve the crime, which was good since Marissa and Connor had their own problems to figure out.

Marissa had hoped working to solve this crime would bring her and Connor together. But instead, he'd told her she'd be safer if she didn't go to the dock and had taken off without her. With as well as Connor knew her, he should have expected her to follow. Marissa was invested in this thing now more than ever. Because either she'd solved the crime, or she'd ruined Valentine's Day. Again.

By the time Greg pulled up at the dock, five cars had already parked, and everyone from the FBI to the sheriff to Joseph Cross to the Thomas family were heading out toward a flat barge with flashlights, most of them from apps on their phones. Marissa's eyes trained in on Connor as if she was wearing night-vision goggles. He glanced up when Greg parked. See? He'd known she'd hitch a ride.

He didn't stop though. He followed his dad toward the barge.

Disappointment deflated her lungs. She needed to take her eyes off Connor and look past him toward the shipping containers. A car would fit in one of those, wouldn't it? Or maybe concealed between them? Though if the Thomas corn exports were part of an entire smuggling ring, there should be more than one car.

Marissa paused to swipe on her own flashlight, except her phone was dead. She rushed to catch up with Greg and Tandy who'd already stepped onto the dock, causing its joints to creak and their footsteps to echo eerily off the water below.

She glanced at the inky liquid in trepidation. She wasn't known for *not* falling into things, just like the river wasn't known for being warm in winter. In fact, the whole Ohio River had frozen over only a few decades ago due to negative twenty-five-degree temperatures. The current temperature wasn't that frigid, but it would feel like it if she got wet. Or so she'd heard…

Tandy looked over her shoulder. "Want me to hold your hand?"

So they could both go down? "Yes."

Tandy waited in her spot, forcing Marissa to suck in her core and wobble out alone. Why hadn't she stopped to put on the ugly snow boots?

These heels weren't worth the risk. She kicked them off and stepped onto the frosty metal planks barefoot. Her toes stung on contact, but she continued forward, eyes scouting for any possible missteps.

The dock rocked, and the tips of large work boots blocked her path. She grabbed onto Connor for balance, knowing it was him before she even looked up to find his dark shadow as disapproving as a dark shadow could be. "Climb on my back," he said.

Aw, he did want to protect her despite being upset with her. But… "What if I knock you off balance and you fall in?"

Connor pulled her hands off his biceps to hold her in place while he pivoted and dropped onto one knee. Hopefully this wasn't as close to another proposal as they ever got. "This dock is wide enough and sturdy enough to drive on with a forklift carrying shipping containers. I'll be fine."

Easy for *him* to say. But Marissa wasn't going to argue anymore if this man wanted to carry her. Maybe it was a truce. She gripped his shoulders and hopped up to wrap her legs around his hips in the classic piggyback position.

Connor looped his arms under her knees and stood. Her skirt fluffed around her, cinched by his grip.

"This isn't a truce," he said. "I just don't want you to get frostbite."

She scrunched up her nose in a pout he wouldn't see and responded with the kind of tone that would keep him from being aware of her displeasure. "Much appreciated."

"And I would have appreciated it if you wore the boots I bought you."

She smiled and wrapped her arms around his neck. She loved his warmth and sawdust scent as much as she loved his banter. "The boots clashed with my skirt."

"Then you should have stayed at the café." He strode down the dock as if she didn't weigh more than a backpack.

Connor's parents, Tandy, and Greg waited at the ramp leading across to the barge. The law enforcement officers must have already gone on with Mr. Cross.

Tandy bounced like a horseback rider instructing her horse to carry her forward. "Let's go."

"We're supposed to wait here." Abigail's tone dropped at the end, indicating impatience. It made sense she'd be upset about their farm being used as a front for car smugglers, but she might also be irritated with Marissa's whole ruining of Connor's proposal. One might argue that Connor ruined it himself, but Connor's mother would not be that one.

Marissa sank down behind Connor, using his body as a shield from his family. Once stolen cars were discovered, they'd all be singing her praises.

Onboard, beams of light flashed from container to container. Mr. Cross, Griffin, and McNeil systematically swung each door open on the dozen or so shipping containers. Behind each door a wooden board blocked three quarters of the space with only a small area at the top where the conveyor belt would pour in the corn. These bulkheads had planks nailed at intervals like a ladder, so workers could climb up and look inside. Griffin climbed up one.

"How do they know there's not a car underneath the corn?" she asked.

Griffin extended something like a broomstick with a handle then poked it inside the freight container.

"Oh." Marissa's stomach clenched in anticipation

Tandy stepped beside them. "Is it long enough?" she asked.

Connor twisted to see Tandy around Marissa. "The containers are twenty feet long, and since most cars are about fifteen feet, the E-Z Reacher should be able to reach it even if the car is parked at the far end."

Mr. Thomas grunted. "If there are cars in with the corn, then I'm not delivering as much corn as was ordered. I wonder if any of my buyers are actually part of this smuggling ring."

Tandy nodded. "You should give the records of your buyers to McNeil to look into."

Griffin climbed down before moving on to the next container.

Marissa peered through the darkness. "Did he find anything?"

Greg snorted. "With our sheriff's eagerness to catch the bad guys, I'd think we'd be able to tell."

"True."

Marissa hung onto Connor and spoke in his ear. "Wouldn't the corn damage cars?"

Connor turned his face to respond, bringing his lips within kissing distance. "I'm sure they protect them with a tarp or something." In the dim light, she couldn't make out the expression in his eyes, but he looked away as quickly as he spoke.

"It's actually an ingenious idea." Abigail sighed. "I just never expected our farm to be involved in something like this."

Griffin stomped to the head of the boat ramp. "It looks like your farm *isn't* involved, Mrs. Thomas."

Marissa's spine stiffened. She hadn't even considered the fact that she might be wrong. It all fit too perfectly.

Connor's shoulders sagged underneath her grip. At least someone was relieved. Though this didn't help their relationship issues.

"Thank you, Jesus," Abigail breathed.

Tandy hugged herself and shivered. "We're back at square one. At least we can go home now."

Marissa squeezed Connor even tighter. Would he take her home? They needed to talk. Plus, she didn't want to be alone on Valentine's.

McNeil and Griffin tromped across the wide gangplank to the dock. Griffin stopped in front of Mr. Thomas. "I'd still like to take a look at your shipping records to make sure there's nothing I missed."

McNeil breezed past. "I'm going to take the records, Griffin. If this is a case of international smuggling, it's a federal matter."

Connor swiveled to watch him pass.

Mr. Thomas moved to follow but paused by Connor. "I'm going to take McNeil to the farm to get our paperwork. You want to meet me there in case he finds something?"

"Sure, Dad."

Mr. Thomas shot Marissa a look before striding away with his wife.

Marissa grimaced. She usually got along super great with Connor's dad, though this wasn't the first one of his son's engagements that she'd ruined. Maybe she'd crossed the line. Or maybe he was under too much stress to be pleasant. She didn't blame him. It was probably a good thing there hadn't been any stolen vehicles on board.

"Does he really think McNeil will find something, or does he simply want you to get away from me?" she asked only loud enough for Connor to hear.

"Neither are good." Connor turned to follow his father and the law enforcement officers.

"I know." Marissa sighed. "But I'm hoping good can come out of it. We need to talk."

Connor paused to let Greg and Tandy pass. Presumably so they could talk right there. She held her breath as the other couple reached land and everybody else climbed inside their cars and started their engines. Now they could talk without being overheard.

"Marissa—"

"Wait!" Mr. Cross appeared at the end of the gangplank, waving a clipboard.

Marissa looked from him to the taillights disappearing around the bend. Only Greg and Tandy remained.

"What is it?" Tandy asked.

"According to my records, we should have five more freight containers aboard."

Chapter Nineteen

Tandy squeezed Greg's hand. Missing shipping containers sounded like a bad thing, but she was new to this whole shipping container thing. She'd always assumed corn was shipped in big piles like she'd seen done on the Ohio River when she lived in Cincinnati. Unfortunately, the freight container method would definitely make getting cars on and off the barge a little easier.

"What does Cross mean?" she asked. If he meant what she thought he meant, she'd need to call the law enforcement officers again. Griffin had to be getting tired of her number popping up on his phone screen by now.

Cross used his flashlight app to study his clipboard closer. "It means either someone lied about loading them or they were removed."

Tandy's stomach cramped. If there really was a car smuggling ring, the thieves needed the cargo to be onboard. The only reason to remove it would be in case they got caught. "Marissa did announce to the whole coffee shop that she suspected stolen cars to be on Mr. Cross's barge. Anyone there could be involved in the ring and contacted the thieves to remove the cars before we arrived. How does that work?"

"It would have to be someone trained in using my forklift." He motioned toward a small vehicle in front of a large storage building with a silo." Mr. Cross rubbed his face. "Who would do this to me?"

"It's not about you, Mr. Cross," Marissa piped up. "If there were five cars on this load, there might have been five cars on the last load too. That's ten cars worth around a hundred grand each. But then double or triple that—because that's what the cars are worth overseas—and you've got a three-million-dollar business."

Greg jerked at the revelations. "That would definitely be motive for killing George."

Tandy's mouth dropped open. She didn't even care that Greg's first thought was about his client. She simply wanted whoever had brought such crime to Grace Springs to be put in jail. "No wonder the Feds are involved."

Connor stomped toward land, his footfalls loud in the quiet of their collective shock. When he reached the end of the dock, he swung both Marissa's legs to one side of his hips then up and over his arm so that she flipped and landed on her feet. Either the couple had taken swing dance lessons together before or Connor turned into a pairs figure skater when stressed. He left Marissa stuffing her feet into her shoes as he ran for his truck. Not exactly Prince Charming with Cinderella.

"You guys take Marissa home." He stopped and waved Mr. Cross toward him. "Joseph, why don't you let Billie take your car, and you can ride with me to the farm. I need you to tell Dad what you told us."

Joseph tromped across the gangplank, pulling out his keys. "Is that all right, Billie?"

Billie nodded.

Tandy reached for Marissa, to keep her friend from losing her balance as she put on her stilettos. And for support, as Marissa's dreams of a Valentine's proposal fizzled out like an Italian soda left on the counter too long.

Marissa gripped Tandy's shoulders and wobbled into her shoes. "Take me to Connor's," she whispered.

Tandy glanced over at Greg who shook his head. She

wouldn't have taken Marissa to Connor's anyway, but now she could blame Greg. "I think Connor has his hands full."

"He needs my help." Marissa let go of Tandy and stood indignantly. "I'm the one who figured out how the cars are being smuggled."

"Yeah, and now it's going to be handled professionally."

Greg joined Tandy. "Is this about the crime or about making up with Connor?"

Marissa tucked her chin. "I'm his Nancy Drew."

Tandy reached for Marissa's hand. "Come on, Nancy. We're going to take you back to the shop. I'm sure you two will solve the mysteries of the heart, but right now his farm could be in trouble, and your presence would only add to the stress."

Marissa let Tandy tug her. "Was I wrong to be upset at Connor about lying?"

Tandy was ready to change the subject. This was *her* Valentine's too. She would get Marissa to the café, then she could spend the evening with her boyfriend. "Maybe not wrong. Just the wrong timing."

Marissa trudged along. "I could be engaged right now."

Tandy opened the door and placed a hand on Marissa's head to push her down low enough that she could be stuffed in the backseat like she'd seen cops do to criminals on television. "Let's do what George did and search out the meaning of things as if we're listening for God's voice. For example, if you had said yes to Connor, you never would have had that fight, and we never would have found out what's really going on here."

She shot Greg a wide-eyed look of desperation over the roof of the car then climbed into the passenger seat.

Greg joined her and started the engine. "Marissa, your mistakes have helped me too. Even if McNeil doesn't catch the real criminals, this evidence will give the jury more than reasonable doubt that Derrick Snodgrass committed murder."

Tandy shook her head and frowned at her boyfriend. She appreciated his skill as an attorney when she'd been the one in jail but getting Snodgrass a not-guilty verdict was not her goal here.

Greg gave her a knowing smile and shifted into drive. "It's good for my career, but not good enough for the community. I hope they catch the real criminal."

"Me too." Marissa sighed from the backseat. "Because I want my boyfriend back."

Tandy rolled her eyes toward the roof. She kept rolling them as Greg practiced addressing the court for his case and Marissa bemoaned her rollercoaster of a love life. Finally, they reached Caffeine Conundrum and let Marissa out.

Was it too late to salvage their night? Perhaps with dinner at Mama's Kitchen?

"Mama's Kitchen?" Greg asked, though he seemed to be focusing on his law office rather than the Italian restaurant across the street.

She could ignore her old insecurities and keep silent out of fear of having them confirmed. Or she could be honest with Greg, knowing that if their relationship was going to work out, she had to improve her communication skills. She opened her mouth to be real.

Her phone rang.

It drew Greg's attention toward her again. "I was hoping Vic wouldn't call you tonight."

He was still worried about Vic? Tandy arched an eyebrow then checked her phone screen. "It's Connor."

Greg blew out his breath, but Tandy didn't know if this was any better. Was Connor in trouble? Had *he* been arrested for the crime? Or worse, had he been caught by the smugglers, and he'd barely escaped with his life? Would they now come after her because he was going to tell her whodunit?

She tapped the green phone icon to answer. "Connor, are you okay?"

"I'm worried about Marissa."

Gah. Tandy dropped her head against the headrest. Were they all back in middle school, and she was the go between who had to pass messages back and forth? "Then you should be communicating with her."

"I need to figure out what to say before I talk to her. Was she right to be mad about me keeping secrets from her?"

Tandy glanced at Greg. If she stayed on the phone with Connor, this could take a while. Though Greg might be okay with that if it meant he could go call his client's daughter with the update or work on putting together his case.

Maybe that's how their relationship needed to be. She'd let him pursue his passion while she pursued hers. They could be a team in the way they supported each other without jealousy. "Hold on, Connor." She leaned toward Greg. "Did you want to talk to your client while I talk to Connor?"

Greg's eyes widened like he wanted to say yes but was afraid to. Like she was offering him a gift too good to be true.

"Is Greg working on Derrick's case?" Connor asked. The eavesdropper. "Because there's no way Derrick is going to jail for murder now. McNeil is calling his whole FBI team in to search for the missing shipping containers."

Tandy jerked upright. Had she heard him correctly? "Are you serious? Why didn't you tell me this first?"

Greg tilted his head. "What didn't he tell you?"

"There's nothing we can do," Connor explained. "They told me to go back to my apartment and stay out of the way while they investigate. So, I'm stuck here with my parents, thinking about how I blew it with Marissa."

"You didn't blow it," Tandy said automatically, her mind whirring with possible scenarios for what happened to the freight containers and if they really were filled with cars along with the corn.

Greg leaned closer. "What didn't he blow?"

She covered the mouthpiece, so Connor couldn't hear as she spoke to Greg this time. "It sounds like the FBI is swarming the area around Connor's farm by the river. If you want to go tell your client the good news, I'll go wait with the Thomas family. Connor's trying to figure out his next move with Marissa."

Greg glanced at his watch then looked out the window in contemplation. "Going to the farm sounds dangerous."

"McNeil is there. There's no safer place." Though she hoped there were some bad guys too. She'd seen Derrick arrested for his brother's murder, and the arrest of a ten-year-old boy, as well as Vic getting a ticket for leaving his unlocked car running. She wanted to see a real criminal pay.

Greg rubbed his chin. "If I let you take my car, will you pick me up in an hour?"

"Yes." Then they could do dinner.

"Do you promise that if you and Connor get into another situation where you either have to make out or be murdered, you'll die for me rather than kiss him?"

Tandy chuckled and punched him in the arm. "I'd rather drink tea than kiss Connor again."

"Hey!" Connor's voice echoed over the phone.

Oops, she'd uncovered the mouthpiece when punching her boyfriend.

"No offense, Connor."

"I might be more offended if I didn't know you drink tea now."

"Shh…"

Greg narrowed his eyes. "What?"

Oh well. Her secret was out. Marissa knew, so the whole town would know soon. Plus, she was supposed to be practicing honest communication. "I like *té con leche.*"

"No. Really."

Tandy laughed. "I do. It's made with warm milk. Very comforting."

Humor faded from Greg's eyes. "Then you'd better rephrase your statement about kissing Connor."

Like there was still a question. "Okay…I'd rather eat shellfish than kiss Connor."

Tandy barely heard Connor's "now I'm offended" as Greg leaned over and kissed her lips.

"Try to avoid all life or death situations, okay?"

"I'll do my best."

Marissa should have been kissing Connor. Instead she was listening to Lauren Daigle on repeat, drowning her sorrows in a cup of tea, and stuffing her face with all the leftover cookies and pastries that didn't get eaten during The Dating Game.

Ugh. The Dating Game. Connor's confessions. The near miss of her dream proposal.

Tea wasn't going to cut it. It left her feeling as lifeless and depressed as when she started rewriting the icing on the conversation heart cookies. She took a big bite out of the sugary Miss Me cookie and stared at the espresso maker.

Why not? She wasn't going to sleep anyway. Better to energize herself to come up with ways to win Connor back than try to give herself a carb coma.

She switched on the machine and scooped rich, nutty-scented coffee beans into the grinder, reflexively checking over her shoulder to make sure Tandy wasn't coming in to find her giving in to liquid temptation. No Tandy, but the realization of what Marissa was doing stopped her cold. She was being dishonest. In the same way Connor had been dishonest.

She was no better. In fact, she was worse. She was a hypocrite.

Memories of her judgement on Connor flooded her mind. Compared to her "lie," he'd actually had an excuse. He was both afraid of her blowing up as well as trying to make his proposal perfect. Whereas, she was simply saving face.

Pride. Vanity. Whatever you wanted to call it. It caused her to pretend she was something she wasn't. And it was destroying their relationship.

Her guts churned at the idea of coming clean. But if they were going to start fresh, she had to. If only there was a way to sweeten Connor's response like sugar in a bitter brew.

She took a deep breath and inhaled an invitation from the coffee beans she'd abandoned. A smile snuck out from the deep inside parts that only tea and coffee could warm. She pushed the button on the grinder as a plan whirled in her mind to the very appropriate whirring sound of the machine. She'd take Connor coffee.

Grabbing two paper cups, she added a shot of espresso to straight black coffee then stopped to pull on the ugly snow boots Connor gave her. They clashed with her fluffy red skirt, but at least they had pockets, and they would also help prevent her from tripping and pouring her peace offering all over Connor. Perhaps even seeing her dressed so horribly for his sake would be a peace offering in itself.

She stuffed her phone in one boot pocket, then, for good measure, stuffed the portable phone charger in the other. If

Connor wasn't impressed by how she'd dressed, she'd impress him with how practical she could be.

With the coffees securely in a drink carrier and her feet securely on the ground, Marissa shut down the shop and headed to The Farmstead. The place was dark with only a few lights coming from the windows of the farmhouse and Connor's apartment, but that helped her with her goal of sneaking in to talk to Connor without his parents noticing. She flipped off her headlights and parked behind the corn silo so as not to be seen from the main house.

As the car engine and coffee cooled, so did her resolve. Was she doing the right thing? When they'd broken up last year, Connor had been the one to pursue her. Having the tables turned was a lot harder.

He could get angry at her about the way she'd also secretly started drinking coffee. He could send her home. Then she'd be even more alone.

Watching the bright orange square of Connor's upstairs window like a stalker, Marissa tugged her phone out of her boot. "Call, Tandy."

The device responded to her voice command, beeping as it dialed.

Marissa wasn't really a stalker. She was going to go knock on his door. But she needed to practice her coffee confession on her friend first and see how that went over.

The phone rang on the other end.

Tandy probably wouldn't answer. She'd made it very clear that she wanted to spend the evening with Greg.

The phone rang again.

The form of a woman appeared in Connor's window. His mom? Consoling him over his messy relationship with Marissa? Good thing Marissa had waited before going up there. That could have been awkward.

The phone rang again. Marissa bit her lip. She might as well go home.

The woman in the window picked up a phone. She pressed a button and held it to her ear.

"You okay, Marissa?" Tandy said over the phone.

Marissa gasped and covered her mouth. Tandy was in Connor's apartment. On Valentine's Day.

"I'm sorry to interrupt you and Greg…" Marissa's voice didn't sound too strangled, did it?

"Don't worry about it. What do you need?"

Yes, Greg had to be there too. They were both consoling Connor after they consoled her. "Is Greg there?"

Pause. Why was Tandy pausing? Had she really been interested in Connor all along, and now that he'd decided not to propose to Marissa, was she swooping in? She *had* kissed him after all.

No, that was a ridiculous idea. But why was Tandy taking so long to answer. She needed to say something.

"Greg went into his office for a bit because of this new development."

Marissa pointed at the woman in the window, though Tandy couldn't possibly see her or even know she was there. "Aha! You got tired of him choosing work over you, so you decided Connor was the better boyfriend. I never would have imagined that you'd tell me not to go to the farm so *you* could swoop in."

"You *are* imagining it."

Marissa's heart hammered like a carpenter at work. "No, I'm not. I can see you in Connor's apartment. You probably kissed him on purpose too, didn't you?"

The woman in the window turned to face Marissa and leaned forward toward the glass. She sighed over the phone. "Come inside, Marissa. We're up here because McNeil is setting up a trap for the car thieves with Abigail's Porsche, and he didn't want our presence in the farmhouse to scare them away. I was about to leave anyway."

Marissa gripped the phone until her fingers cramped. She wanted to believe her friend, so she'd go see for herself. "Fine."

She jabbed at the red phone icon to disconnect then shoved the device into her boot. This night had gone from bad to worse. All the coffee she'd drank on the way over was not enough to handle the possibility of another betrayal. She grabbed Connor's coffee and guzzled it down like Thor. She would have liked to shatter a mug on the ground like Thor too, but then she'd have to clean it up, and she already had enough messes to deal with. Not to mention that the mug was made out of paper.

With a surprising calm, she tugged at the door handle and stepped into the cold night that would probably sting her face had she not gone numb. She didn't want to break up with Connor. Especially on Valentine's Day. She'd never hated the holiday more.

She clicked her door shut then looked up to the lighted window as she walked. What was she going to do when she got up there? If only she hadn't drunk all the coffee, then she could have used it to splash in someone's face. Whose face would she have splashed it in? Tandy or Connor? They both deserved it.

A chain jangled from the barn. If someone was over there, they could see her now. But what did it matter if she got caught by Connor's parents? It wasn't like they had a relationship to mend now.

Feet crunched on rock and some kind of electronic beep gave the farm a sci-fi feel.

Marissa paused and squinted through the dark. Two

shadows stood on either side of a car. Abigail's car. Someone was stealing her Porsche.

"Hey!" The word burst from her lips before she had a plan for what to do after she interrupted the burglary.

The shadows jolted, and more rocks crunched. The doors swung open. The ignition turned over, and headlights blinded her.

She shielded her eyes and yelled. "Stop!" They probably wouldn't, but her yelling could attract help.

No help came before the driver slammed his door and stepped on the gas, heading directly toward her.

Chapter Twenty

COLD PIN PRICKS EXPLODED DOWN MARISSA'S arms and legs, rocketing her into action. She pumped her arms and legs, her only focus that of reaching the stairway to Connor's apartment before the car reached her.

The Porsche sped forward and swerved to cut her off course. These thieves weren't trying to get away. They were trying to run her over. And she'd thought ruining her boyfriend's proposal was bad. If only getting out of this life and death situation was as simple as kissing Connor.

With renewed energy, and the warmth of the engine fanning her exposed calves, Marissa pushed off the hard ground and dove for cover on the side of the shop. Her roll ended with frozen gravel lodged into the flesh of her legs and in her skirt. The Porsche peeled past.

She propped herself up on her elbows and heaved in oxygen with the gratefulness of someone aware that it might have been her last breath. Red taillights dimmed when another light appeared overhead. Connor and Tandy clattered onto the landing.

"Marissa?" Connor pounded down the stairs and knelt beside her like the devoted boyfriend he used to be. "Are you okay?"

Was he talking about her body or her heart? They both throbbed against an attempt at destruction. And they both would survive. "Yeah."

"I'm so glad you wore the boots I bought you."

Marissa narrowed her eyes. Did it make him feel better

for cheating on her if he thought he saved her life? Now she wished she'd worn her heels to spite him. Only, in her heels, she would have definitely rolled an ankle then been run over. She smirked. She'd survived worse.

Tandy joined them, but only took a second to check on Marissa before looking past toward the taillights shrinking in the distance. "They stole your mom's car. Where's the FBI?"

Connor supported Marissa's head and shoulders so she could roll to a sitting position. He shot a glance down the road then reached under Marissa's arms to heave her higher. "I don't know where McNeil is, but we can't let them get away. Call him now."

Marissa tested out her appendages slowly. She was able to stand without the ache of any broken bones, but her legs did burn where her tulle skirt brushed against scraped skin. Nothing that a hot bath wouldn't cure. And she'd be taking many, many hot baths to soothe her bruised emotions.

Connor raced away like he was aware of the direction her thoughts had turned. She should have expected as much. He'd been racing away all day.

Except this time, he raced to her Jeep and jumped behind the wheel. He'd taken her keys. He was a car thief too. Good riddance.

The headlights blinded her, and her pulse reverted to her earlier fight or flight mode, ready to outrace all attempts at hit and run. Whether it was the caffeine or the adrenaline, she had the energy to sprint a marathon.

Only Connor turned the wheel and spun the car to a stop in front of them. He popped his door open. "Get in. We're going to see where these guys go and report to McNeil."

Marissa didn't know whether Connor was more intent on getting his mom's car back or wanting justice for the attempt on her life, but she was in either way. Without thought, she grabbed the handle nearest her, yanked, and dove into her backseat.

Tandy only froze for a second before racing around to the front of the vehicle and hopping in the passenger side. She already had the phone to her ear when Connor gunned it. "Agent McNeil, this is Tandy Brandt."

Marissa righted herself against the force of propulsion. She buckled loosely into the middle so she could lean forward between Connor and Tandy. Connor had driven her car before, but never with her in the back. Had she made herself the third wheel?

Oh well. There were bigger problems at stake. Like the wheels that had almost ran her over.

Tandy explained it better. "We just witnessed Abigail's Porsche get stolen for real this time. They even tried to run over Marissa."

Marissa rocked side to side and finally gripped the inside edges of the front seats as Connor took corners like a NASCAR driver. The Miss Me cookie churned in her stomach.

"No, I didn't see the thieves. But it looks like they are headed toward the dock."

Marissa glanced around in surprise at their location. If the taillights ahead took the next left, they'd be headed to the barge owned by Joseph Cross. She'd been right about the smuggling.

"Have you found any of the other cars?" Tandy asked the law enforcement agent on the other end of the line.

Had he been looking?

"Okay. Well, if you can catch these guys with Abigail's Porsche, then maybe that's all you need."

The taillights took a hard left.

Marissa leaned forward and pointed in case Connor had

missed the road they'd turned on. "Did you see that?"

"Yes." Connor slowed and flipped off his headlights.

Marissa's heartbeat pounded in her ears as the world outside slid silently by.

"They turned toward the barge. What do you want us to do?" Tandy said over the phone then waited a moment before motioning toward the turn. She hung up and whispered over her shoulder. "McNeil wants us to wait until his team gets here so they can take our statements."

Marissa nodded. She needed to tell the FBI agent about the attempted hit and run. The cars didn't matter as much, but if these guys were the thieves, they'd also killed George. They needed to be stopped so they could never kill anyone else.

Connor slowed as they got closer. Did the thieves know they'd been followed? Would they go about their business like they'd gotten away or were they currently setting a trap and waiting for Connor and Company to arrive. No silhouettes the size of little European cars emerged from the shadows of surrounding trees and brush. Her Jeep continued to creep forward until they could make out the glint of moonlight off the river and the outline of the barge bobbing by the dock.

Connor pulled off the main road and shifted into park. He kept the engine running, either for heat or a quick getaway, but Marissa didn't see any movement that might be a threat. She combed the woods with her eyes before her gaze settled on the two people in the front seat. "If our lives are threatened, you two better not pretend you're here to make out and expect me to hide behind the seat."

Tandy shot Connor a look she couldn't decipher. "I told Greg I would rather eat shellfish than kiss Connor. I'll call him now."

Marissa watched skeptically. Did Greg know Tandy had been at Connor's house?

Connor twisted to face her. "Tandy came over to talk to me about you, Marissa. Because I'm really confused about our relationship."

Marissa did a double take. She'd take confusion over betrayal any day. But this wasn't any day. This was Valentine's. "Me, too," she said with more sarcasm than intended.

"Greg, we're at the docks. The thieves stole Abigail's car for real this time and tried to mow Marissa over. McNeil is on his way down now. We're waiting here."

Marissa couldn't see as well as she could hear, but if Tandy's expression was as sincere as her tone, there was no aloofness between her and her boyfriend. Which meant Connor could be telling the truth.

Connor tapped Marissa on the shoulder and pointed the direction of the side road they'd come from. A dark SUV rolled past toward the river. McNeil?

Her belly flopped. This was the moment they'd been waiting for all week. This made her glad she'd found the fancy device in George's coveralls and had the blowup with Connor that helped her connect the corn shipping to the car smuggling. Maybe this was how it had to happen so George could have justice.

She wasn't ready to fully trust yet, but she could lean back in her seat with relief.

A knock on the window reignited the pulse throbbing underneath Marissa's jaw. She jerked upright, reaching for anything that could be used as a weapon. Normally her stilettos would work but getting hit with a snow boot wouldn't pack the same punch.

Tandy had seen McNeil's big, shiny forehead before he knocked on the window and lifted a flashlight. Marissa must not have noticed him with the way she jumped, but Tandy didn't blame her. The tea lover had been through the wringer that night, and Tandy's assessment didn't even include the way the car thieves had tried to run Marissa over. She reached back to smooth a hand over the bunched muscles in Marissa's forearm.

Connor rolled down his window to get the FBI agent's next direction.

"We got 'em," McNeil said curtly. Probably all in a day's work for him.

Marissa flopped to the side with such dramatics that Tandy almost expected her to hold the back of her wrist to her forehead and whimper, "My hero."

Enough joy bubbled up inside Tandy that she felt like a hero, as well. They were all heroes. She'd called the police, Connor had tracked the enemy, and Marissa had made it all possible by having a very public fight with her boyfriend.

Tandy leaned toward the window. "You should call for EMTs to come look over Marissa. She got banged up when avoiding the hit and run."

McNeil's beam of light crossed over the seats to pinpoint Tandy's friend. She laid there relaxed enough to be a corpse except for the rhythmic puffs of breath that escaped her lips. "Yeah, she looks like she needs help. Is she capable of hiking down to the dock to I.D. the criminals before you leave?"

Marissa popped up like a Jack-in-the-box. "I don't know that I can I.D. them because it was so dark, but I want to give my statement so the men you caught don't get away. Who are they?"

"We arrested a couple of farm hands from The Farmstead."

Connor smacked the steering wheel with his palm. "I knew it!"

"Well, now you can prove it." McNeil's flashlight beam roved from Marissa's face to Connor's then dropped as he moved to open the rear door. "I'll need your statement too, sir. I'll have you all come down to my vehicle while I make the report."

Now that Tandy could relax, exhaustion hit like a weighted blanket. She wanted to curl up in her bed and sleep for days. They were so close. Only a few more lose ends to tie up.

She tugged on the door handle and stepped into the frigid air. "Greg borrowed his partner's car and is coming down too. He'll want to know if you think the farmhands are also the ones who killed George."

McNeil led the way down a trail. "That's my guess. They probably knew about Derrick Snodgrass's chop shop, so when they got caught with the Corvette, they killed George to cover it up and pinned it on his brother."

Tandy's chest tightened, and her eyes burned with unshed tears. She was sad for George, but she was also angry. At least Marissa had survived, and these men would never be able to kill again. She needed to thank McNeil for that. "How long have you known about the smuggling ring?"

McNeil tromped through the snow into the parking area where his Suburban sat next to Connor's mom's Porsche. "It was the tip on stolen keys that brought me here a week ago. When Derrick Snodgrass turned out to be doing nothing more than selling parts, I left to let local law enforcement handle the issue. Then Vic Whitaker arrived in town. That seemed to be a little too convenient to be coincidental."

Tandy's chin jerked up. "He had nothing to do with this. He came to see me."

McNeil smirked. "Oh, I know that now."

Tandy didn't like his tone, but she wasn't going to let it rile her. She'd found closure with Vic, and she'd worked things out with Greg. "Well, Greg will be thrilled to hear you say his client is not a killer."

Connor and Marissa joined them, slower and more subdued. Connor nodded toward the Porsche. "And Mom will be thrilled her car is still in the country."

McNeil tilted his head toward the large metal building on the other side of the loading dock. "It looks like they were planning to drive her Porsche right into a freight container then cover it with corn like you girls suspected. In fact, we found Randon's Corvette already in one."

Tandy raised her eyebrows at Marissa. She'd been absolutely right.

Marissa didn't seem proud over the revelation. No "I told you so" or victory dance. She only peeked at Connor who was too busy pulling out his phone.

"I need to call my dad and tell him about this."

"Sure." McNeil waved them forward. "Why don't you come see first so you can tell him exactly what's going on?"

Tandy looked for Greg's headlights. He wasn't there yet, which meant she still had time. "We can do that?"

McNeil scowled. "I hate to admit it, but you ladies solved another case."

She grinned. It was nice working with a law enforcement officer who didn't have any problems with giving her credit. If Randon was as grateful as McNeil, then maybe she could persuade him to create a phone app for their café as a thank you gift.

She pulled her phone from her back pocket. While she could call Randon now, he'd be even more excited if she could send him a photo of the car. "Can I take a picture?"

McNeil took off toward the building. "Yeah. My crew will be doing that all, as well, but since you're here now…"

Tandy jogged after him and called over her shoulder. "Come on, guys."

Marissa's teeth chattered. She did have bare legs.

"There won't be any wind inside." Tandy beckoned them forward.

Marissa hugged herself and followed. Connor put his arm around Marissa, probably torn between seeing what had been going on with their farm shipments and making sure Marissa was okay.

They entered through big sliding doors to find a variety of crates that looked like train cars and equipment designed to lift and move the crates as well as a conveyor belt to fill them with corn. The air smelled sweet and earthy like a maze at Halloween.

A shipping container with a blue tarp inside caught her attention. "Is that it?" Of course, the smugglers would have to cover the car for protection before dumping corn all over it, though a photo of the tarp wouldn't be as exciting for Randon.

McNeil nodded.

"Unbelievable." Connor's forehead wrinkled. "Dad is going to freak."

Tandy strode closer to get a better angle with her camera. Maybe Randon would recognize a tire.

Connor joined her then walked past into the container, his footsteps clanging. He'd probably seen all this before, apart from the car smuggling.

Tandy looked back at McNeil. "Can I go in?"

McNeil crossed his arms like a bouncer, nodding her through. She stepped up into the metal box and dropped low to really show off the tires.

Connor lifted a corner of the tarp. Sure enough, the polo white vintage sports car could only belong to Randon.

"Hold that there," she said.

Marissa stepped in hesitantly. "You guys, it's really cold. We should go wait in the Jeep."

Tandy snapped her photo then stood. "Yeah, Greg will be here any moment."

Footsteps drew her attention toward the warehouse entrance. "I'm here now." He stopped outside the container and frowned from Tandy to McNeil and back. "What are you guys doing in there? You're contaminating evidence."

McNeil drew his gun and aimed at Greg. "No, they're helping me get rid of the evidence. Particularly, the witnesses. Join them inside, Greg, then everyone toss your phones out here."

Chapter Twenty-One

Marissa's heart drummed against her chest. McNeil was the smuggler. Was he also the one who had killed George?

She wanted to scream "No!" and charge him, but he had a gun, and though she'd outrun a car earlier, she couldn't outrun a bullet.

She could pull out her phone and hurl it at McNeil's head. But what was the worst a phone could do? Possibly distract him for a moment? That wasn't nearly enough to outweigh the dangers of it angering him enough that he'd shoot her.

Greg held up his hands like he was under arrest. If he, a guy who'd just arrived and was probably still warm from his ride, didn't think he had a chance against an FBI agent with a gun, then it was even less likely that she could do anything in her state of being frozen—both literally and in fear.

She sucked in an icy breath and turned to Connor for help.

Connor widened his eyes her way. That had to mean something. But what?

He nodded at his phone before tossing it into the dirt outside the container. Tandy and Greg did the same with the phones in their hands. Marissa was struggling to even compute McNeil's request. But now that she was the only one left with a phone in her possession, she was their only hope. Maybe that's what Connor had been trying to tell her.

"My jacket doesn't have any pockets to hold a phone," she said. That was the truth, so hopefully she wouldn't look guilty. She lifted trembling palms. "See? No phone."

McNeil's facial expression didn't change. It didn't twist into an evil scowl or turn crazed or fearful. It was as if threatening to kill innocent citizens was as routine for him as arresting a murderer. "You could be telling the truth, Miss Alexander. But in case you're not, I'm going to shoot your boyfriend here if you don't throw a phone on the ground in the next five seconds."

The barrel of the gun swung Connor's direction. Connor took a step backward, deeper into the freight container. So much for the possibility that they could gang up on their enemy.

Connor's jaw hardened but the look he shot Marissa was as soft and warm as a caress. Was he saying he was willing to take a bullet so that she would later have the opportunity to call for help? Would she even get such an opportunity? McNeil had the power to shoot them all right there.

If McNeil was only planning to lock them up in the shipping container and let them freeze to death so he could claim they died of natural causes, that would give her a chance to text Griffin for help. In such a scenario, hanging onto her phone gave the rest of them a chance to get away, but she didn't want to live in a world without Connor.

The gun clicked.

Marissa jumped.

Thankfully, McNeil had only been taking the safety off his weapon, not shooting anyone.

"Wait!" She yelled.

One corner of McNeil's lips curled. He might have been a handsome man if not for his black, black heart.

Connor sent her a warning look.

She frowned and shook her head. Should they somehow survive this, he may still leave her, but she wasn't going to let him die for her.

Tipping over, she dug in the pocket of her snow boot and pulled out the phone with its sparkly pink case then tossed it in the dirt. But that didn't mean she couldn't still call for help. She had it set to audible dialing. Once McNeil locked them up and left, she might be able to yell, "Call Griffin," loud enough for her phone to dial the sheriff.

McNeil grunted his approval. "That's what I thought." He kept the gun trained on Connor but looked past the freight container. "Felipe, Bruno, come on out."

Who?

The farmhands that McNeil had claimed to have in custody walked out to join him. They were his accomplices. They'd tried to kill her once, and now, with McNeil's direction, they could succeed.

"You won't get away with this." Greg spoke with the authority of a defense attorney.

Tandy's fists balled. "*You* killed George, didn't you, McNeil?"

McNeil kept the gun trained on them, but even if he didn't, his henchmen probably had guns too. "I didn't want to kill George. I'd only been planning to pin the thefts on him and his brother, and I used the excuse of investigating them as a way to get out here and run the operation. Then these geniuses got the Corvette stuck in the snow and left the relay attack unit behind. I thought I'd cleaned up their mess, but George must have found the device and stuck it in the coveralls for you to find."

Marissa's heart surged with awareness. George had purposely entrusted the device to her. Had he been suspicious that Randon's car had been stolen? If so, he might have suspected his brother, and getting rid of the device could have been a way for him to force Derrick to stop stealing. The part that made her stomach turn was how McNeil considered ending someone's life the way to clean up a mess.

The farmhands avoided eye contact as they swung one of the container doors closed and locked it into place. The bolt clanged a death toll.

The frosty grip of fear surrounded Marissa the way Lake Erie pushed mountains of ice to shore in winter. She pushed through the cold to face McNeil on the other side of the open doorway. "How many people are you going to kill to keep your smuggling operation in business?"

McNeil lifted a shoulder. "You should have left the investigating to the law."

"Some law," she bit back.

Connor stormed past her toward their only escape route. "I'm not going to let you lock us—"

A gun fired. Lead pinged off metal.

Marissa ducked instinctively. Her pulse halted as if her brain thought she might be dead, but when no pain followed, she jerked back to life, looking for Connor.

He'd jumped away from the door, as well. No red spots of blood revealed a wound, so he was okay too, but a little more hesitant to attempt escape without a plan.

She gripped his arm to hold him back in case he changed his mind.

Connor twisted to lean his forehead against hers. "You should have kept your phone. Then I would have known I wasn't dying in vain."

She gripped even tighter and whispered. "My phone has voice dial activation. Once these guys close the doors and leave, I can call for Griffin."

The idea of waiting to call felt as reliable as calling for a lifeguard when drowning, but what other choices did they have? McNeil had made it clear he wasn't afraid to shoot.

"Hey." Greg huddled with them. "McNeil is okay with hurting us, but he doesn't want to hurt the car. What if we put it in neutral, get behind, and push? We can use it as a shield and maybe even block the door open with it."

Tandy ran to the vehicle and ripped off the tarp, revealing a black convertible top. She pulled at the door handle, but it didn't budge.

Without pause, Connor strode to the car, whipped a hammer from his toolbelt, and smashed the corner of the window. Shards of glass rained down. "Hurry, before they close the second door."

"Hey, boss," a Hispanic accent rose from outside the container. "They're breaking into the car."

The dude spoke English. Probably even wrote the note on Abigail's car.

McNeil growled. "Another mess I'll have to clean up. Just keep going."

Connor pulled the driver's side door open and bent inside to shift and disable the parking brake.

Marissa rushed behind the bumper and prepared to push. Her heart ticked out the milliseconds of time left before the second crate door would swing shut and leave them to either freeze or suffocate.

Except the men didn't swing the door shut. They slid a panel of wood inside the opening, leaving only a foot of space left at the top and blocking out much of the light.

Tandy and Greg flanked her, hands planted against the trunk. They would have to ram the panel.

"I got it," Connor called from where he'd bent inside the car. "Start pushing." He stood up to race and join them, but the sight of the plank stopped him in his tracks. "Oh no."

"Come on," Greg prompted as if Connor was being lazy.

But Marissa knew better. If Connor had stopped, then something was seriously wrong. "What?"

His answer was interrupted by the rumble of hydraulics, and the front of the container rose higher, rocking them all on their heels. The traction on Marissa's boots kept her in place, but both Tandy and Greg tipped backwards and smashed into the far wall.

"What's happening?" Tandy yelled.

Connor held onto the car for balance and looked around as if seeing their surroundings for the first time. "They are lifting us up to pour corn in from the conveyor belt."

Marissa gasped at the air. She really was going to drown. Unless she called Griffin now.

She turned to walk sideways uphill toward the small opening like people did when wearing skis. "Call Griffin. Call Griffin!" she yelled. Would the phone be able to hear her voice over the noise of the machinery?

Connor joined her, pressing one palm into the wall to hold himself against gravity while he pushed her forward with the other.

The incline continued to rise. There was no way to keep herself from toppling backwards.

"Grab onto the bulkhead," Connor instructed, then before she could even fathom what he meant, he scooped her into the air high enough for her to reach the top of the plank blocking their exit.

She curled her fingers over the rough wood moments before Connor dropped out from underneath her. Her feet dangled. But as this was as close to freedom as she might possibly get ever again, she strained through her shoulders and biceps to pull herself closer to the opening. It took much grunting and wiggling, but at the same time her mouth reached the opening, the machinery stopped lifting her, and only silence rang in her ears.

"Call Griffin!" she yelled.

Derisive laughter rose from the ground below. "I'm pretty sure you're not talking to me, princess," McNeil mocked her. "But if you're trying to get your phone to dial the sheriff, you should know that your cell battery is dead."

Dread punched her in the gut. She dropped out of her pullup, and the sudden shift of weight pried her fingers from the wood. She screamed as gravity tugged. Her stomach fluttered, wind lifted her hair, and the back of the freight car rushed up to meet her. Strong arms caught her then both she and Connor sank to the ground.

"Oof."

They sat there motionless, her insides trying to catch up with her outsides. Connor's body heat felt nice, but the heat of Tandy's gaze not so much.

"You didn't charge your phone?" Tandy deadpanned.

Marissa hadn't known the mistake was going to cost them their lives. Guilt weighed down her shoulders. All she could do for an excuse was reach into her boot pocket and pull out her portable charger.

Connor tugged a flashlight from his toolbelt and highlighted what was now a useless cord.

Tandy's mouth fell open. "You had that in there too? You could have been charging your phone this whole time."

Marissa had planned to get around to it, but she'd been too distracted by thoughts of Connor. She looked up at him with regret. Yeah, she was in his arms now, but they'd wasted not being together because they'd failed to communicate. "I'm sorry," she said, lowering the cord to the ground.

His sad smile offered forgiveness. "Unless you have another phone in your Mary Poppins boots, don't worry about it."

If only.

A memory nibbled at her thoughts. What was it? Surely, she didn't have another cell phone that she'd forgotten about. So what good could her charger possibly do?

Marissa narrowed her eyes and scanned the area as if she'd find the thought that evaded her. All she saw was Randon's car, shining in the spotlight of Connor's flashlight beam. It was very pretty, but Randon was never going to enjoy it again simply because he hadn't charged his tracking device.

That was it! From her angle below the bottom of Randon's car, she could see the dark silhouette of a little black box. She scrambled to her hands and knees, then crawled uphill. Could it be?

She used the rear tire like a step stool and pressed herself higher so that her belly was flat against the freezing metal floor of the shipping container. Rolling carefully to her side without losing her footing, she reached underneath the car and gripped gritty plastic. With a tug, the box pulled away slowly at first then freely as if it had been connected by a magnet.

Connor stood to spot her on her way back down.

"What did you find?" asked Tandy.

Marissa jumped off the tire and cupped the box like The Holy Grail. "It's Randon's tracking device."

Connor peered closer.

Tandy jumped up. "If he has a tracking device, why didn't he use it to find the car?"

"Because it wasn't charged."

Greg crawled over the trunk of the car to get a closer look. "Does it use the same kind of charger you brought?"

Marissa caught her breath and turned the box over to study the shape of the charging port. Her only hope was that with as technologically advanced as Randon liked to consider himself, the fact that she'd bought the latest phone would put their gadgets on the same level.

The small rectangle hole had rounded edges on one side exactly like her phone's charger. She let her breath out in a huge whoosh. "Yes!"

Another whirring sounded from overhead, and what felt like a mosquito bite pricked the back of her neck. She reached to rub the sting away.

Another bite stung her shoulder despite that area of skin being covered in layers of clothing.

"Oh no." Connor moaned.

A melody like that of handbells rang out around them.

Marissa looked up to find reality raining down in the form of corn. Kernels tapped against her cheeks, and she quickly ducked and closed her eyes to keep out the sticky, sweet dust. The light sprinkle turned into a shower before she could even squat to find her phone charger. The cord was swallowed up by what was known as a "corn pool" during harvest events at The Farmstead pumpkin patch.

Marissa dug in, feeling around for the cord in the waves of dry kernels. "I lost it."

"You what?" Tandy waded through the rising tide.

Marissa looked up to yell louder, but the corn pelted harder and faster.

Connor ripped off his jacket and held it over her head. "The charger is buried," he yelled to Tandy.

Greg dropped down next to her and frantically flung heaps out of his way. "Here it is."

Marissa's guts untangled in relief. "Plug it in." She held out the box for Greg to make the connection. She didn't trust herself not to drop it and lose it again.

Greg connected the device. They all watched as if the

simple connection would bring the police busting into the warehouse, sirens blaring. Naturally, nothing happened except the corn was now reaching their knees.

"I powered it on," he said weakly. Because Sheriff Griffin might arrive eventually, but they could all drown before then.

Tandy gripped Greg's hand as the shipping container filled with corn. She'd seen the movies where people fell in corn silos and died. That would be them if they didn't do something quickly.

Connor pointed to the car. "Get in."

He would know more about corn drownings than anyone, but even in the car, they'd eventually die of suffocation. That is, if they could keep the corn from coming in the broken window. "The window's broken."

Greg ushered her toward the door and stooped to grab the tarp. "We'll block the corn with this."

It would be better than just standing there. If the police were really going to come, this would give them a little more time.

Tandy waved Marissa forward. Connor would want to make sure she was safe first. "I'll hoist you up."

Connor climbed onto a tire so he could pull from above, and Tandy laced her fingers for a step for Marissa. Her friend's rubbery snow boots threatened to break Tandy's hands apart, and her fluffy skirt scratched Tandy's face, but on the count of three, she gave Marissa a boost. Connor yanked her hand then grabbed her legs to direct her headfirst through the window. Marissa's big skirt fluffed around her and her boots kicked a few times before she disappeared inside.

Tandy looked for Greg who was now on the other side of the car, climbing up to the windshield to drape the tarp across. His side of the freight container was clear from the corn storm, so he was able to climb a lot quicker.

"Come on, Tandy." Connor reached down for her.

She gripped his hand.

He hoisted her high enough to grab the handle of the car. Her feet dangled for a moment before she found something solid to step on. Probably Connor's shoulder.

If they made it through this alive, they were all going to be a lot closer to each other. Especially considering the Corvette was a two-seater.

With a mighty shove, she pushed off whatever it was she was standing on and cleared the window to collapse on the seat back. She spun around to reach out for whoever was next. Connor's fingers locked around her palm. With one big tug he appeared then let go of Tandy to hold himself up like a gymnast on the uneven bars. He rocked in head first and dove over Tandy to share the passenger seat with Marissa.

Greg's face peaked in from over the top of the windshield now covered in tarp. He was going to make it.

He waved Tandy deeper inside. "Scoot towards the gearshift. I'll slide into the driver's seat then you can sit on my lap."

Tandy shifted and made herself as skinny as possible. Greg's face disappeared for a moment before his feet swung in followed by his legs and torso. They didn't stop until he was sitting in the seat like an astronaut, prepared for takeoff. He reached underneath the seat and pulled a lever to make the seat slide back as far as possible.

Tandy lifted her hips and scooted in front of him, but more importantly, the tarp fell into place over the hood of the car, blocking out the kernels but not the rushing sound. The white noise brought images of being buried alive. They were fine, but only for the moment.

She gripped the steering wheel and sighed. Had Cupid only worked his magic to bring them all together for them to die together on Valentine's? Of course, Cupid was a myth, while God was real. And if she was ever going to learn to communicate with him the way George had, now was the time.

I'm about to die, God. That's about as vulnerable as I can get. If there's a way to get us out of this, I'd really love to be able to understand. If not, I'm gonna meet you real soon…

Her mind whirled through images of her life, focusing on the events that had led her here. Randon's Corvette. The mystery had begun with this car, and it was going to end with this car. If only Randon was there with them to give them his keys. Then they could turn the ignition and…

Tandy jerked upright. She didn't need keys to start the ignition on an old car. Vic had taught her how to hotwire. "Connor, do you have a screwdriver on your toolbelt?"

"Uh…yeah."

Tandy thought back through the process. If the screwdriver didn't start the car, she'd have to actually connect wires. "Do you have any wire clippers?"

"I have my Leatherman with a knife. I can cut with that. Why?"

She grinned over her shoulder. "Put your seatbelts on because we are going for a ride."

Chapter Twenty-Two

TANDY TOOK A DEEP BREATH TO steady her hands and inserted the screwdriver into the ignition. If the ignition turned over, she would know that she had received direction from God. Talk about a lesson in communication.

She twisted the handle. Nothing.

She tried again. *Come on, God.*

Nothing. But she wasn't giving up.

She pulled the screwdriver out of the ignition. "Now I have to pop off the panels on the steering column. Randon's going to kill me."

Connor aimed the flashlight below the steering wheel to the recessed area under all the giant gages. "He's going to kiss you."

Tandy let the joke relax her. "I've kissed all the men I ever want to kiss."

"And more," Marissa added for her.

Greg chuckled. Because none of that mattered anymore. And because they were all a bit giddy with hope.

Do or die. Tandy jabbed the tip of the screwdriver into the seam of the panel and pried it back. The material popped and ripped, not coming off as one piece, but in a jagged chunk.

Greg reached around her to rip it off. Connor angled his beam of light for her to find the bundles of wires. She unwound them and slid her fingers up the different lengths to pinpoint the two main wires, then, with a flick of her wrist, she sliced them apart.

Connor leaned closer. "You want me to do it? I've worked with electrical wires before."

Tandy would have loved help, but Connor was in the passenger seat, and for him to trade places would take more time. They had to get out before the kernels built up enough to impede their traction. "I've got this."

Vic had explained the method to her, and though his lack of communication is what had ended their relationship, he'd improved by being honest and respectful. That change could very well save her life.

Sinking the knife blade into the rubber coating of the first wire needed, she scraped the end clean. Not too hard.

Something clattered inside her door. A trickle of corn.

Greg jostled her as he tucked the tarp in tighter, but he wouldn't be able to hold it forever.

Tandy reached for the second wire, scraped it, and twisted it together with the first. Now the brown one.

The bottom of the tarp ripped from the pressure. Corn spilled in. If she didn't hurry, it would weigh the car down. Or bury them.

"Hurry," Marissa prodded.

A trace of brown caught Tandy's eye. She tugged out the hidden wire and repeated her process, stepped on the clutch, and then touched the wires together. "Pump the gas."

Greg jabbed the screwdriver back in the keyhole and twisted. The engine roared to life.

Marissa whooped.

"Go, go, go!" Connor yelled.

Tandy reached for the gearshift. She wanted to jam it into first and bust through the bulkhead to freedom, but the whirring sound started to die. Hadn't Vic said that she might need to rev the engine to really get it going?

She stepped on the accelerator a couple times. Fumes

filled the air, overpowering the corn scent with the smell of gas. Great. If this plan didn't work, they could die from carbon monoxide poisoning. So many options for their demise. But she was going to choose Option D—none of the above.

Tandy yanked the gearshift to the top left corner and stomped on the gas.

The tires squealed, the car shot forward, the engine thundered, and the door loomed closer. Despite the corn pouring thicker against the windshield, Tandy only pressed harder. The car connected with metal, lurching them all forward. Had there been airbags in the 50s, they would have exploded like balloons. But instead, there was only one Corvette in the world made of steel. And this was the one.

Wood splintered, metal screeched, rubber burned, and the bright light of freedom momentarily blinded her. The car burst from its cage to land on the conveyor belt, ten feet off the ground.

Tandy stepped on the gas to drive to the ground, but the tires whirred uselessly. Only the undercarriage fit on the conveyor, and with the way the car rocked backwards, they might get dumped right back into the freight container. Her foot eased off the clutch and the car died.

At least, if they went down, they'd go down fighting. They'd created an even bigger mess for McNeil to clean up. And hopefully that mess would eventually lead to his arrest.

Metal joints creaked from below, followed by what sounded like the popping of pins and the echo of zipping cables. Her stomach fluttered as the Corvette crashed toward the ground and the bottom of the conveyor belt shot towards the ceiling like they were on one end of a teeter totter.

Marissa screamed, Greg wrapped his arms protectively around Tandy, and her body tensed for a hard landing. The impact jolted through her bones to her jaw. She wasn't sure which hurt worse, the bruised tailbone, jarred spine, or bitten tongue. But at least the blood in her mouth, like the taste of a lucky penny, told her she'd survived.

She twisted to make sure the rest of the passengers had experienced the same fate. Marissa gave a schoolgirl giggle. Connor whooped like a winning athlete. Greg squeezed her in a hug.

The safety of a gun clicked off.

Tandy stilled. Her heart shuddered. This wasn't over yet.

McNeil appeared outside her window, the barrel of his gun aimed at her nose. The farmhands had them blocked in from the other side. She looked past McNeil's weapon to find the man's stance as nonchalant as usual, with only a twitch in his cheek and flicker in his eyes to give away the depth of his anger. "You done?"

His coolness, more so than the temperature of the air, made her shiver. Like he believed he had all the power, and she was only a naughty child that needed to be taught a lesson. The idea couldn't be more backwards.

Movement at the door to the warehouse caught her attention. Men in black. With guns. Creeping closer.

She wasn't alone. She never was. Someone was always listening. Always ready with an answer.

Tandy slid her hand smoothly down the inside of the door panel until her fingers caught the cold metal of a handle. "No, McNeil. You're done." She jerked the lever and slammed the door open against his knees. He stumbled backwards.

At her action, a S.W.A.T. team poured inside, shouting out communication to each other so they could work together in surrounding the enemy. The farmhands dropped their weapons in surrender.

McNeil regained his balance, spun, and took off the opposite direction. The special forces unit gave chase, but before they could catch him, he leaped into a forklift and gunned the engine, powering the machine forward with enough force to split the men like bowling pins. They evaded being hit but didn't turn in time to catch him before he sped past. The forklift careened toward the exit.

Tandy gripped the doorframe and leaned through the open window. "He's getting away!" she yelled.

Surely McNeil couldn't return to his old life of pretending to be an FBI agent, but he could continue his life of crime if not caught. How many more people would he steal from or kill to make a buck? And how much terrorism would his stolen vehicles support?

Not to mention his attempt on her life. Would she ever feel safe again if this man wasn't behind bars?

"Freeze, McNeil," an officer yelled through a bullhorn to no avail.

The S.W.A.T. team raced to catch him, but if he made it through the doors, he'd have the head start to his car where he could definitely get away. And as a former law enforcement officer, he'd know how to work the system to evade capture.

McNeil's laughter floated back as the vehicle left his pursuers in the dust. A few more feet and he'd be free.

Metal clanged, and the door slid shut in front of him. Sheriff Griffin stepped out from the shadows by the control panel and aimed his weapon at his enemy.

McNeil stomped on the brake and spun the wheel. The machine swerved wildly as the driver fought to keep from hitting the door. It slowed for a moment before spinning as if to take out the sheriff.

Tandy gritted her teeth. Marissa gasped from behind.

Griffin held his ground, playing chicken with a killer in a forklift. The S.W.A.T. team all dropped into position to take aim, as well. McNeil's head swiveled around as he took in his situation and probably looked for another out. His gaze landed on their group still in Randon's car. He scowled and spun the wheel toward them. Like this was all their fault.

Tandy's heart leaped into her throat. Greg wrapped his arms around her from behind. Marissa's ice cube of a hand found hers and squeezed.

The forklift pivoted their direction, lost traction on a layer of corn, wobbled, and tipped over onto two wheels.

McNeil's face contorted in fear as the vehicle continued out of control. He yelled and covered his head before crashing to the ground. The vehicle landed hard enough to spray corn against the Corvette's windshield.

Griffin stepped forward. "Nathan McNeil, you are under arrest."

The man lay on his belly. He lifted his head, jaw slack. A chewed-up wad of gum fell from his mouth.

Tingles of relief radiated warmth through Tandy's body. She melted into Greg's chest, not sure she could comprehend everything that happened. Not sure she wanted to.

Marissa and Connor joined them for one giant group hug. Connor released her, but Marissa didn't let go. The poor woman was probably freezing from wearing a skirt in February and needed the body heat, so Tandy continued their embrace despite the gear shift in her ribs.

"You did it, Tandy. You saved us." Marissa gushed. Ah…this hug was a grateful-to-be-alive hug.

Well, then Tandy should squeeze just as hard. "I got us out of the freight container. Your phone charger saved us. Without it, the police never would have arrived in time."

Marissa laughed and finally let go, looking down at her

feet. "These boots really did save my life, didn't they?"

"Told you," said Connor with a smile.

"Good thing I've been working on my communication skills and finally learned to listen." Marissa made the statement sound like a question as if hopeful that would be enough for Connor.

"Good thing," Connor repeated noncommittally.

Tandy knew they had stuff to talk about, and that they'd be better off discussing it alone. "I say we give Griffin the credit for this one. Look at him."

They all watched through the windshield as the sheriff had McNeil lie face down in a puddle of corn so he could handcuff his arms behind his back.

Marissa nodded. "This has to be Griffin's best Valentine's day ever."

Greg nuzzled the back of Tandy's ear with his nose, and for the first time she was aware how close they were. Very cozy. Of course, it helped that neither of them was headed to the Emergency Room with an allergy or gunshot wound or anything. "It's *my* best Valentine's ever," he said.

"Really?" Tandy twisted to smile at him over her shoulder. "Because I find it a little corny."

Despite the cold and the near-death experience, Marissa didn't want to get out of the Corvette for three reasons. One, it now felt safe like a security blanket. Two, Tandy's bad puns made her laugh. And last but certainly not least, Connor held her in his arms. Unfortunately, the owner of the car had arrived and was storming through the warehouse like he thought they'd gone for a joyride and crashed his car rather than having rescued it from real thieves who'd been trying to ship it out of the country.

Randon's arms waved in the air as if he were conducting a symphony. "What did you do?"

Connor gave a small growl, his chest rumbling behind Marissa's back. "Tandy, think you could hotwire this thing again and get us out of here?"

Tandy clicked her tongue. "That might give him a real reason to be mad at us."

Greg stepped a foot outside the car. "I'll handle this."

Tandy climbed off his lap. "This is when I'm glad I date a lawyer."

Marissa watched the other couple get out, leaving her alone with Connor. She twisted around to face him. "We can't get in trouble, can we?" she asked, but when she looked into his solemn gray eyes, the remaining adrenaline from fight or flight mode kicked back in. Yes, she was in trouble.

"No," he said simply, and she wondered if it was because he also had trouble thinking when their lips were in such close proximity.

Could she kiss him and pretend everything was better? She pouted at the answer she already knew. If she really wanted to communicate better, she needed to be vulnerable.

His gaze dropped down to her pout, and he grabbed for the door handle. Before she knew it, he'd propelled her out onto the cement floor. If only she was wearing high heels, then she'd have an excuse to trip so he could catch her.

No, no, no. That's not what she wanted. She wanted a secure foundation. Not only for her feet but for their relationship.

Randon stalked around them to look at his car from every angle. "Oh man. You even broke a window and ripped off part of the dashboard? Do you know how much I paid for this thing? I hope insurance…" He shook his head and looked down as if he couldn't handle anymore. His gaze snagged on Marissa's feet and traveled up to her face. "What are you wearing, Marissa?"

She smiled hesitantly at Connor. "It's the latest fashion."

Randon rolled his eyes then continued on with his rant.

A fireman Marissa dated in high school brought her a blanket.

She wrapped the stiff and scratchy material around her legs. "Thanks, Troy."

"Sure." Troy gave his boyish grin. "Though I heard it's nothing compared to what Connor gave you."

Marissa tilted her head. "The boots?"

"No." Troy laughed like she'd told a joke. "Let me see your rock."

The rock? As in diamond? As in engagement ring? Her stomach churned with a mix of disappointment and dread. She should be wearing Connor's engagement ring right then, but instead she feared she might never wear it. She glanced at Connor to see if he was going to explain. Because she didn't really know where to begin.

Connor made a slashing motion in front of his throat. He stopped when she caught him.

"Oh. Uh…" Troy took a step back. "I guess Valentine's Day isn't over yet. But it's certainly a memorable one, huh? I'm going to go…uh…try to put out fires instead of starting them."

Marissa sighed. If the whole town knew Connor had been planning to propose, then they were certainly all going to hear about The Dating Game disaster.

Griffin strode over as Troy left. "Let me make sure I got my facts straight."

Law enforcement officers and emergency workers continued to pour in. Greg and Tandy joined their circle.

Marissa stepped closer to Connor to make room for them. And because she wanted to.

He rubbed her back. That was good, wasn't it?

Griffin held his stylus over his phone. "McNeil is in charge of the car theft ring. When the ports on the East Coast started cracking down, he used his knowledge of Snodgrass's and Knibbs's history as an excuse to investigate out here, only instead of investigating, he was actually smuggling his cars in shipping containers with the help of the two newest hires at the Thomases' farm."

Randon kept shaking his head in disbelief. "The farmhands stole my car?"

Connor nodded. "Yeah. If McNeil was telling the truth about that, when they got it stuck, they accidentally left behind the attack relay unit that they used on newer cars."

Griffin scribbled furiously. "But it was McNeil who attempted to steal the car off George's tow truck, and when George caught him, McNeil killed him, knowing he could pin it on George's brother?"

"Yes." As Marissa connected the pieces in her mind, more fell into place. She scrunched her nose. "And he was probably the one who broke into Billie's shop and destroyed the video footage."

Tandy pursed her lips to one side. "That means he was never really suspicious of Vic. That was simply bad timing. Though if Vic hadn't come, I never would have learned how to hotwire a car."

Randon muttered something indiscernible under his breath.

Marissa nudged him with her shoulder. "And you never would have met Susan."

He quit muttering.

She smiled up at Connor before remembering that they

weren't a happy couple at the moment. Though… "If we hadn't had a fight, we might never have caught McNeil."

Connor smirked. "Happy Valentine's to us."

Griffin paused in his writing and raised his eyes to look at them without lifting his face. "Connor, I'm going to be keeping your mom's Porsche a little longer until evidence is collected, but you're free to go. I'll find an officer to give you a ride unless Marissa wants to drive you home."

"I do," she blurted. Hopefully, if she ever got to say those words in a wedding ceremony, she'd be a little more eloquent. She peeked at him to see how he'd taken them.

Connor stuffed his hands in his pockets. "That's fine."

He was giving her a chance.

Her pulse skipped a beat in the same way it had when she'd been hanging from the inside of the shipping container. Choosing to be vulnerable in a relationship was almost as scary as being captured by killers.

Chapter Twenty-Three

MARISSA HAD ALREADY CLICKED THE REMOTE to start warming up her Jeep, but as she climbed behind the wheel, she still had to adjust the settings and turned on the seat warmers. Her teeth chattered from cold, though the shivering could very well be her nerves.

Connor dropped in beside her. He motioned to the empty coffee cups snuggled in the console. "Too bad those aren't full of something warm."

Ugh. He would have to bring up the coffee.

Rather than shift into drive, she closed her eyes. "Connor, I have a confession."

"Okay…"

She took a deep breath and peeked an eye open. "I've been drinking coffee."

He didn't move, only stared at her. She opened both her eyes to try to better read his expression in the dim light, but it was as legible and stony as hieroglyphics. "What are you thinking?"

She braced for the worst—for their relationship to go the way of those hieroglyphics.

"I have a lot of thoughts."

"Such as…?" Now that she was vulnerable, she needed to be understanding. She'd listen to whatever he had to say.

"Well, my first thought is that in a normal relationship, this would be the most ridiculous confession ever."

Hope warmed her heart and stilled her shivering. She'd be okay with writing off their conversation as ridiculous.

Except… "We've never had a normal relationship, so…?"

"So, it is a big deal. In fact, it's so big, I'm having trouble believing it. When did you start drinking coffee?"

Marissa curled her toes in a cringe. "The day George died. I grabbed your cup that I thought was tea and took a sip. When I realized it was coffee, I figured it must have been Billie's. I was grossed out at first, but remember how much energy I had that day?"

Connor rubbed his jaw. "That makes sense now. You still hate the taste, but you like how the caffeine gets you going."

"Yeah, it kept me too busy to think about my sadness for George."

His eyes warmed. He was much better at this communication thing. In fact, what kept them together was probably how understanding Connor had been.

"Why did you hide it from me?" Connor's lips twisted on one side.

A good question. Too bad she didn't have a good answer. "It was more about hiding it from Tandy. I mean, we had this rivalry thing going where we were competing to see how many customers we could sway to our side, so I didn't want her to know that *I* was on her side."

Connor lifted a shoulder. "Well now that she's confessed to drinking tea, it sounds like you're on the same team."

Marissa could understand her best friend and business partner without agreeing on everything. Billie said so. "Tea tastes better."

"I disagree." Connor gave a sad smile. "That's our biggest problem, isn't it? I was afraid to disagree with you, and when you blew up at me, it seemed I was right to be afraid. And now that you confess to also hiding what you've been drinking, I can't help thinking how hypocritical that is."

Marissa didn't like admitting she was wrong. It took

vulnerability to a whole new level. It was always easier for her to get angrier at the person who was angry with her, or twist things around to make it seem like she was really the victim. Or, and she hated admitting this even to herself, but she'd been known to toss her long hair and charm her way out of an argument.

This was where Billie's final key to communication was either going to open or close the door to their relationship. "You're right. I expected you to be vulnerable and understanding, but I didn't want to have to do the same. I made my needs and desires more important than yours. I didn't treat you as an equal, and…" Her throat clogged in an attempt to block the words from coming out. She swallowed it down. "If I don't change, you are better off setting up boundaries and moving on without me."

Connor leaned his head against the seat and stared at the roof of the car, but his hand reached across the console and encircled hers with power and warmth. The lump in her throat came back, but for a different reason this time. He was choosing connection.

"Have you been reading *How to Win Friends and Influence People*?"

"What? No." Was the whole vulnerability thing that powerful? "I've been talking to Billie."

Connor rolled his head to the side and gave her his lopsided grin. "What else has Billie said?"

Did he want the whole lesson or just an object lesson? "She said to be honest with you and to appreciate your thoughts even when they differ from mine. So, I wore the boots." She motioned toward her feet. "And I was headed to your house to bring you coffee." She pointed at the cups.

Connor lifted his head in delight. "You were going to drink coffee?"

She pressed her lips together and nodded.

"With me?"

She nodded again. No words were needed.

"You must really love me."

A laugh burst out. "More than tea," she admitted.

Connor turned to face her, his smile fading into sincerity. His eyes narrowed to peer into hers. "You were right about me needing to put up boundaries."

Oh no. She squeezed his hand tighter. She didn't want to let go.

"But that's different than a wall."

Marissa blew out her breath. She'd lost Connor once before, and she didn't want to do it again.

Connor squeezed her hand in return. "With a wall, I would block you completely out of my life. With a boundary, I step out of the dirt of dysfunction and through a gate into a healthy lawn, and I invite you to join me."

He was inviting her into something better. "I want to join you."

"I was hoping you would say that." He leaned forward and nuzzled her nose.

The feather light tickle of his touch was more than skin deep. It soothed her soul like only his touch could.

His lips hovered above hers, warm and magnetic. "I also need to apologize."

For what? "For not kissing me already?"

He pulled away far enough for her to see his lips turn up. "No. For making a scene at the grand opening of your tea loft."

Oh. That. She'd practically forgotten about it in the wake of almost dying a bunch of times. Hopefully the town would too. "Well, do you want to know how I would have answered the question about a perfect wedding proposal?"

He studied her. "I thought I knew, but it hasn't been working out so well."

Time to start afresh. Being together was all that mattered anymore. Especially since she'd almost lost that opportunity. Twice. "You've really gone all out in the romance department. Your first proposal on the cruise was magical. And today would have even topped that. But I don't think I need a show anymore. You are enough. I'm good with simple and heartfelt, like Greg figured Tandy wanted."

"I will keep that in mind." He leaned in. Finally. And after the kind of kiss that could steam up the windows if they continued, he pulled away slightly. "You still willing to drink coffee with me tonight?"

She smiled. "Are you asking me out?" Now that Valentine's Day was getting good, she didn't want it to end. She stepped on the brake and shifted into drive.

"Always." Connor turned toward his window, but not before Marissa spotted his huge grin. "Plus, I want to be at the shop when Tandy sees you drink it."

"You brat," she said without any anger. Probably because being vulnerable had freed her from the fear, pain, and frustration that Billie said was always behind anger. She stepped on the gas and followed the path lit by headlights. "That's truly why you want to drink coffee tonight, isn't it? You want to see if I'm going to humble myself even more and confess to Tandy."

"Maybe," he said. And she loved him for it.

Tandy handed Greg a cup of cocoa. Except it didn't look like hot chocolate or even something she would serve. It was pink.

Greg took the drink with one hand and felt her forehead

with the other. "You okay there, Tandy? Did you hit your head a little too hard on the steering wheel when driving the Corvette out of the shipping container? Should I have you checked by the EMTs again?"

Tandy pulled his hand down and smiled up at him. Now that the adrenaline had drained away, she'd begun noticing some bumps and bruises, but nothing as ER worthy as Greg's first kiss. "No, I just thought I'd serve you a cup of cocoa to thank you for hiring Connor's mom to paint that picture of my dog. The only cocoa Marissa made today is from white chocolate with half and half. If you can ignore her addition of red food coloring, you'll find it really quite palatable."

Greg sipped, leaving a tiny whipped cream mustache on his upper lip. He licked it off. "Mmm…palatable."

She picked up her own mug and let the sweet cream coat her tongue. Not a bad way to end the day. She circled the counter to sit beside her boyfriend. After the Valentine's Day they'd had it was simply good to be alive, but, as much as she hated to give in to the cheesiness of the holiday, the truth was that love is what made life worth living.

Greg was there for her when it mattered. The trick was that he wasn't going to be able to read her mind and know when it mattered to her. That's where Billie's little communication advice came in. Tandy would have to speak up about her needs, and when they weren't met, she'd have to give Greg a chance to explain his intentions rather than assume the worst. Otherwise, they'd be no better off than she'd been with Vic.

"I want to thank you again for the painting you had made of Cocoa. It showed me how much you really do care." She met his gaze with an apology in her heart. "If Connor hadn't accidentally told me about it, I might have written you off as indifferent about our relationship and gotten back together with Vic. Not because I cared for him more, but because I thought he cared for me more. I'm glad I didn't."

Greg set his mug down. "I'm glad you didn't too. And I need to apologize. When Vic showed up, I retreated. I was afraid you were going to leave me, so I busied myself with work, when I should have told you how I felt."

Tandy's lips parted in new awareness. "So you aren't always this busy?"

Greg shook his head. "Nope."

"What a relief." Tandy sighed. "Of course, if you hadn't been so busy trying to prove Derrick Snodgrass innocent, I wouldn't have worked so hard to try to find him guilty, and we never would have solved George's murder."

Greg took her hand. "I've always enjoyed being with you as friends, but now that we're more than that, we're going to have to remember that dating isn't always going to be roses and…pink hot chocolate. It's going to take work. But, as you know…" He stood and pulled her to her feet. "I've got a pretty strong work ethic."

Tandy wrapped her arms around his neck. "Workaholic," she whispered against his lips.

The bell over the door rang. Tandy spun to find Marissa leading Connor through with hands clasped. They must have done their work as well. Or perhaps life and death circumstances had a way of bringing people together.

"Hey." Connor's tone dropped. "Just because you guys won The Dating Game doesn't mean you get the whole place to yourself for Valentine's."

"It should." Greg's chest pressed against Tandy's back and he wrapped his arms around her waist. "You two are interrupting what was a very sweet moment."

Tandy hugged Greg's arms closer. As this was only the beginning of many sweet moments to come, she didn't mind sharing. "Yes, Greg was enjoying your pink cocoa, Marissa, but there's plenty left for you guys too."

Marissa strode toward the side of the counter, but Connor snagged her hand and swung her toward a stool. "You sit," he said. "I'll make our beverages, while you tell Tandy what we're drinking."

Tandy glanced back and forth between the couple. Marissa sank sheepishly onto her seat as Connor headed toward the espresso machine. She did a double take. "I know what Connor likes to drink, but what are you drinking, Marissa?"

She covered her face then peeked between two fingers. "Coffee."

The smile started on Tandy's face then spread through her whole body. Had she heard correctly? "You're drinking coffee?" She checked on Connor again, who was indeed making two Black Eyes.

Marissa pulled her hands down and pointed. "You drink tea."

So she did. She even drank pink cocoa on occasion. She picked up her glass mug. "This calls for a toast. Though words cannot espresso how much Marissa's coffee drinking means to me."

Marissa narrowed her eyes. "How brew-tiful."

"Wait." Connor looked over his shoulder from where he stood at the grinder. "Tandy, help me finish these drinks first, then we can toast."

He'd already ground the beans and poured the shots. She surveyed his mess as she squeezed behind the counter next to him. "What do you need?"

He dipped his head and lowered his voice. "I'm looking for the spoon."

She pivoted to point at the stir sticks. "You can use—"

"No, I want a spoon."

Weird. The only spoon she had was…

Her eyes widened. Her heart tripped. She wanted to giggle and jog in place and clap her hands. The giggle escaped but Connor stopped the rest with a warning look.

"What's so funny, Tandy?" Marissa asked.

Tandy peeked over her shoulder to see if Marissa suspected, but her business partner kicked her feet from her seat on a stool and gazed into space like she was half asleep and, thankfully, oblivious. "I must be on a sugar high from the hot chocolate."

Marissa rested her elbow on the counter to prop up her chin. She gave a relaxed smile.

Tandy pinched her lips together to keep from any more giggling as she pulled open a drawer and dug behind coffee sleeves to retrieve a metal spoon engraved with the words: Will you marry me?

She turned sideways so she could wave it for Greg to see while keeping it out of Marissa's line of site. Greg shot her a thumbs up.

Marissa almost caught him. "You really are excited to see me drink coffee, aren't you?"

Tandy handed the spoon to Connor and hurried around the counter to Greg's side. She wanted a good view, and she also wanted to share the moment with her own sweetheart.

Greg slung an arm around her neck and kissed her cheek. "Stop grinning. You look suspicious," he whispered in her ear.

She shivered at the warm brush of breath on her skin and kept grinning.

Connor stirred the coffee, picked the mug up with both hands, and ceremoniously turned to set the cup in front of Marissa.

The bride-to-be looked at the mug and shook her head. "I can't believe I'm drinking coffee. You know this will keep me up all night, don't you?"

"I propose it will," Tandy said before she could stop herself.

Greg pinched her side.

Connor's head jerked her way with a semi-scowl that he barely wiped off in time. "I'll stay up with you," he said. He picked up his own mug. "Now let's toast. Here's to a Valentine's we'll never forget."

Tandy lifted her cup to her lips but didn't tilt her head back because she didn't want to miss Marissa's big moment. Connor and Greg did the same.

Marissa pulled the spoon from her mug and stuck it in her mouth. Probably to lick it clean before she set it down. Tandy hadn't expected that. But when sliding the utensil through her lips, her gaze caught the rest of them watching her.

She held the spoon to the side and looked down at her shirt. "Did I drip? I should have put on George's brown jumpsuit before trying to drink coffee from a mug."

Tandy and the men held their breath collectively.

Marissa shook her head at the silly people she now considered her best friends. Had they never seen anyone drink coffee before? Well, okay, they'd never seen *her* drink coffee before. She might as well give them what they were waiting for.

Setting the spoon down, she reached for her cup handle. She raised the mug, smiled at the weirdos still not drinking their own drinks, and sipped the bitter concoction that would give her enough energy to bake crumpets all night if she wanted to.

Blech. So nasty. It was weird that Connor had served her mug with a spoon when there wasn't any cream or sugar in it. Even if there was, Caffeine Conundrum usually used stir sticks. But he'd specifically asked for a spoon, hadn't he?

A thought struck her. A thought so delicious and creamy that it might as well have been pink and only served on Valentine's Day. But it couldn't be.

Connor had been planning to propose in the carriage, not over a cup of tea. Though he had gotten so upset during The Dating Game when Greg mentioned the spoon he'd fallen out of his chair. Could Connor have been the one who brought it into the shop?

She lowered her mug, her eyes zeroing in on the inscribed utensil. It was inscribed! Did she mention that it was inscribed?

She picked up the spoon so she could read the four little words again and again and make sure she wasn't imagining things. More coffee dripped to the floor, but she didn't care.

Will

You

Marry

Me?

She spun her stool to face Connor who had dropped down on his knee and pulled out a ring box. Had he been carrying it this whole time?

He gave his famous half smile. The one that melted her like a marshmallow—even when she'd been intent on never dating him again. "I'm going to set another boundary, Marissa. This is the last time I propose."

The thrill of surviving death didn't compare to getting to spend the rest of her life with this man. "This is the last time I say yes."

Marissa held out her left hand, and he slipped a familiar vintage ring on her finger. It had a round solitaire in a square setting. It wasn't the one he'd given her before. No, this one looked like the one her grandmother used to wear.

She exhaled in awe. "Where did you get this?"

"Billie bought it at your grandmother's estate sale and saved it for me. Do you like it?"

She covered her mouth. Grandmother's estate was what had torn their first engagement apart. But now it was uniting them together. A true symbol of how they could overcome any obstacle. And of Connor's love for her. How could she possibly reciprocate in kind?

"I love it." A tear streamed down her cheek. She wiped at it then laughed and waved her hand so her friends could see the ring. "Did you know he got me my grandmother's ring?"

Tandy held her hands to her heart. "That's one secret I wasn't keeping."

Greg shook his head. "Way to set the bar high, Connor. There's no way I'll ever be able to top a proposal like this."

Marissa's cheeks burned from a smile her face couldn't contain. She reached down to grab Connor's hands and pull him up with her.

Connor rose into a lunge and stepped his back foot forward to come closer. Only that foot slipped on a wet spot from the coffee. His leg shot past her and he pitched forward, sure to send them both to the ground.

Marissa braced herself, planting her feet, closing her eyes, and wrapping her arms around Connor's waist, hoping she didn't break a leg and would still be capable of walking down the aisle on her big day.

Nothing happened. The ground didn't rush up to meet them. She didn't even bump into the stool. In fact, she was still standing.

She peeked one eye open to find Connor leaning against her. Her boots had held their traction. *She'd* caught *him.*

Tandy's eyebrows arched. "Did that just happen?"

Greg wrapped an arm behind Tandy's shoulder. "I wouldn't believe it if I hadn't seen it."

Connor righted himself, as sheepish as he was elated. "Shall we make it a fall wedding then?"

Tandy chuckled. "That's appropriate."

Marissa laughed along and leaned into Connor, wrapping her arms around his neck. She'd marry him anytime, but autumn on The Farmstead would be perfect. She might even wear cowboy boots, since boots were working out so well for her. "Pumpkin spice and everything nice. That's what fall weddings are made of."

Tandy lifted her mug. "I'll start practicing my toast."

Connor swayed with Marissa like he wanted to practice for their first dance. "You girls and your beverages."

Greg sipped from his mug. "They're both a cuppa trouble, aren't they?"

Marissa grinned over at Tandy. What mattered on Valentine's Day was not that they lived happily-ever-after, but that they knew the important people in their lives were committed to working through their troubles with them.

AUTHOR NOTE

Dear Reader,

As ridiculous as this story is, I hope you'll hear a ring of truth in it. I really wanted to use the holiday of Valentine's to take a closer look at the importance of communication in building healthy relationships. When we're wounded, it's so easy to try to protect our hearts with unhealthy behaviors that only cause more pain, but since we're responsible for our own actions, it's up to us to focus on what we should be doing to create connection.

With help, I pondered the basics of communication and came up with understanding, vulnerability, and equality. Think about how our whole world might change if we all made these our goals.

I wanted to take this even farther into the idea of communication with God. Think about how *we* might change if we make time to speak to our Creator and listen for His voice.

I'm thankful God helped me finish this book. I had to research more than I've ever researched to make the plot work, and I got really stuck, but I'm thrilled with how unique the ending turned out.

The most interesting thing in this book is that these grand theft auto stories are all true. There really was a ten-year-old who stole a car from a car lot. There really was a carjacker who got stuffed in a trunk. There really was a vehicle that the owner chained up to keep from getting stolen, and he found the vehicle chained up backwards the next day with a note from the thieves. It really is illegal in Ohio to leave your car running when it's not locked. Not even authors can make that stuff up.

Tandy and Marissa's adventures will continue in two more books. As you know, there's now a wedding to plan, and it might get just a little more complicated if, say, Marissa is sent to a safehouse or Connor is arrested right before the big day.

Find my other stories at www.angelaruthstrong.com or join me for discussing all these crazy characters on my fan page at www.facebook.com/groups/1557213161269220/.

Thirsty for more,
Angela

Now, A Sneak Peek at Book Three

A Latte Difficulty

Chapter One

"BLACK IS A GOOD COLOR FOR coffee, not bridesmaid dresses."

Tandy Brandt turned away from the bride-to-be in order to hide her smile while grinding more nutty-scented coffee beans. She knew Marissa Alexander, a reformed Midwest beauty queen, would never use black as a wedding color, which made it all the more fun to suggest. "Black will be *my* wedding color," she declared.

"Ugh." Marissa pulled yet another wedding magazine out from under the counter at their shop, Caffeine Conundrum. For the last five months, she'd spent every free moment obsessing about her upcoming wedding.

Their shop was finally starting to clear out after a morning of pouring iced coffee and sweet tea. Customers trickled out to the street for a parade that would kick off the weeklong Americana Festival leading to Independence Day.

Besides Greg St. James and Connor Thomas, who were at the shop to assist their girlfriends, only Randon, the local hipster millionaire, remained at a table, waiting for his order.

"Greg," Marissa addressed Tandy's childhood sweetheart with a huge sigh. "Please tell me you won't let

Tandy make me wear a black dress when you two get married."

"Can we talk about this after there's an actual engagement?" Greg suggested, though it was hard to take him seriously when he was dressed like Abraham Lincoln. He tugged his fake beard low enough to sip from a straw then grimaced. "Though I can tell you that if I let Tandy dress me like this to hand out coupons during the parade for your Red, White, and Brew booth at the fair, then I'm not going to have much say in wedding planning."

Things were getting more serious between them, but there was no rush. Especially since Tandy would never want to overshadow Marissa's time as the bride-to-be.

Tandy grinned over her shoulder from where she filled the espresso machine with fresh grounds. "I didn't really think you'd wear that costume, Greg. I suggested it as a joke."

Greg stood taller and straightened the lapel on his long black suit jacket. "Oh, I don't joke about our 16th president. He's the reason I decided to become a lawyer in the first place."

Connor casually sipped from his mug. "You wish you were wearing a shirt like mine though, don't you?" He puffed up his chest to better display the image of Captain America's shield screen-printed on the front of his t-shirt.

"So badly." Greg replaced his beard with a snap of elastic.

Marissa waved away her fiancé's interference. "Don't listen to him, Greg. You look fabulous and should really get some pictures of yourself in costume."

Tandy combined two shots of espresso with steamed coconut milk. "He's already been in your photo booth, Marissa."

Connor crossed his arms and leaned against the counter

to face Greg. "I'd think after what happened to President Lincoln at Ford's Theatre, you'd want to avoid Booths."

"Not cool, Captain. Not cool."

While Connor was taking the Lincoln jokes too far, Marissa was taking the photo booth thing too far. Just because she'd gotten a good deal on renting the booth for her wedding reception in the fall by advertising it in their shop during Americana Week, that didn't mean she had to force everyone to use it.

Tandy grinned at her friends and left them to their banter so she could deliver Randon's latte. It warmed her fingers. He'd ordered a hot beverage despite the fact the temperature was already into the 80's. Not to mention the guy had grown a full beard. Not the best way to keep cool during the summer.

She set his mug on the stainless-steel table with a clink. "Aren't you going outside for the parade?"

He didn't glance up from his laptop. "Nada."

For a know-it-all, he'd been unusually quiet today. Probably designing another phone application. One of these days she'd get him to make her an app for their business where customers could pre-order drinks.

"Working on something important?" she asked.

"Always." This time he did glance up but only to make sure she wasn't looking at his computer screen when he angled it away from her.

Fine. If he didn't want to talk, she wouldn't waste her time. She rolled her eyes and turned back toward her friends, but they'd all disappeared.

A light flashed from inside the photo booth set up next to the stairs leading to the tea loft. Had all three of them crammed inside? Marissa's laughter spilled out. Yep.

Tandy changed directions and pulled back the photo

booth curtain to get a peek. Marissa sat in the middle of the bench, wearing the Statue of Liberty crown and holding Lady Liberty's torch. She'd somehow gotten Connor to put on sunglasses and hold a sign on a stick that read "All American Dude." Greg, of course, was already in costume.

Grinning, Tandy tugged a little flag from a jar on the prop table and squeezed in to sit on Greg's lap.

The group grunted and shifted to make room for her while the camera snapped shots at the most awkward moments then flashed their images on the screen. The whole booth shook with Marissa's laughter.

Greg wrapped an arm around Tandy's waist to keep her from sliding to the floor. "This really isn't very presidential behavior."

Marissa wiped at her eyes. "But it's so fun. Aren't you glad we got one of these for our wedding, Connor?"

Connor shook his head but couldn't keep from smiling. "As fun as this is, we should probably head out to the parade or we'll miss the float I built for The Farmstead."

Tandy clicked her tongue. "I hate to tell you this, Marissa, but Randon isn't planning to leave the shop. We're not going to be able to close down."

Marissa frowned and pulled back the curtain to see for herself. "I'd kick him out, but I'm hoping we can get him to build us an app one of these days."

"Me too." Tandy arched an eyebrow. "Plus, I'm a little scared of him. Do you remember when he mentioned the Ohio Power outage like he had something to do with it?"

"I remember." Connor slid his glasses to the top of his head, messing up his messy do. "I've also been wondering if he's had anything to do with the new computer virus that everyone's talking about."

Marissa looked around the crowded space in confusion.

"What virus?"

Greg stroked his beard. "That could be how he's making his millions."

Marissa turned to Tandy, eyebrows pinched. "He's making money off a virus?"

Connor wrapped an arm around her shoulder. "No. Though if you don't know about the virus, you might be spending a little too much time planning our wedding."

Marissa held her hands wide, knocking Tandy in the face with her torch. "I only have three more months before the big day. I have to make sure nothing goes wrong."

"I know, I know." Connor humored her with a grin. "If you want to know about the virus, it's a form of ransomware. You've heard of ransomware, haven't you?"

"I've heard of a ransom."

"Right. It's like that." Connor snapped and pointed. "Hackers hold all the information on your computer for ransom unless you pay them a fee to return it. It can really affect big businesses. Like Ohio Power for example."

Her eyes widened. "You think Randon is a hacker?"

Tandy lifted a shoulder. This wouldn't be the first time she suspected him of a crime. "When I took him his coffee, he did turn his computer away from me so I couldn't see what was on his screen."

"Then we certainly shouldn't leave him alone." Greg cleared his throat. "We could watch the parade from the windows."

Tandy twisted to grin at him. "You just don't want to go outside in your costume."

"I don't blame you." Connor shifted his weight to stand without knocking anyone else off the bench. "But if I stay inside, the crowd on the sidewalk will block my view of my parents' float." He ducked out of the booth to give the rest of them room to move.

Tandy smoothed Greg's fuzzy beard. "And you're supposed to hand out our coupons."

Greg sighed and scooted her off his lap onto the bench next to Marissa so he could stand as well. "You're right. Both Abe and I are men of our word."

"Thank you." Tandy grinned up at him. He was normally as polished as George Clooney, which made his ridiculous costume that much more endearing. "I'd come with you if I could, but one of us has to stay here to ensure Randon doesn't hack our laptop and hold Marissa's precious wedding plans for ransom."

Marissa shooed her away. "They're my wedding plans. I'll keep them safe. Plus, Greg needs you."

Greg nodded solemnly. "I do."

Tandy let herself be pulled away. It was probably time to back off before Marissa's wedding obsession got even worse. If that was possible.

Marissa waved goodbye then smiled at her image in the photo booth's computer screen. She'd earned herself more free time to plan her wedding.

The bell over the door rang a couple of times, joining in with the music from the band and announcing her friends' exit. She didn't envy them at all. While they were going out into the crowds and heat, she got to stay in the cool and the quiet. Not to mention, having the whole photo booth to herself.

She removed Lady Liberty's crown from her head and set down the torch, as well. The next time she was in this booth, she'd be wearing a wedding dress, and all the photo booth strips would be taken home by guests as mementos of her big day. She twisted her long, blond hair up to imagine how she might want to style it. Though Connor liked her hair down. She released it to cascade over her shoulders.

Should she make a strip of photos for Connor? She could hold out the engagement ring for a closeup on one then blow him a kiss in another. Or she could spell out the word LOVE with her hands by forming one letter in each of the four photos taken. That would be cute.

She practiced her poses then reached for the button to start the countdown.

"Give me the file." A deep voice boomed through the room.

She froze in place before pushing the button. A shiver slid down her spine. Who was talking?

She leaned forward and pulled the curtain back a few inches. Across the shop, a man in jeans and a white t-shirt stood over Randon, gun drawn.

Marissa covered her mouth to keep from gasping aloud, but that didn't stop her heart from quivering.

Randon glared up at him. "How'd you find me?"

He knew the man? He knew what file the man wanted? Then why didn't he hand it over so he wouldn't get killed?

"I traced your computer location. What? You thought you would be safe in this crowd?"

Randon snapped his laptop shut.

Marissa wanted to scream, *No, Randon! Your stupid apps are not worth dying for!* But then she might also get killed. Was there any way she could save them both?

She fumbled through her jean pockets then apron in search of her phone. All empty except for one of her "Save the Date" cards she'd been planning to give to Tandy. She must have left her cell with her magazines. If she didn't do something fast, she might not even make it to her own wedding.

"You won't get away with this," Randon growled.

The man laughed. It was a low and menacing sound that would haunt Marissa's nightmares.

What else could she remember about this guy? Jeans and a white t-shirt weren't that memorable. If he killed Randon, how would she ever be able to describe him to Sheriff Griffin?

From the back, she could see the perpetrator had dark skin, but that wasn't unusual in the summer. What else?

There wasn't much hair on his head. He was either bald or buzzed cut. And he seemed to be in pretty good shape. She'd guess six foot and 180 pounds—a little leaner than Connor. She needed more.

He lifted the gun. Hopefully it was only to make a threat that Randon would take very, very seriously. "Ironically, this crowd is what will allow me to get away with whatever I want. I could shoot you, and nobody would hear it over the bang of those drums."

As if on cue, a heavy drumbeat broke through the white noise of festivity.

Marissa tugged the curtain open a little farther to see the people on the street. Every back was turned her way. If she ran and screamed for help, she'd never make it. She could be shot and killed within feet of her friends as they obliviously sang Yankee Doodle, laughed at Shriners in little cars, and caught candy.

Randon lifted his hands as if being arrested by the cops. "How do I know that, if I give you what you want, you'll let me go?"

That was such a good question. But not worth the risk of

refusing to obey.

The gunman shook his head. Ooh, he had a mark on his neck. Like a tattoo.

Marissa narrowed her eyes to decipher its shape. She leaned sideways to get a more direct view. Her elbow bumped the front of the booth.

Had the gunman heard the thud over the sounds from outside? Her heart jumped to her throat as she waited. The man didn't even move. Whew, that was a close…

A flash lit up the photobooth.

Oh no. She'd bumped the button.

The gunman turned. His jaw hardened.

"Run, Marissa," Randon yelled as he splashed the contents of his coffee mug over the man's white shirt.

The gunman turned to retaliate.

Marissa charged up the staircase. It was closer than the front door, and that way she wouldn't have to pass the guy with the gun.

Her feet scrambled. Her arms pumped. Her pulse pounded louder and faster than the drums outside. She dared to look over her shoulder to see if she needed to duck bullets.

The man brought the butt of his gun down against Randon's head. Randon crumpled. The gunman jumped over his body and bolted toward the stairs.

Tingles shot down Marissa's arms and legs. She couldn't run fast enough. Feeling the pressure as if swimming upstream, she dodged ornate tables and chairs to reach the metal exit door.

She burst into the warmth of sunshine on the roof and the jovial tunes of a marching band below. It felt like breaking the surface when drowning—igniting a surge of hope mixed with the fear of being sucked back under.

She spun and faced off with the man who'd cleared the stairs and was close enough that she could make out not only his light green eyes but the symbol on his neck. Then with every millisecond stretched into a lifetime, she slammed the door in his face and slid the bolt into place.

The door rattled against his weight but held. She'd survived. Though she didn't know if she could say the same for Randon.